# Smoke and Mirrors

mirror series *book one*

# Norma Marie

*For my other half.*
*Thank you for not walking away.*

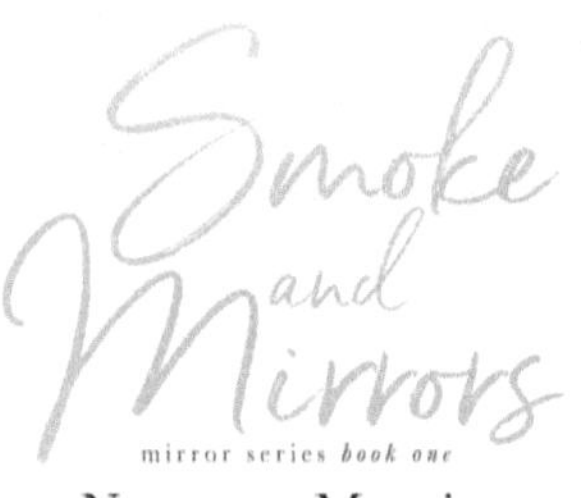


Norma Marie

Natalie
When my supposedly perfect life falls apart, I turn to my best friend Lucas and relocate to BoothBay Harbor with my sole reason to push on; my daughter Savannah. Being around Lucas again makes the voices that tell me I'm not good enough fall quiet. But just as I start to heal, my past and his present threaten to tear us apart.

Lucas
In high school, Natalie was my best friend... and my secret crush. With her back in my life, she's reawakening feelings I thought were long gone. When things start spiraling, it takes all I have to prove to her that I won't walk away again. The further I fall, the more she pulls away. I want it all, but she has to want it too.

Can I be enough to show her that this is real, or is she living in a past filled with nothing but smoke and mirrors?

## Chapter One

NATALIE

ears blur my vision as I pull out of the driveway I once called home, my grip on the steering wheel turning my knuckles white as every moment over the past hour flashes in my memory. I knew my husband was cheating. *Husband, what a fucking joke.* Finding him buried to the hilt in the nanny, while our daughter screamed down the hall was the final straw. The rose-colored glasses I once wore have been torn off, revealing a life that I didn't want any part of. The sound of Savannah, my six-month-old baby girl, cooing in the backseat pulls me from having a full-on breakdown. *She's my reason.* I shake the thoughts of what I walked in on from my head and make my way out of Galveston—the place I grew up in, the home I couldn't escape. I refuse to look back; the past is nothing but smoke and mirrors. But the pain of everything I've endured over the past few years is crushing me, threatening to destroy me, even as I run away from it all.

As I cross into the next town over, I pull into the parking lot of the first hotel I see. The adrenaline seems to be wearing off. My eyes are drifting closed and my stomach is turning in knots. I won't make it much farther without getting some rest

1

and feeding my girl. I get us a room on the first floor, making it easier to pull everything we need inside. As I situate us into the space for the night, the events of the day crash into me, my reality becoming nothing but blurred vision as the tears fall freely from my eyes. I could turn a blind eye when the cheating wasn't right in front of me, but to come face-to-face with it, it was like something inside of me finally snapped. *Turn a blind eye*, I roll my eyes at the words my own mother spoke to me when I asked her how to handle Ethan's cheating. I can't believe I was so naïve, but it was all a façade. Closing my eyes, the memories play vividly across my thoughts. No matter what I do, I can't forget what I saw. Tears mark trails down my cheeks as the aching in my heart takes over all my senses. Hanging my head in shame, I do my best to rid myself of the thoughts. I don't have time to wallow when my daughter needs me.

Once I get myself under control, I dry my cheeks with the sleeve of the hoodie I'm wearing and open my eyes. The hotel is nothing too fancy, the fading yellow color on the walls making it look more dated than it is. There are two queen-size beds, a small table with a cute little chair tucked in the corner. The desk is by the wall closest to the closet and what I can guess is the bathroom, a phone and a bible sitting on top. Placing the bags I brought in on the bed closest to the entrance, I start the mundane task of going through everything I brought into the room.

Setting up Savi's belongings on the bed farthest from the entrance, my thoughts turn to my parents, more tears falling as I think of them. Based on how I left, I know they won't accept me back into their home. Ethan was their golden boy and my pairing off with him was the highlight of their life. My father was enamored with him from the day I started dating him, quickly discarding me in favor of having a son to bring into his line of work. *I was nothing more than a piece on a board, a pawn in their game to rise through the pillars of society.* The thoughts in my head flay me, cutting to the quick as I play over every instance where my father pushed me aside for my husband, where my mother turned to drinking instead of being there for her own daughter. Just as the thoughts try to take over again, Savi giggles. Hearing her pulls me from the recesses of my mind and back into the moment.

Grabbing Savi, I move us to where we can get her feeding started while I siphon through the numbers I know by heart. I don't even know why I'm thinking about calling anyone, but the thought of being alone is breaking me. There aren't many people in my life since I got married, his controlling ways made it so I lost contact with anyone who wasn't considered worthy of our social status. I easily dismiss my parents and my husband, scoffing at the term he's been graced with. Just as I'm about to give up trying to figure out who I can call, my childhood best friend's name pops into my head. *Lucas.* I shake my head at his name. He probably changed his number the minute he left after my engagement was announced. Last I heard through the social grapevine was that he's a successful model, and according to his mother, he's been paired off with another model in the business. The last thing he needs is me butting into his life. As much as I want someone to talk to, the thought of him knowing everything only deflates me.

Savi falls asleep during nursing, so I shift her off and settle her into the middle of the pillows on the bed closest to the bathroom. She shifts and rolls a bit, before finally getting comfortable and falling deeper into slumber. Going over to the phone at the desk, I sit in the chair and stare at the phone, willing it to tell me who to call, who to reach out to. My mind keeps going to Lucas, no matter how many times I try to tell myself that he isn't going to answer, that he changed his number and forgot about me. I have no one else in my life that I can turn to, no one else that will just be a friend. That's all I really need right now, a friend. Bracing myself on the desk, I grab the phone and dial his number. It goes to voicemail after a few rings and I hold my breath, praying it's not some random number I called.

"You've reached Lucas Moreno. You know what to do." His voice instantly soothes the pain in my chest, the breath I was holding releases as I try to figure out what to say. The beep coming far too soon.

"Hey, Lucas. It's Natalie. Um, Natalie Conaway. I don't know if you remember me, or even what to say, except to ask if you can call me back." I rattle off the hotel number along with the room number before hanging up. Hanging my head, I walk over to the bed Savi's laying on and give in to the feeling of being on my own. Kissing her softly on the forehead, I lay beside her, my thoughts driving through my brain at what feels like a thousand miles per hour.

Turning on the TV, I set the volume lower, so I don't wake her. As much as I want to give in to the demons in my head, I can't break, not yet. Sitting still is only making things worse, so I start cleaning up the mess around the room, packing up everything that isn't needed. This hotel isn't a long-term plan, even if Lucas doesn't call me back. I have no idea what I'm going to do, but the reality is, we can't stay here. I need to get the hell out of Texas, start somewhere new. Just me and my girl.

Grabbing some of my toiletries, I head into the connected bathroom and start prepping for a shower. I haven't had a shower since last night and with Savi sleeping, now's the best time to handle my business. Staring into the mirror, I take in everything about my appearance. My blonde hair is lifeless and dull, the natural wave hangs flat, much like my self-esteem these days. My blue eyes no longer sparkle with happiness. My shoulders slump forward, like the weight of the world is sitting directly on them. Bracing on the counter, tears form in my eyes as I try to figure out what the hell I'm going to do.

Turning away from the sight of myself, I start undressing. Just as I start pushing my pants down my hips, the phone in the room rings, making me jump at the loud noise. Pulling them back up, I dash out of the bathroom, crossing to the other side to the desk as quickly as I can. I grab it before the noise can wake up the sleeping baby on the bed.

"Hello?" My voice comes out barely above a whisper.

"Natalie? Is that you?" Lucas' voice on the other end brings tears to my eyes, not of sadness, but because the feeling of being alone in this world isn't as tangible as it was just a few moments ago.

"Lucas." Just saying his name brings a sense of relief I wasn't prepared for.

"Nat, what's going on? Why are you calling me from a hotel number?" I smile at the nickname that he gave me when we were kids. No one has called me that in so long.

"I just needed a friend." My voice shakes as I utter the words. I don't want him to know the ugly truth I'm hiding. The thought of him finding out has me hyperventilating, the shortness of breath clawing at my lungs as they panic to get air into my body.

"I can hear you panicking Natalie, so before we get into anything, I'm gonna need you to take a deep breath for me." I do as he asks, his words penetrating the fog in my head. "Now let it out and do it again." I let the breath out and continue breathing for him as he listens on the other end of the line. As the fog clears with each new breath, I realize what a huge mistake I made by calling him. *Why did you call him? He has his own life, a girlfriend. You're too broken for him.*

"You know what, this was a bad idea. Just forget I called. I'm sorry for bothering you." The words fly out of my mouth.

I go to hang up the phone, but I hear him yelling through the other end.

"Natalie." Pulling the phone back up to my ear, I brace myself. "Don't hang up. Please don't hang up."

"I'm still here." My voice is soft, his yelling hurting me more than he'll ever know.

"You're not bothering me. And I think you're full of shit for saying you just needed a friend. We've been friends since we were kids. I haven't changed my number because I was hoping you'd call me. Just because I left and never looked back didn't mean that I could forget you. I just couldn't stand there..." he cuts himself off but quickly recovers. "Where are you?"

"Just outside Galveston, in a hotel in Ellisboro."

"What's going on?"

"I can't be here anymore." I wish I could tell him what happened, why I left, but I can't.

"Ok. Listen to me, Natalie. You're going to be okay. I don't know what's going on, but you'll always have me in your corner." I hang my head as he reminds me of the words he used to say during our youth. "Come to BoothBay Harbor." His words interrupt my train of thought.

"Where?" I have no idea what he's talking about. *Where the hell is BoothBay Harbor?*

"It's in South Carolina." My eyes widen. He didn't just walk out of Galveston, he ran clear across the country.

"I can't just come there, Lucas. It's too far. I'm driving. I have my daughter with me." As much as I'd love to be around him again, I can't let him see just how broken I've become.

"You can come. Those excuses aren't stopping you. You're stopping you." I hate when he calls me out on things. He's been doing it since we met. But it's also why I knew I needed to call him. Of all the friends I had, he was the one who always had my back.

"It's going to take me a few days, maybe a week. Like I said, I have my daughter." I give in. Maybe a new town will be just what we need to get our fresh start.

"That's fine. I'm finishing up a job, so I can be there to meet you." *I'm interrupting his life. Oh God. I can't do this.*

"Oh, you're working. I'm interrupting your life." He cuts me off again.

"Natalie, stop." I slam my mouth shut, causing me to bite my tongue, the copper flavor of the blood hitting my taste buds. "You're not interrupting anything. I was planning on heading back home after this was done anyways." The tears start falling even more as I listen to his words, the reality of everything settling deep into my chest as the memories crush into me. "I don't know what happened, Nat, but I promise you have me."

I nod even though he can't see me through the phone.

"So back to my first question, why did you call from a hotel phone?"

"Um, my phone broke." I lie, but based on his deep breath coming through, I know that he knows I'm not telling the truth. Luckily, he doesn't call me on it. The phone is back at *that* house. It wasn't my phone anyway. It was another way for Ethan to control me, watch me. I make a mental note to get a new phone before I leave town.

"Natalie, I know you're hurting. I can't tell you how much I wish I was there right now, but you're the strongest woman I know. Get some sleep, and in the morning, I want you to call me when you're on your way out of town."

"Okay."

"Promise me, Nat."

"I promise, Lucas."

"Goodnight, Natalie."

"Night, Lucas."

The next few days are hard as I push forward to South Carolina. We finally crossed the state line an hour ago and I know Savannah's about to lose her mind if we don't stop soon. I have no idea what I was thinking when I called Lucas, but somehow, he convinced me to come out to where he's living now. *Don't get too comfortable, he'll see how broken you are*. The voice takes another stab at me as I pull off the highway. Savi's cries get louder as I do my best to find somewhere, anywhere, to stop so I can feed her.

"I know, baby girl, I know. We're stopping soon. I promise." I do my best to calm her as I drive further down the road. *You would pick an exit that has nothing within a mile*. The voice is taunting me further and further down the rabbit hole and the more it jabs, the more I want to succumb and just give in. The high pitch wail of my daughter interrupts my train of thought. "Almost there, Savi girl."

Just as I am about to give up, a small gas station shows up. It's pretty much empty, but there isn't any other place that I can see. Pulling off, I get out and quickly maneuver myself into the backseat, locking the doors before I make a move to grab Savi out of her car seat. Her face is contorted into the most adorable scowl as she looks over at me, her cheeks red from anger. Doing my best not to giggle at her, I unbuckle her and pull her out. Grabbing the cover just in case, I cover my chest while working at my shirt, so she can get fed. As soon as she latches, I feel her entire body relax into me as she starts to feed.

"Oh, Savi. What are we doing?" I start speaking out loud, knowing she won't answer, but desperately needing someone to talk to. Looking up, I notice my reflection in the rearview mirror. The woman staring back at me is a stranger to who I thought I would be. Turning away from it, I peer through the blanket and to my daughter who is still suckling away. "I'm so sorry, baby girl. I imagined so much more for you than this, so much more for me. I wish I could go back and change it, but I wouldn't. Because then you wouldn't be here." Her eyes catch mine as I watch her. The beautiful blue in them holding me with her gaze.

Caressing her cheek, I watch as she slows down her feeding, her eyes getting heavier and heavier. Just as she closes her eyes, a tear escapes my own. "I promise, I won't let you down, baby girl. It's me and you, kiddo. Us against the world."

Crossing into the town that will be our new home, I feel a sense of peace wash over me. It's like a tiny little island here, right off the coast of South Carolina, with one highway that connects it to the big city on the other side of the harbor.

## Welcome to BoothBay Harbor
Population 662

My eyes widen at the small number under population. As a city girl, I don't know much about small towns, but the idea of not being surrounded by thousands of people feels like relief to me. Just as I pass the welcome sign, I pull up my Bluetooth and press the call button for Lucas.

"Hey, Nat. Where you at?" He laughs at himself, making me roll my eyes.

"Just passed the welcome sign. GPS says fifteen minutes."

"Sounds about right. I'll see you in a few." I nod, even though he can't see me. *He isn't going to want to stay around someone as broken as you. You may as well turn around now.* I feel the sting of tears in my eyes as the voice penetrates through, stealing my sense of reasoning. "Get out of your head, Natalie." I roll my eyes again, hating that we haven't even seen each other, but somehow, he can still read me like a book.

"Yep, see you in a few." I end the call before he can reply. Rolling my neck, I do my best to relieve the tension. I can hear Savannah in the back making cooing noises as she wakes up from the nap she succumbed to after her last feeding. I smile at her noises, knowing that she is the only reason I am still going.

"Turn left and your destination will be on the right." The GPS interrupts my train of thought. Taking the left it indicated, I watch as the house numbers slowly pass by as we get closer and closer to the beach at the end. Seeing the gravel driveway, I no longer fight the tears that have been threatening to fall since we entered the state. Every single emotion that I've been holding back is now pummeling me, washing over me like a waterfall, making it hard to breathe as I make my way slowly down his driveway.

"Almost." I'm talking to myself as I set the car in park, tears not stopping. Taking a deep breath, I shut the car off and turn towards the back, refusing to even look at the house.

"We're here, baby girl. I don't know if this is where we'll stay, but for now, we can call this home." She coos at me some more, the sound bubbling hope in my chest. Turning back, I mentally prepare myself for this reunion. Stepping out of the car, I can feel his eyes on me.

Looking up, I see him standing on his porch, watching me. He looks the same, but so different. I take a minute to take him in. His usual crazy dirty blonde hair, emphasis on the dirty, that he sported in high school is now faded on the sides with some length on top. There's some highlights added as well. *Holy shit, he grew up.* I shake the thoughts from my head and prepare myself to get out. I lift my eyes to him and give him a tight forced smile. I see his eyes narrow as he takes in my smile, but I don't give him any more than that before I turn away, my thoughts now going to the baby in the backseat.

Pulling the door open, I unlatch the seat and pull out the carrier Savi is in. She continues to coo as I pull her out. *This is for her.* Turning back to Lucas, I see him staring at the car seat in confusion. *Did he not know?* His eyes bounce back and forth between the seat and my eyes, his fists clenching at his sides. *Is he angry that I brought a baby here?* He notices me watching him and instantly releases his fists, moving towards me. I haven't moved an inch since I turned around, terrified of what's about to happen.

*This is it, he's about to tell you that you must go.* I hunch my shoulders, ready. The defeat I feel is rolling from me in waves. *I should have never come.*

I watch the waves crashing into the beach from our location. Today's session is for a new bathing suit company. Unfortunately, the waves are a bit too rough for us to shoot in. We've been delayed twice now, once for weather, and now for turbulent water. Rolling my neck, I watch as the crew and photographers try to figure out what we're going to do.

Their bickering annoys me, mainly because there's a solid solution for the problem we're having. But I'm just the pretty face, meant to be seen and not heard. It doesn't matter that I have a degree in marketing, or that I took classes in public relations. They don't see the degrees I busted my ass to get, because it doesn't do a damn thing for the pictures they want.

I may have a hot body, washboard abs, and a smile that people say can drop panties from miles away. I may not look like I have much going on beyond my looks, but I'm so much more than they ever give me credit for. One day, I'll prove it. I'll be the one they come to when they need someone to figure shit out, the one they turn to as more than just a body for a picture that may or may not sell whatever products they've decided on.

"What's with the face?" I look up to see my agent Justin staring down at me.

"Delayed again. And the solution is really fucking simple, if they just opened their eyes to it." His eyes go out to the scene I'm watching, the photographers still arguing about what to do.

"What solution?" I trail my eyes down the beach a little further than where they are set up to shoot, a spot where the waves are still rough, but they aren't enough to take you out. His eyes follow mine and he quietly laughs.

"They want this location, but they don't really see past their minds' eyes." I retort as he goes back to watching the scene unfold below, the photographers and crew continue to argue.

"Lucky you don't have anything else booked for a few weeks then, huh?" He smirks before taking a seat beside me on the sand. The area we're in is surrounded by beautiful beaches, but also some of the deadliest waves. When the water is rough, there's no opportunity to really enjoy it, unless you find spots like the one down the beach. "Where's Lauren?" I bristle at the mention of my so-called girlfriend. When I first started modeling, my agency thought it would be a good fit to pair me with someone else who was starting out. We've been "together" for three years now, but I wouldn't call it a real relationship, more like a working one, a convenient one.

"Don't know." He nods his head, looking at me. He thinks my relationship with Lauren is solid, that's how I know I'm doing my job. But what he doesn't realize is that when we aren't working, she's off doing her own thing, while I'm at home doing mine. We both know this is just to better our careers, nothing more and nothing less. As long as we deliver and do our job, they don't pay much attention to us.

"Let me go find out if I can figure out what the hell's going on, maybe even talk them into moving down the beach a little." He winks before standing and makes his way over to the photographers. They talk a few minutes before he sends a thumbs-up my way, signaling that I'm good to get out of here, it's too late in the day to try a new set up now. Grabbing my bag, I head up the walkway that leads me toward my guesthouse.

Walking into my cottage, I throw my bag to the bed before heading to the shower. Stripping down, I stand under the hot spray of water hoping it gets rid of the slimy gunk they sprayed all over me for the shoot, the makeup on my face, the massive amount of styling product they used in my hair. By the time I'm done with this shower, I'll look like a watered-down version of all the ads I've ever shot. This is the part of modeling that no one sees. They see the pictures and never know what kind of work goes into making it all happen. I'm tired of the entire process. Tired of being nothing more than a model with a nice body and some good facial features. Hanging my head, I let the hot water continue to beat on my back, relaxing my muscles as I stand here.

Grabbing the loofah off its hook, I scrub at my body and watch as the slickness rolls off with the suds from my body wash. I grab my shampoo, lathering it in my hands before washing my hair and grabbing the conditioner the crew handed me this morning after I got done with hair and makeup. My usual dirty blonde hair has been highlighted for this shoot, which means using special conditioner, so it continues to look natural. You'd think I'd be used to this by now, but honestly, I hate this part of my job.

I wrap the towel around my hips, walking out into my

bedroom. The room they got us isn't too bad of a setup. Each room faces the beach, with beautiful French doors that open to the sand and waves beyond the small deck outside. The room is done in light blues and whites, matching the look outside. It's cozy, but it's not home.

Grabbing my phone, I sit on the edge of the bed and look through the notifications. There are several text messages, but it's the missed call that sticks out to me. It's an area code I know well, considering I grew up in the area. I rarely hear from people back home, especially when I'm working. I pull up the voicemail, bring the phone to my ear and my breath drops at the voice coming through the line.

"Natalie Conaway. Holy shit." I whisper, even though no one's in the room to hear me. I nearly drop the phone as I go through all my childhood memories. She's in all of them, not a single memory doesn't include her. Our parents are both members of the same country club, our mothers are best friends. We've been inseparable since the age of eight. She became my best friend, at least until high school. I was a typical ladies' man, always had a girl on my arm. Natalie didn't date. Well, until Ethan came into the picture. The day they started dating was the day I realized that I was in love with my best friend. I haven't seen her since I walked out of her high school graduation party. The same day her father announced their engagement.

Putting the phone down, I grab some clean clothes and get dressed, all while replaying the voicemail over and over in my head. *Why would she call now? Why does she sound so defeated? Why a hotel room? What the hell happened?*

Once I'm dressed, I grab my phone and a beer. Heading out to the small deck that overlooks the beach, I see the photographers from today's shoot are still out there arguing about something. Some of their voices reach me, but I can't tell what they're saying. Rolling my eyes, I sit in the lounge chair and prepare myself to make this call.

The minute I hang up the phone, I'm rushing back into the bedroom. I need to pack and get back to BoothBay Harbor. I know it will take her some time to make the drive, but I have a lot of things to get done before Natalie gets there, including cleaning the guest house that I hope she'll stay in.

"What are you doing?" Lauren's voice pulls me from my thoughts as I watch her walk into the room.

"I'm heading home." I shrug her off and go back to what I'm doing.

"What do you mean you're going home?" There's a sound of annoyance in her voice, something that bristles against me. I hate that she thinks she has any power over me just because we're being marketed as a couple.

"Just what I said."

"The shoot isn't over, Lucas. I was coming to get you to let you know they called a meeting, something about moving the location a little further down the beach or something." She goes to stand in front of me as I make my way to the bathroom to grab my stuff from in there.

"I have something more important to take care of." I brush past her. She stomps her foot and turns towards me.

"What the hell is more important than our job?"

"My best friend from high school called. Something happened and I need to get home so I can meet her there." I'm moving around the bathroom, collecting everything that's mine, so I don't have to make multiple trips in here.

"What do you mean *her*?" she screams at me. "Who is she? Why haven't you told me about *her* before?" I look over at her, her face is red with anger as she watches me.

"Because it wasn't any of your business. Now, if you don't mind, I need to finish packing." I walk back around her as she tries to block me. She stomps her foot again, clearly agitated that I'm not changing my mind.

"Are you fucking kidding me right now, Lucas? We have a job to do." The annoyance in her voice is like nails on a chalkboard. I don't know who she thinks she is, but this is one of the main reasons why I barely hang around her unless we're working.

"I don't know what you want me to say." I finish up packing and zip my bags. I need to get to Justin and have him get me a ticket home. Walking around her, I look around to ensure I grabbed everything. She stands there with her arms crossed staring at me, watching me.

"We have work, Lucas." I roll my eyes. I know we have work, but right now, Natalie is more important than any modeling gig. Something happened, I don't know what, but that voice didn't belong to the Natalie I grew up with.

"And it's been delayed twice already Lauren." I watch as she turns away from me, her eyes going to the double doors that look over the beach. She's a classic beauty. Blonde hair that she keeps chopped to her shoulders, emerald-colored eyes that sparkle when she's happy, high cheekbones, a cute nose, a tight fit body. But underneath all of that is someone vain, only ever concerned with herself. She takes one more look at me and then walks out, muttering something under her breath.

Grabbing my phone, I send a text off to Justin asking him to get me a flight home. Instead of replying, he calls.

"No. Fuck that, you're not going home, Lucas. You need to finish this photo shoot. You signed an agreement." His voice gets higher as he bellows at me through the phone.

"Justin, either book me a flight home or I'll do it myself and you can find someone else to yell at." Usually, I'm all about the job. It's what pays the bills, but at this moment, there's nothing more important than getting home.

"What the fuck is going on?" He's no longer yelling, but I can still feel the anger in his voice. I know Justin well, so I know right now, his fingers are massaging the bridge of his nose as he tries to calm himself down.

"I just gotta get home." That's all I'm giving him. I know he won't accept what's really going on as a valid excuse.

"Fuck, Lucas. You're one of my closest friends. We've been working together for years now. I don't know what has your panties in a twist, but I'll get you home and then you better pray like hell that I can pacify these people. They're gonna be pissed that Lauren's here and you aren't. They didn't just sign her, they signed both of you as a package deal. They called a meeting to discuss moving down to the location you spotted earlier and were planning on shooting early." He sounds defeated, his voice deflating as he finishes his speech. And honestly, the last thing on my mind is the stupid photo shoot or Lauren.

"I know that Justin. But I can't explain why I need to go home. I just know that I need to be there. So, I'm telling you, do whatever you need to do to make that happen." There's a deep sigh on the other end of the line.

"I'll book your flight. Do you need me to book you a cab to get back to the house or are you good?"

"My car is in long-term parking, so I got it." I take a deep breath, my mind no longer racing with thoughts of needing to get home. "And, Justin, thank you. I know this is a huge ask of you."

"Whatever, man. I got it. But do me a favor? Call me when you can explain, just so I know you're okay."

"Got it." He hangs up as soon as the statement is said and two minutes later, my flight information is in my e-mail.

I got home with a day to spare. I called a cleaning company to come clean the guest house and air it out since it hasn't been used, well, ever. Then, I stocked the fridge and pantry, knowing they've been on the road for a while and the last thing Natalie needs to worry about is going shopping. I don't know how old her daughter is, but I know Natalie's favorites, so I made sure to grab anything she may want. Once I get a read on the situation, I can make sure they have what they need.

She called just a few minutes ago, saying she passed the welcome sign for this small town. I know I have about ten to fifteen minutes before she gets here. I pace the window, waiting for the car to show up, willing it to show up. I won't relax until I see it. Getting that phone call from Natalie rattled me. I hadn't seen the girl in just under four years, but the minute I heard her voicemail, I felt my heart shatter for my best friend. Her voice was soulless, lost, despondent. Even through a phone, from states away, I could feel the pain in her voice.

I hear the crunch of the gravel in my driveway before I see the car. And then there it is, making its way slowly down the drive. The car is nothing like I expected. I know Natalie comes from money, but I never expected her to flaunt it so exuberantly. The new model Lexus looks out of place in my driveway, my own Jeep looking like a run-down piece of shit in comparison. The car is a four-door sedan, candy apple red, and completely out of my league, even with my own fortune sitting in my bank account.

I walk out the door without a second thought to the car, but instead the woman behind the wheel. The need to see her with my own eyes pushing me onto the porch, where I stand and wait. I watch as she puts the car in park, tears marking her cheeks as they escape from her eyes. She takes a deep breath, cuts off the car, then turns to the backseat. I can see that she's talking, probably to her daughter. I don't talk to my parents all that much, wanting nothing to do with their world, so I hadn't even known that Natalie had been pregnant. I wonder how old this child is, why she left Galveston. *What happened?* The unknown angers me because it's partially my fault. Although I kept my number the same, I never took the time to reach out to her. She was my best friend, once upon a time.

She gets out of the car, her movements slowing the minute she sees me standing there and offers a small smile, but it's nothing like her normal beams of happiness. Her smiles have always been my favorite part of her, they just radiated so much joy that you couldn't help but smile with her. This one is weak and looks almost forced. She turns to the back door and opens it. I watch her for a few minutes, wondering if I should help her, but not sure how to even try. And then out comes a car seat. For a baby. *Jesus Christ, she has a small baby.* My fists curl into themselves without thought. The anger at her ex clouding me. The forced smile's gone as she stares at my fists, the tears steadily streaming from her eyes again. She doesn't move, stuck to the spot she's currently in, her eyes on my curled fists. The last thing I want to do is scare her. Shaking the anger off, I unclench my hands and make my way off the porch.

Walking down the short walkway between my porch and my gravel drive, I offer a small smile of my own as she watches me. Her beautiful eyes aren't as bright as I remembered, the usual spark I long to see is now missing. Her shoulders are hunched like she's holding the weight of the world. Her hair's in a messy bun on the top of her head, the clothes on her are baggy, hiding her body from the world. Without saying a word, I can feel her defeat. It's radiating off her in waves, hurting me deep within my soul. It's in this moment that I know that I'd made the right choice in telling her to come here.

"So, who do we have here?" I motion to the car seat in her hand. She looks at it, and then back at me, letting more tears fall from her eyes. It takes all I have not to reach over and dry those tears and pull her into me. That's the last thing she needs, me manhandling her, so I stay rooted to the spot I'm in.

"This is my daughter, Savannah." Her voice is barely above a whisper as she turns the seat to where the opening faces me. The baby girl nestled inside blinks a few times and then looks up at me, her beautiful blue eyes that match her mother's pulling me in. She's watching me with such intensity that I'd swear I'm being judged. I look at this sweet, innocent girl; she looks at me. And then she smiles, a toothless gummy smile that melts my heart the minute I see it. I grin back at her, she coos at me and I fall in love with a tiny baby.

"Let's get you both settled." My eyes move to Natalie as I speak. I watch her as her eyes widen at my remark, her face showing confusion to what I said. "Come on, you both must be tired from that drive." I put my arms around her and instantly feel her tensing up. I release her immediately, hating that she feels like this with me of all people.

"I'm..." I put my hand up to stop her. I don't want her to apologize for something she didn't do wrong.

"Can I grab her for you?" She nods and I grab it slowly from her, my hand gently brushing against hers. The minute our skin touches, it feels like I've been shocked from head to toe. It's like my body comes alive just from a single small touch. Walking off, I carry the car seat to the guest house, noticing that she's walking behind me. I can see the weight on her shoulders, the defeat in how she walks. This isn't the Natalie I knew in high school, but I'm going to do everything in my power to bring her back.

*Chapter Three*

NATALIE

## THREE YEARS LATER

I watch as the afternoon sun hits the water just right, creating the perfect moment in time. Lifting my camera, I focus the lens and take the shot, plus several more. Sunsets are my favorite time of the day to capture on film. There's something inspiring about the colors and beauty that comes from a perfectly captured sunset, especially on the water. I adjust my footing, kneeling to find the perfect shot and adjust my lens again. Using my camera has focused me, helping me find my happy place after years of not knowing if I could ever find it again, especially after everything Ethan put me through. *Turn a blind eye, it's what we do.* My mother's voice breaks through my calm, forcing me to take a deep breath and channel my energy again. I close my eyes and breathe deeply, a coping technique my therapist taught me when I first settled here. I knew that if I wanted to be the mother Savi deserved, I'd need help. Lucas was a huge help to me but having someone who didn't know me listen to everything I endured was like lifting a weight from my shoulders. I

23

never told him everything that happened during those years, but somehow, he knows just how to make everything better.

Shortly after starting therapy with Dr. Hart, I made the decision to finish my certification in photography. When everything fell apart, I was only two classes away from finishing, so instead of letting Ethan steal something else from me, I took the time to finish. I've since started a home business with my photography, and it's slowly grown to the point where I've been looking at a studio downtown. Focusing my lens one more time, I take another shot of the sunset and smile as the colors come through perfectly on my screen.

"Momma, look." I turn my head to look down the beach a short way where my Savi's playing with a puppy in the sand. Bringing my camera up, I take some quick shots of her. Her beautiful smile brings peace to my heart, seeing it helps me know that I'm doing okay, even if some days I don't feel like I am. Her blonde hair is in cute pigtails and I know there's sand embedded in every braid. She's my other happy place, and the reason I fought through all the ugliness of the past few years. *Ugliness you could have prevented had you just left sooner.* I dismiss that thought as quickly as it enters. I got Savi out of that ordeal, and she's worth every single bad moment. Smiling, I watch as she continues to giggle and play.

"I see you, baby." I watch as the owners walk down and stand off to the side, also watching the silly playtime their puppy's having with my baby girl. The happy couple's smiling at the antics going on in front of them. *That could have been you, but you're nothing now. Worthless. Useless.* Tears prick my eyes, but I refuse to shed them. Moving a little closer to my daughter, I stop and take a few more shots wiling the voices in my head to go away. Turning to the sunset, the sun is working its way down to the point that it cascades a beautiful array of colors on the water. I take a few more shots of it before calling it a day, letting it rest against my stomach as I approach my daughter. The owners of the puppy call him over to them, wave at me and then head off to wherever it is they call home.

"Time to get home, bug." I smile down at my extremely messy girl. She stands up, dusts herself off and then puts her hand in mine as we make our way to the little guest house along the beach that we call ours.

"Mama?" I look down at my sweet girl and see her chewing her lip, like she's contemplating something. Stopping, I kneel in front of her, pushing the hair that's fallen out of the messy braids out of her face. Cocking my head to the side, I find her eyes and smile at her.

"What is it, bug?"

"Is Lucy coming today?" I giggle at the nickname Savi gave my best friend. She couldn't say his name properly no matter how hard she tried, so she just started calling him Lucy.

"No, baby, Lucy isn't coming. He'll be back in a couple days though for work, so I'm sure he'll make time to see you." She looks as though she's about to cry, so I shift my camera to my back and pick up the sweet girl. She buries her face into my crook of my neck, sniffling. Since showing up on his doorstep three years ago, Lucas became a staple to both of us. His unfailing strength helped me get through the worst of my depression after leaving Ethan. Even after all the years apart, it was like we didn't miss a beat. He's still the same best friend I had growing up. Ethan never approved of my friendship with him. Never wanted me to be friends with anyone except who he believed worthy to be in my inner circle. The memories of introducing them pulls at me. The minute Ethan found out I was best friends with a male, it was like something snapped in his head. He started commandeering all my time, making it hard to hang out with the one person in my life who cared.

With Lucas being a model, he's always jet-setting off to some location to work. Sometimes he'll fly in for a weekend, but for the most part, he's off working with his girlfriend. This time of year, though, he's hardly around. As we get back to our little home, which happens to be the guest house on his property, Savannah takes off to her room to add to her ever-growing shell collection while I get my camera put away.

Just as I'm finishing up getting everything put where it belongs, Savannah comes rushing in, throwing herself into my arms. Her energy is something I always wished I could bottle up and sell. Even with a full day at the beach, she has so much energy left. She giggles as I pick her up and swing her around.

"Mama, I hungry."

"Okay, baby. Wash up and I will start dinner." She giggles some more as I lay kisses all over her face before setting her down, letting her rush off to do what I asked. I've been so blessed that she's been so easy. There are times that her sassiness is out in full swing, but for the most part, she's a very easy going, sweet child. The past three years haven't been the easiest, but she's the reason I keep going and the force driving me to get up each day. *You're broken, how can you be any good for her?* I squeeze my eyes shut, forcing myself to find the calm in the madness going on inside my head.

Of all the things Ethan did, she's the best thing that came out of my marriage. She doesn't ask about him much, and for that I'm thankful. The only piece of him that she has is his dimples. The rest is all me, from her cute button nose to her bright blue eyes. I know the day will come that she asks about the man who fathered her, but for now, she hasn't. He signed away all his rights to that precious girl without a second thought, all so he didn't have to pay me a dime. The minute he found out he didn't have access to my trust fund, he discarded us like we were yesterday's trash. It saddens me to think he could give up something so beautiful so easily, but the Ethan I fell in love with disappeared shortly after we started dating, and although there were times I saw the old him there, he never came back. I watched the hope of him die before he slammed out of the house that last day, the final parting words just before he walked out of the divorce hearing creating a chasm so deep that I couldn't believe what he just said.

*"Your father was right. Having a kid doesn't change anything. In fact, all it did was make you fat and undesirable. I'm happy to be rid of you and that little shit."* I shake off his words as I hear her running back into the kitchen, ready and willing to help me make our dinner.

The rest of the evening is quiet. We eat, play our matching game, and at the end of the night, we read her favorite story before bed. As I lay her in her bed, kissing her forehead, I whisper the same thing I've been telling her since we left that house, "We are going to be just fine, you and me. Us against the world, kiddo."

I pour myself a glass of my favorite Moscato and take a seat at my desk in the corner of the living room. Taking a sip, I set the glass off to the side as I wait for my pictures from today to upload to my editing studio. I don't like working when Savi's awake and tend to get my best work done when she's asleep. Our time together is ours, so editing is my way of escaping after a long day. I click through each of the pictures, making my way through the ones I know are definite keepers and moving them to their own folder before moving the rest into another folder.

Pulling open the first picture, I smile at the scene in front of me. It's a shot of Savi with the puppy at the beach. Her smile is so big, dimples set in each cheek. I can hear her laughter in my mind. The hair that escaped her braids blowing wildly, but all you see is the pure joy radiating out of her. Her eyes are a picture of unhindered happiness. That smile is how I know I made the right decision for us. No matter how hard it may have been, I can rest easy knowing that my daughter is happy. It's all I can ever ask for. My marriage was nothing but a string of affairs on Ethan's end. The memories threaten to take over as I sit here looking at the smile on my daughter's face, but I refuse to give in to them, not when all the proof I need is sitting right here staring at me from my computer screen.

I click through the sunset pictures, notating the light and any adjustments I may need to make. Our main reason for the beach trip today was to scope out the location for my next session. It's not my normal type of session, but Lucas begged me to help him out when a photographer they had backed out at the last minute. After getting some details and ensuring I wouldn't have to travel, I made it work. I rescheduled all but one of my clients for the day. I owed him for everything he's done and even though this isn't my wheelhouse, it'll be nice to see Lucas in work mode. After finding out that it would be a sunset shoot on the water, I knew that I'd need to get the timing right for the perfect lighting for the scene I'd be capturing. I work through each of the shots, adjusting and touching up as needed. I can see tomorrow's shoot coming alive before me as I work through each edit, picturing the moment in my mind as if it were happening right here and now. I'm so focused on my work that I don't notice my phone buzzing beside me.

**Madison:** Hey girl hey. Do you need me to grab Savi tomorrow?

Smiling at the text, my thoughts go to Madison. She's my best friend, other than Lucas. I met her shortly after I moved here, and she's become my saving grace. We ran into each other, literally, while I was scoping out a location for a photo shoot with Savannah. I'd been staring at my camera instead of watching where I was going, and then the next thing I knew, we were both on our ass staring at each other. Savi was off to the side laughing at us as we sat there. Madison always said our friendship was our very own "meet-cute", if only we were lesbians. Her sense of humor's one of my favorite things about her, not to mention, her love for my daughter. Those two are as inseparable as Lucas and Savi are.

**Natalie:** yes please. The session goes into the evening.

**Madison:** no problemo, you know I love that little bug.

**Natalie:** and she loves you.

I'm still smiling when I put my phone down and get back to editing.

I work later than I intended, the wine going down easier with each sip I take. Finishing up the last picture, I notice I'm also on my third glass of wine. I normally don't drink as much as I did but the thought of doing a high-profile magazine shoot has me feeling nervous. I sit back, my eyes going to the ceiling.

The day starts like it always does, with Savannah rushing around trying to find her shoes, again, while I rush around trying to get my gear together for today's clients. It took me a couple of years, but I finally gained a solid foothold when it comes to my photography. I own my business, full and clear, and my client list continues to grow steadily. It's gotten so busy that I had to put Savi in daycare because I couldn't keep up and I couldn't keep pushing her on to Madison, even though she kept insisting that it was okay. I don't honestly know where I'd be without her friendship in my life. *She will get sick of you too.* I shake off the nasty voice in my head. I even have my eyes on a studio downtown that I could use when I can't do outdoor shots.

"Savannah Marie, we have to get going, baby." I grab the last of my things and turn around to find her standing behind me. Her eyes are cast down as though she's ashamed to even look me in the eyes. I set my stuff back down again. Taking a deep breath, I prepare myself for another Savannah moment. I wouldn't trade these moments ever, but sometimes, I just wish she'd use them when I wasn't needing to leave the house in a hurry.

"Momma, no shoes." Her voice is trembling, thinking I'm about to yell at her for doing something wrong. Taking a deep breath, I do my best to make my voice as calm as possible.

"Oh, honey, they're in your cubby." Her sweet little face looks up at me with tear filled eyes as she shakes her head.

"I looked there already." Groaning in frustration, I walk over to her cubby and mentally curse as I realize she's indeed right, there are no shoes in her cubby. I run a hand through my hair as I turn to her.

"Baby, I would like to know where your shoes are. Why didn't you put them away where they go?" I can't expect much from her, she's only three. But there are days that her sass comes out, and I wonder if I'm dealing with a teenager instead. Today though, she's just a three-year-old who didn't put her shoes away and can't find them.

"I sorry, Mommy. I so sorry." She starts to cry, knowing it always goes straight to my heart. I lift her up and hold her close, soothing her tears as we walk back through the house. Walking into her room, I sit her on her bed and start the process of looking around.

"It's okay, baby. Did you check under your bed? Or in

your closet?" I dry the tears under her eyes as I look around the room, eyeing the closet.

"The closet has monsters, Mommy, I can't go in there." I suppress a smile and sneak over to the closet as she watches me with wide eyes. I grab her closet door and jump out at the same time I open it.

"Rawr." I yell, "Go away monsters!" Savannah giggles on her bed as I look around the messy closet, the sound making me smile.

"Found them." Grabbing the shoes, I go over to her and put them on her feet as quickly as I can.

"Thank you, Mommy. Monsters are so scary," she whispers as she hugs me tight while I finished lacing her up. Smiling at her sweet little face, I note that the tears are mostly dried up, her smile now taking residence on her face, dimples popping. I wish I could be as innocent as her again. *You'll never be as innocent as her again. You're nothing but a washed-up single mom who has nothing going for you.* I sigh as I stand up from my kneeling position and put my hand out to her, refusing to let the voices take over.

"Let's go, my little Savannah bug, it's time to get going." She takes off across the room and slams the closet door. She quickly takes my hand again before leading us out of the room.

Driving into BoothBay Harbor for work feels weird. When the photographer of our last shoot canceled, Justin went nuts. This was supposed to be one of my solo campaigns without Lauren. I don't do many throughout the year because we're more marketable as a couple. But lately, I've been wanting more and more jobs on my own, without my supposed girlfriend hanging all over me. When the photographer canceled, the first person I thought about was Natalie. She's not in the scene for this kind of job, and more of a life photographer, but her work's amazing. After the photographer walked out on us, I went to the ad manager for the company we're shooting for. After showing him her website, he told me to reach out to her and hire her.

It took some convincing, but she finally agreed, once she was able to confirm that she could move her other appointments around. Part of me feels bad for doing that to her, especially since her calendar is already booked out for months, but I needed this job. I must admit that having the ability to fix the photographer issue for the campaign gave me a thrill. It's not my place to make those kinds of suggestions, but I saw the opportunity and grabbed at it with both hands.

Pulling into my driveway, I watch as the waves crash on the shore on the other side of the guest house. Being away from Lauren this week is good for me. Ever since Natalie came into the picture, all Lauren does is harp on the fact that I haven't asked her to get married yet. It's fucking ridiculous. We aren't even in a real relationship, so why the hell does she think I'm going to marry her? We don't even see each other outside of the jobs we have, or when we are needed for some social engagement where having her on my arm is needed. We've never even slept together.

Grabbing my bags, I head into my house and drop everything off in the bedroom before heading into the kitchen. The shoot with Natalie isn't until later this afternoon, so I have some time before I need to be down at the beach on another part of the island. BoothBay Harbor is considered an island since it has water on three sides, but it's connected to the mainland by a highway bridge. I live on the west side while the shoot location is on the south side. It's not too far from my house, but one of the stipulations of doing it here was that we didn't do it near where I live. My home is my sanctuary away from the public and the last thing I need is the paparazzi or anyone finding out my address and stalking me.

Staring out the window above my sink, I take notice of the darkened windows in the guest house. Natalie must be doing her morning shoot that she told me she couldn't reschedule. It was a surprise engagement shoot for one of her first couples that she ever booked. I totally understood and we worked around it so she would be doing the job for me in the evening.

I spend the rest of the morning lounging. I don't get many opportunities for a break when I'm working, so I'm taking full advantage of this while I can. Sitting back on the recliner in my living room, the thoughts of stepping back from modeling take hold. I never intended modeling to be a full-time thing. It was just a way to help me get to the next level, a way to pay for college without having to rely on my parents' money. But then they paired me with Lauren, and I was getting booked for advertisements months in advance.

Since the day I talked to Natalie, and later met her daughter, I've been thinking about stepping back more and more. But the fear of failure stops me every single time I start making moves to step back. Then there's the whole thing with Lauren. Stifling a groan, I sit up and run my hands through my hair. How the hell do I even begin with that shitshow of a relationship that isn't even real? I know I need to end it, especially if I'm stepping away from modeling.

Grabbing my bag, I head for my walk-in shower to wash away the nastiness of the drive and maybe figure out what the hell I'm going to do.

Stepping out of the shower, I rotate my neck, enjoying how loose my muscles feel. The first thing I did when I made it in the modeling scene was install a massaging waterfall shower head. That thing is a masterpiece. Wrapping the towel around my waist, I make my way out into my bedroom. Just being here has me relaxed more than usual. I usually don't mind being away, but lately, it's felt redundant. The hotels all look the same, the jobs are all the same. I look forward to coming home more than I do working. Once upon a time, I couldn't wait to be on a plane to a new destination. But these days, I hate that my schedule has me leaving more than staying.

Pulling on my briefs, I also grab shorts and a beater to wear until it's time for me to leave. The red blinking light on

my phone has me rolling my eyes at the number of notifications I missed from Justin. I was only in there for fifteen
minutes, but he hates being kept waiting. I rotate my neck one
more time, steeling myself from what I'm about to see. Sitting
on the edge of my bed, I quickly dismiss the five missed calls
and open the texts, reading through them one by one.

**Justin:** hey, just got to the location. Looks good. Crew
should be arriving soon.

**Justin:** crew just checked in. When will you be on
your way?

**Justin:** Paparazzi is swarming, get your ass down here!

*Fuck. How the hell did they find out?* I exit the notifications
without answering him and log into social media. I'm not a
huge fan of the apps, but they help me touch base with my
fans and keep an eye on things. Tapping the notifications, the
first thing I notice is that Lauren tagged me in a photo. *I'm not
even with her.* Taking a deep breath, I click it.

The photo shows her at the beach of our last location
together before I left for my solo shoot. She's got her
sunglasses on, her lips puckered into a sad face as she holds an
umbrella drink with an empty lounge chair beside her. The
caption reads *'all alone on the beach... what's a girl to do?'*
followed by who knows how many hashtags. My tag is clearly
sitting in the middle of the empty chair.

I force close the app and lean forward onto my knees.
Lauren inadvertently let the press know we weren't shooting
together, even though this has been scheduled for months.
Hell, she should be on her way to do one of her own shoots
without me. *Why would she tag me like that knowing that she's
off doing her own thing?* And then it hits me. I'm in at home,

with Natalie. Ever since the whole argument when I left the job after our phone call, Lauren has been playing the 'woe is me' card.

The minute Natalie's name enters my brain, I realize just how bad this is. *Fuck. She's not going to like this.* Rushing to get myself dressed, I grab my shoes and slip them on, nearly tripping on my own feet in the process. I'm really hoping Natalie isn't at the location yet. I need to get these paparazzi out of there before she sees them. The last thing she needs is them terrorizing her or making implications that aren't even there.

The moment I pull up to the south beach entrance I can see the place is swarming with press and paparazzi as they try to get any picture to make a story out of. I don't see Natalie anywhere around and breathe a sigh of relief that she isn't here to see this craziness. Getting out of the car, I run a hand through my hair trying to calm myself. The last thing I need is for one of these assholes to get a story highlighting my temper.

The paparazzi is one of the biggest things I dislike about my career, other than always being gone. They like to weave stories together without any real proof. They take pictures of compromising situations and twist them to fit their agenda. I have nothing against the profession, because a guy must make money, but I do have something against their moral system. They tear apart families and couples, not caring because it's all about the bottom line.

Coming into the entrance, Justin sees me and starts waving at me to join him. His wave doesn't go unnoticed and soon I'm swarmed with people putting cameras in my face, yelling at me. *Why aren't you with Lauren? What's with this new location?* Question after question is fired at me and it takes all I have not to punch the next guy to shove a camera at me.

"Everyone, please calm down. Lucas here is going to set up a small talk with y'all while the crew gets the location ready. If you'll follow me, I'll lead you on over." Justin takes control of the crowd and pulls them down the beach, away from the crew and out of my face.

Taking a deep breath, I try to push the stress off before heading off after them. Just as I go to stand in front of them, they start firing off rapid questions one right after the other. Justin steps forward, putting himself between me and the cameras.

"Alright. We don't have much time so if y'all could please quiet down." Justin yells over the crowd, using his hand in the air to get their attention. They instantly quiet, making me glad I have him in my corner.

"I wasn't exactly expecting this, so I'll be quick." I start, noticing a few people grab out pads of paper like I'm the president giving a notable speech. "I'm doing a solo shoot today here at the south beach of BoothBay Harbor. Every so often, Lauren and I do these to help keep ourselves relevant outside of our joint shoots. This in no way reflects upon my relationship with her. I'm simply here to do a job." Justin smiles and nods at my impromptu speech.

"Why isn't she here supporting you? According to her social media feed, she's at a beach in Florida." One guy asks from out in the crowd.

"As I said, we both do our own shoots. Lauren is currently working on her own solo campaign currently. We'll be meeting up again in a few weeks for our next joint job." Smiling, I step back, and Justin takes charge again.

"Alright everyone, we don't have any more time for questions as the crew needs to get Lucas into hair and makeup. This is a closed set so I need you all to pack up and get out of here or we will have to call the cops." The press moans and groans but slowly, they head out.

"Fuck man. What the fuck was that? All because Lauren posted that picture on the beach?" I put a hand on his shoulder as I watch them all walk away.

"You know them, bloodhounds trying to sniff out any story they can find." He rolls his eyes and walks off. I trail behind him, thankful as fuck that Natalie wasn't here for that circus. Pulling my phone out of my pocket, I scroll through until I find Lauren's contact info.

"I'll be right there." I call after Justin. He waves me off and I move to a secluded area to make my call.

"Hey babe." She yells into my ear, the music in the background so loud I can barely hear her. I hear a few whispered words, but I can't make anything out and then everything goes quiet. "Okay, that's better."

"What the hell were you thinking?" I hear her gasp at my outrage, but I know all this shit started because of her stupid post on social media.

"I don't know what you mean?" She tries to play innocent, but I'm so fucking sick and tired of her doing this. It's like Natalie coming into the picture set her levels on psycho. I don't know how I didn't see this shit coming when we first got together.

"The fucking picture, Lauren." I'm doing my best to keep my voice down, but I'm drawing looks from the crew. The same crew that usually works with the both of us.

"Oh that." I can feel the dismissal in her words. "That was just me having fun." She giggles and hiccups, indicating that she's intoxicated.

"I don't have time for this shit Lauren. I came to my location and was swarmed by paparazzi questioning me because of that fucking post." She giggles again, clearly not listening to a word I'm saying. "Are you even listening?"

"Something about pizza, right?" She laughs so hard she snorts. I'm seething at this point, my phone so close to cracking from the pressure I'm putting on it as I hold the phone to my ear.

"I'm done with this fucking shit." I hang up on her, breathing deeply as I try to calm myself before going down to the hair and makeup tent.

O nce I get Savi settled at daycare, I head out to start scoping today's first location. The clients I have this morning are a couple I've been shooting for a while. I did their college graduation pictures, back before this became a real business, and now today, I'll be shooting a surprise engagement. The boyfriend contacted me not too long ago asking if we could do it. He knew that his girlfriend had already arranged a couple's shoot with me, and he wanted to use this as his special moment. Even though I'm no longer married myself, these kinds of shoots have a special place in my heart. *It's as close as you'll get to real love without having it for yourself.* My inner voice stabs deeper than usual.

The first location I arrive is where they did their college graduation photos. We're recreating a timeline for them, and then the final location will be a whole new setting for them, a secluded beach on the other side of the island, which also happens to be where I'll be shooting Lucas' campaign this afternoon and into the evening. I'm glad that Madison is picking up Savi for me since the daycare will close before I'll be finished. The couple I'm shooting should be arriving any minute, so I start taking out all my equipment and getting myself ready to work.

I can already see where I want to stage them, how I want to pose them as I take in my surroundings. It's all coming to life in my head, each shot forming before they even arrive. I know we'll be recreating some of the pictures, but also taking new ones as well. I start taking practice shots, without the clients, so I can adjust my settings for the current natural light we have. I'll have to do this with each location, so I'm glad to have a little bit of time to myself before they show up.

After a few minutes, they show up and look just as in love as they did when I first met them. *The first day I met Ethan enters my head, his radiant smile drawing me to him that day.* Shaking it off, I send them a small wave. Thomas shares a knowing smile with me, and I start the process of getting them in position and posed. They're smiling and laughing, doing what people do when they're young and in love. I remember those times, but I don't remember being as carefree as these two are. They're everything I wanted to be when I was younger and in love. *But my young love was a foolish sham, a delicate piece of wool covering my unsuspecting eyes, blinding me to the truth of it all.* I get more shots than I need, trying my best not to let my own thoughts get in the way. These two make my job so easy, and to capture their love, and I don't know if I can classify this as work.

We move to the next location, each one coming together just as beautifully as the last. Their smiles are everything. The laughter Thomas gets out of Britney is so perfect that I can't help but get shots every time she laughs. There is something so pure about it, so happy, that you can't help but want to smile at the sound of it. *I never laughed as carefree as she does. I don't think Ethan ever looked at me the way he looks at her.*

As we get closer to the beach, I can see Thomas getting more and more nervous.

"I'm going to get some shots of Britney on her own." I bring her down to the waterline, having her take off her shoes. The lighting coming in is perfect and I know these shots will probably be some of my best work to date.

"What if she says no?" Thomas asks me as I come back to him, kneeling to get the perfect shot.

"Thomas, she loves you. Her smile and laugh, everything coming out of her today is pure, unfiltered joy. She won't say no." I talk him down as I work the camera, the clicking of the button the only other sound between his labored breathing and my pep talk. He smiles as he watches her pose, as I take shot after shot as she walks along the waterline. She turns towards me and seeing Thomas, the smile on her face becomes so blindingly beautiful. I can feel the love radiating from her as I focus in on her with my camera. I make a motion for Thomas to join her.

I take picture after picture, the love between them so transparent that anyone can see it, even from miles away. And then the moment happens. The sun is at the perfect setting to where the lighting makes them almost ethereal, casting a glow around them that makes the photographer in me squeal with delight. Thomas drops to one knee. *Visions of my own forced engagement filter into my head.* Squeezing my eyes shut, I will the scene in my head away. Opening my eyes back up, I capture the look on her face as she watches him, as she listens to each of the words he's expressing to her. I'm far enough away that I can't hear him, but the tears of joy slipping down her cheeks and her smile gives away the happiness she's emoting. She nods her head at him, and he slips the ring on her finger. I capture each moment throughout the entire thing, tears falling from my own eyes as I watch their love unfold before me. *You were never good enough to experience a love like that.*

Walking towards them from my shooting spot, I can see

the smiles haven't left their faces. They are so happy and so in love, they don't notice me approach.

"Congratulations you two. I just want a few more shots, up close, and then we can call it and you guys can go celebrate." I smile at them and then pose them. I take shots of her ring being held out from them as they smile at each other. Shots of her hand on his cheek as they look each other in the eyes. I capture moments that I know they'll want. The ones that they can look back on and smile, remembering today as a beautiful memory in time.

Smiling, I put down the camera, and I head back over to them. "You're all set."

"You knew about this, didn't you?" Britney asks me, still staring at her ring finger in shock.

"I did." Her blinding smile causes a smile to take over my face as well. She comes in and gives me a big hug.

"It was perfect. Thank you, Natalie." She whispers in my ear. I can feel the joy in her voice and for a moment, I revel in it. Releasing me, she takes Thomas' hand.

"I should have some sneak peeks up soon, and I will get your gallery up by the end of the week." She hugs me again before Thomas steps up and gives me a quick hug and then they are on their way back to their car, off to celebrate their moment, and I smile as I watch them. Their love and joy make today one of my favorite shoots to date. *This is the only way to experience true love these days. Through the lens of my camera.*

Walking back to my stuff, I finally allow myself time to breathe. On shoots, I try to stay professional, keeping myself to a strict way of being. I refuse to allow my own baggage and thoughts get in the way of creating any moment. But now, with the shoot done, the thoughts are invading my head again. I find myself going back to wondering where everything went wrong with my own marriage. Ethan's cheating being the one thing that broke our marriage. *Why wasn't I enough? When did the love die? Was there ever any real love there? Was I just a name to him?* The questions beat themselves into my head as I sit by my camera bag, staring out at the waves.

Grabbing my stuff, I take one last look at the waves and walk down the road to the coffee shop. I need all the caffeine if I want to get through this shoot with Lucas.

Walking into the secluded area of the beach feels like I'm entering a secret world. The crews are bustling all around as they get things set up. There are several tents set up for wardrobe, one for makeup. Each tent has a crew working in it on its own. Seeing all this hustle makes me slightly happy that I work for myself and don't have to deal with all this craziness daily.

"Ma'am, may I help you?" A younger man walks up to me. The first thing I noticed is that he's about my age. He's good looking but his suit throws off the vibe that he's pretentious. I've dealt with these types all my life, so I paste a fake smile on my face and reach out to shake his hand.

"I'm Natalie Conaway. I'm filling in as the photographer for this shoot." He takes my hand with a look of shock on his face. I don't know who this man is, but he clearly wasn't expecting me to show up.

"Ah. Well, let me show you to your tent. We have all the equipment you may need in there." He starts walking off, expecting me to follow him. I hesitate for just a minute before taking a deep breath and getting in step behind him.

"And your name is?" I ask as we approach the tent appointed for me.

"Oh, my apologies. I'm Justin Hammond." He says this like I'm supposed to know who he is. He reads the confusion on my face and shakes his head before continuing. "I'm an agent." Nodding my head, I don't say anything. *Whose agent is he?*

"Natalie. You made it." I turn around to Lucas running up to me. He's stripped down to a pair of board shorts and nothing else. My breath catches as I watch him make his way over. All I see are shiny abs, like he's been covered in baby oil. I can't even avert my eyes away from him. I can count eight prominently displayed on his stomach. "I see you met Justin," he says as he reaches us. My eyes immediately go to the man I was just standing with, who is watching me with curious eyes.

"We just met," Justin says, his eyes never leaving me. "Natalie just got here, and I was showing her to her tent."

"I'm glad you could do this, Nat." I turn to Lucas and smile at him. I refuse to let my eyes move down from his face. I didn't realize he looked like *that* under his clothes and now the image is forever burned into my memory.

"It's my pleasure. Let me get my camera out and get set up and then we can get started." I move to enter the tent and place my bag on the table set up for me. Taking a deep breath, I look around at everything they provided.

"What the hell were you thinking?" Justin's voice interrupts me as I start pulling together the lenses I'm planning on using.

"What the fuck are you talking about?" Lucas shoots back. I'm frozen as I listen to them argue just outside my tent.

"You didn't tell me *she* is who you hired for this." Justin's voice is dripping with disdain. My shoulders slump forward, wishing like hell I'd said no when Lucas asked me to do this. *You're not good enough to be a photographer for a high-end shoot like this.* The inner voice pulls me down even further.

"She's an amazing photographer and my best friend, asshole." Lucas sounds pissed but I'm too lost in my own self-sabotage to really let his words reach me.

"You're asking for trouble." I hear Justin say. Going to the other side of the tent, I wipe the tears off my face. *What the hell am I doing here?*

"Nat?" I turn to see Lucas at the entrance of the tent, his eyes full of concern at the sight of tears on my face.

"I think you need to find someone else." I start packing my stuff back up, but his hand finds mine and stops me. The tingle I feel every time he touches me intensifies as my eyes find his.

"You're the one I want to do this job. Justin's a dick, so don't let his words affect you. I know how good you are, let's go prove it." I shrug him off, not wanting to be here anymore. When I first took this job, it was mainly to settle that feeling of debt to Lucas after all he's done for me and Savi.

"I don't belong here." My whispered words have his shoulders slumping slightly. I turn back to my bag, wishing like hell I could be strong enough to do something like this for him.

"I swear I'm gonna kick his ass. He may be my agent but he's also my friend and he should trust that I know what I'm talking about." I give him a small smile before I start trying to pack up again. "Natalie, I need you to do this." I turn to face him again, opening my mouth to speak but one word has me stopping. "Please."

Nodding my head, I grab the lenses I want to use and my bag. I wave him ahead of me to exit the tent.

"Natalie, this is Mr. Arnold Rainier. Arnold, our photographer, Natalie Conaway. I'm going to finish getting ready, and should be good to go shortly." Lucas introduces me to the ad manager for the company, giving me a big smile before running off.

"So, Lucas tells us that you own your photography business? What kind of photography do you do?" Arnold is an older gentleman, also wearing a suit. Considering how Justin reacted earlier, my guard's up.

"I mainly do lifestyle photography with emphasis on families and couples, but I also do landscape and nature when I'm able to." I give him a tight lip smile, which has him grinning wide.

"That's quite a feat for such a young woman. I've looked over your shots on your website and I have to say, I'm impressed." My smile widens as he starts to tell me what they're looking for today from the shots I'm taking. I can see everything in my mind as I work through each shot he says must happen. "The shots on your site are beautiful, Natalie, but I have to say, they pale in comparison to you." A blush rises onto my cheeks. *He's flirting with me.*

"That's very nice of you to say. I'm excited to get started." The guard I had up when we were first introduced lowers as we continue to chat.

"I'm equally as excited to see what you can do, my dear." He winks at me. *This man is a shameless flirt.* By the time Lucas is done, Arnold has me giggling and laughing like we've been friends for years.

"Ah, the man of the hour has returned." Arnold shakes Lucas' hand. "I'll let you two get to work. I can't wait to see the magic you both create." He winks at me before walking off.

"I'm happy to see that smile on your face, Nat." I turn to Lucas and shake my head at him as we head down to the water's edge.

Shooting with Lucas was probably the most fun I've ever had doing a non-lifestyle shoot. I had to do these types of shoots for some of my classes, so I knew exactly what was needed of me. The crew were all amazing, working with me when I wanted to change things up to get a better shot. Lucas had me smiling and laughing at his antics the entire time.

"That was awesome, Nat." Lucas comes up behind me and wraps me in his arms. I sigh in his arms. I've always loved getting hugged by Lucas. His arms have a way of making me feel protected when everything around me feels like it's falling apart at the seams. *He'll realize how broken you really are, don't get too used to this.* The voices in my head have me pulling away from him.

I give him a small smile before turning away. I steel myself against the tears I know are about to fall from my eyes and grab my phone out of the pocket I keep it stashed in during my shoots. I trust Madison to watch after Savannah, so I never feel the need to check it when I'm working. I unlock the screen and watch as notification after notification come streaming in. Seventeen missed calls from Madison, two voicemails and four text messages. Before I even try to listen to the voicemails, I open the text messages first.

I have no idea what's going on but something's wrong, I can feel it. She never calls while I'm on a shoot, much less this many times, all she ever does is text me to let me know what's going on with my handful of a three-year-old. All four text messages are from her. Scrolling to the top, I start from the beginning, not even paying attention to the last message.

**Madison:** Just picked up bug. I know you're at a shoot, but I wanted to let you know. I was a little late picking her up, so she's on a sass kick. No worries, I got her though.

I smile at this message. When Savi has a sass kick, it's like dealing with a hormonal teenager, except with feet-stomping and all the things that come with being a three-year-old.

**Madison:** We are going to the park. Savi's wanting to play and I have no toys here.

**Madison:** Come by my house when you are done. I'm making tacos and margaritas.  Savi begged for tacos and you know we can't have tacos without margaritas. *wink*

My stomach growls as I read that message, pushing me to get back to the tent and grab my stuff a little faster. I stretch myself from all the kneeling I did today. Realizing I didn't read the last message, I stop and look at my phone. Time stamped thirty minutes ago, the message glares at me as I drop to the ground, knees hitting the soft sand, phone slipping through my fingers as I replay the message repeatedly in my head.

**Madison:** Get to the hospital Nat. Savannah got hurt!

## *Chapter Six*

LUCAS

The minute her knees hit the sand, I'm at her side. I don't know what just happened but seeing her break like this is shredding me.

"Nat, what happened?" I kneel beside her. Her eyes haven't left her phone since she hit the ground. Grabbing her phone, I maneuver it so I can read the last message. Without even thinking about what I'm doing, I pull her into me, both of us collapsing on the sand as my knees give out from the weight of adding her.

"I need to go. I need to get to Savi." She tries to push off me, but I hold her to me.

"I know. Just let me make sure you're calm before I let you go." She nods and lets me hold onto her. The shirt I put on after we finished is being soaked by her tears, but I don't care. I can't help but notice how small she feels against me. When she first got to town, she always wore baggy clothes, hiding her body from the world. But as time passed, she started wearing clothing more fitting. The first time I saw her in anything other than a baggy sweatshirt, I nearly lost it. She has a beautiful body, even if she refuses to see it that way. Today is no different, she showed up in an off the shoulder t-shirt that highlighted the delicate curve of her neck. It wasn't form fitting, but the way it sat on her made me wish I knew what she looked like underneath.

"I'm calm, Lucas. Thank you." Her voice pulls me from the thoughts of her without clothing and I mentally punch myself for allowing my mind to get away with me, especially when she's dealing with what's going on. "I'll call you once I know more." I watch as she pushes away from me and looks toward the tents where her stuff is. I want to go with her, but I need to meet with Arnold and the rest of the agency he's working with. I feel stuck in a no win situation.

Standing, I help her up and pull her into another hug. "I'd be on my way with you if I could be. I just need to finish up some things and then as soon as you tell me where you are, I'll be there." She nods into my chest before pulling back from me.

"Thanks, Lucas." She gives me another small smile before turning and walking off. Seeing her walk off hurts more than I can say. I want to say fuck it and run after her.

"What was that?" Justin asks as I walk back to the tent where my stuff is waiting.

"Not that it's any of your fucking business, but her daughter got hurt." I shrug him off and move into the tent.

"Oh shit, that fucking sucks." Turning to him, I notice a look on his face that I've never seen before. His eyes show genuine concern that has me questioning so many things. Justin's an amazing agent, but his humanity is a rarity to see. I say we're friends, but I've never actually seen him be anything other than the asshole he was outside Nat's tent earlier.

"She's going to call me later to update me." He nods at me before moving into the tent with me.

"I'm sorry about earlier." He pulls up a seat and sits, his shoulders slumping forward as he looks at me. "She was completely professional today and what I said was completely out of line."

"Yea, it was. You're an asshole. And it's not me you have to apologize to, it's Natalie. She heard you, fucker." His eyes get big as my words hit him.

"Fuck." He puts his face into his hands, which only causes more questions to formulate in my head. *What the fuck is going on with him?* I shake the question off. I don't have time to worry about him with everything else going on.

"Yea, fuck is right." He nods into his hands as I grab my shit and get ready to meet with Arnold and go over the shots from today to figure out which ones the campaign will be using.

All I can think about is Savi being hurt the entire time I'm sitting there listening to them go back and forth over which photos to use. We moved from the tent we were in, to an outdoor cafe so the crew could tear everything down. I should be paying attention, considering this is the side of modeling I want to be on, but I can't get the image of Natalie breaking on the beach out of my head.

"Lucas, are you listening?" Justin's voice pulls me from my thoughts.

"My apologies, what's going on?" He smiles at me, knowing I'm doing my best to be present, even if my mind's somewhere else.

"I was just saying that Natalie did amazing work today and we have more pictures than we can possibly use. There isn't one shot that she took that isn't worthy of our campaign." Arnold says, his smile genuine and reaching his eyes.

"She'll be pleased to hear that." My honesty has him smiling wider.

"Speaking of, where is she?" he asks, looking around the table.

"She had to get going." I say, knowing it's not my place to give any details about what's going on.

Arnold nods his head at me and continues speaking with the rest of the team about the session from today. I look over to Justin and he has a glazed look in his eyes, like even he has checked out of the conversation.

"Well, gentlemen, if that's all there is, I need to be going." I stand and excuse myself. I don't even know why they ask me to be a part of these things. I never get final say in what shot's used but Justin says it's better to be present, so they can build that relationship with you. The better the relationship, the more bookings you get. It's how we've always worked.

"Thanks for your time." Arnold shakes my hand and I give Justin a small nod of my head as I walk out. Grabbing my phone, I notice I missed a call from Natalie, along with a text.

**Natalie:** heading to Charleston.

*Fuck, that's not a good sign.* Pulling open her contact info, I hit the green button. The phone rings several times before going to voicemail. I hang up and try again. Same thing. *Shit, damn it, fuck.* All the curse words are rolling through my head like a tsunami.

Getting into my car, I make my way home. I don't know where they are in Charleston since there are multiple hospitals so until I have more information, the last thing she needs is me barging in. Just as I pull into my driveway, my phone ringing pulls me out of my daze. Nat's name is flashing at me on the screen.

"Nat?"

"Lucas, where are you?"

"Heading home."

"You need to come to Charleston Pediatric, room 423. Please hurry." Her voice is barely a whisper, almost like it was the night I called her back at the hotel when she first left Texas.

"What happened?"

"Just come, please. I'll see you soon." She hangs up on me and I sit staring at my phone in shock for a minute before her words hit me. *Pediatric unit.*

Walking into the hospital feels like I'm living in a dream. Until I see things for myself, I'm in a state of denial in my head. Opening the door to the room Natalie told me, I walk in, and immediately drop my bags as Natalie flings herself into my arms and breaks down. Her arms are wound so tight around me that I don't even know how I hadn't fallen over when I caught her. I just hold onto her as tight as I can, knowing that when she's ready, she'll be the strong woman I know that she is. Walking us across the empty room, I sit us on the chair in the corner with her in my lap. Savi isn't here and I have no idea what's going on so I hold onto her, hoping she calms down enough to tell me.

After about ten minutes, her sobs finally subside enough for her to pull back from me. Her tear-stained face breaks my heart. She untangles herself from me but doesn't leave my lap.

"Where is Savi? What happened, Nat?" I whisper to her, which has her looking at me and then back down at her hands.

"Savi fell while she was playing at the playground with Madison. She hit her head on a rock and lost consciousness. Madison had been trying to get a hold of me, but I was at the shoot with you. I leave my phone on silent while I'm working. I didn't know until they were already at the hospital in town." She takes a deep breath and looks me in the eyes. "They were prepping her for transfer here when I got there."

Placing a soft kiss to her forehead, I ask softly, not wanting to cause her anymore pain, but I need to know the extent of what is happening. "Where is she?"

"CT. They are measuring the swelling to see if surgical intervention is needed." Her lip is quivering, and I know she's about to fall apart again. I pull her into my chest and rub her back as she quietly cries on me. I keep rubbing her back, but my mind is running a million miles per hour. *Why is Natalie here by herself? Where's Madison? If this happened during her watch, why the hell isn't she here with her?* The questions keep shooting, and soon I can't contain myself anymore. Before I can say anything, she continues. "She has a large contusion on the right side of her head that is causing her brain to swell. When she landed, she landed full force on the rock." The tears are steadily streaming out of her eyes and all I know is I'd give anything to take this pain from her.

"Nat, where's Madison?" My voice is a little harsh, but I'm trying hard to rein in any anger I might be feeling right now.

"I sent her home when I found out you were on your way. I've been holding it together this whole time because she felt horrible that it happened. I didn't want her to see me falling apart because it would've only made things worse." Her voice is still barely above a whisper. Hearing that she stayed strong until she saw me simmers my anger, but only slightly. I'll deal with the other shit later, the only thing I can focus on is that she knew she could fall apart with me.

"Baby, I wish you hadn't sent her away until I got here." Her entire body goes stiff at me calling her baby, and I wonder where the hell that even came from. I hadn't called her that, ever. It was either Nat or Natalie. There were no pet names between us, not even years ago when we had been closer than ever. Just as she's about to say something, the door opens, and the nurses are wheeling a bed into the room. Natalie jumps from my lap and goes to the bedside, grabbing Savannah's hand as they wheel her in.

"I see your friend made it in," the nurse gives me a soft smile. Natalie looks up at me and then quickly back down. I smile softly at the nurse and just give a small nod. I wait patiently while they get the bed in place, working around Natalie as they get the wires and everything where they need to be.

My breath's taken away as they turn the bed to where it's facing me. I can't move, the sight in front of me rooting me to where I stand. The only thing I see right now is my sweet little Savannah. Her little body looks even smaller in this giant bed. There are wires coming from everywhere. She has a tube down her throat, bandages all over her usual crazy curly hair. I choke on tears as I see the little girl that I've come to love in so many ways looking so much tinier and more fragile than the day I met her. Her eyes are closed, but you can see bruising and cuts on her sweet little face.

The pain in my chest is radiating as I struggle to make my lungs work. I force myself to take a breath. I wasn't sure what the hell I was expecting, but it sure as fuck wasn't this. My feet are stuck in place as I take in everything, staring at the bed, willing it to be a bad dream or I am hallucinating. Something besides this harsh reality being placed right in front of me. I don't want any of this to be true.

Once the nurse finishes, she lets us know that the doctor will be in shortly to discuss what's going on. I'm still stuck in the same position, barely registering the words she's saying. As soon as she walks out and shuts the door softly behind her, my strength fails, and I'm falling to my knees. A loud sob rips out of my mouth as I hit the ground. *Fuck.*

I can't see past my tears as I crumble into myself. The pain in my chest feels like it's trying to tear me apart from the inside. All the anger from before disappears, as I feel myself succumb to complete and utter misery. Every sound in the room has faded into the distance and the only thing I can hear is myself sobbing, but even that sounds foreign to me. My breathing's becoming erratic, but I'm frozen in my spot. I can't even register the pain that is shooting in my knees from landing on them on the hard floor here in the room.

"Lucas, I need you to try to breathe for me." Natalie's voice cuts through the fog. And it's then that I realize she's sitting beside me, pulling me into her, just as I had done with her when I helped her on the beach. But I can't look at her right now, I can't even think straight. I push her off me, but she just comes right back in, her arms pulling harder, forcing me to topple over. My head lands in her lap and she's looking down at me, tears coming down from her own eyes.

"Breathe, Lucas. Please. I need you to breathe." I take in her eyes, they look so sad, but they also look scared shitless. She's right. I can't break when she needs me. I need to be strong for her right now, and I can see in her eyes that she needs me to be. I take a deep breath, as deep as I can, pushing past the pain that emits from forcing my lungs to work. The tears are still coming down, both from my eyes and from hers, but our gazes stay locked as she takes deep breaths with me, exhales with me.

It's been three days since I got here. The only time I've left the room is to get us some food or coffee from the cafeteria. Natalie refuses to leave at all, so it's on me to make sure she takes care of herself, even if she doesn't want to. I haven't broken again since that first night, and I won't. Not when I know that both of my girls need me to be strong for them. *My girls?* When did I start thinking of them both that way? Savannah has always been my girl, but I haven't dared think of

Natalie that way in a very long time. *Now isn't the time to dwell on this shit, get it together, Lucas.*

Heading back from the cafeteria with coffee, I had just gotten off the phone with Justin and told him to reschedule all my stuff for the next month, just until we knew what was going on. He didn't like it, but he knew I wasn't changing my mind on this. Lauren has tried calling several times since I've been here, and each time, I send her straight to voicemail. I don't have the energy to deal with her right now, on top of everything else going on. She's the last person on my mind. I'll deal with all the drama going on with her when things here settle down and I can find time to breathe again.

Savannah hasn't woken up yet, but the swelling's been going down, albeit very slowly if you ask me. The doctor told us yesterday that if it continues to go down, there will be no need for surgery. For now, they're just keeping her on sedatives to let her brain heal on its own. There's a CT scheduled for later today to see if we can start the process of weaning her off and removing the breathing tube, but until then, it's just the beeps of the machines and Natalie's off-key singing of every boyband in 90s history.

Walking back into the room, I stop at the entrance and watch as Natalie sings to Savi. It's what she does every day around this time, right before they wheel our girl off to CT. She puts on her favorite 90s playlist and sings all their favorite songs to her. If it came out in that decade, Natalie knows it. It's her playlist for cooking, cleaning, editing, everything. Savannah knows these songs just as well as her mom, seeing as she was raised on it. I can only laugh at her favorite music. If it was my choice, we'd be playing some rock or country. But these moments, watching Natalie be silly with these songs, I wouldn't trade them for anything. Except maybe watching Savi dancing and singing with her.

As if realizing someone's watching her, Natalie looks up to

me. She gives me a tight-lipped smile and motions for me to come all the way in. She turns the playlist off and grabs the coffee from my right hand as I offer it to her.

"Thank you. You know you don't have to stay, right?" She takes a sip from her cup and looks at me.

"As long as y'all are here, this is where I am. Don't even try to make me leave, Nat. It's not happening." I give her my own tight-lipped smile as I take a drink from my own coffee. My face scrunches at the taste and I realize I gave her my cup. A giggle comes out of her mouth as she watches my face contort in horror as the sweetness of her coffee attacks every taste bud in my mouth. Hearing that giggle is like hearing the water crest on the shore, it's everything to me, but fuck, this tastes like straight sugar.

I glare at her. "You seriously just let me drink this frou-frou shit? You took a sip of that and knew it was mine and didn't say a thing?" A wide smile breaks on her face and she giggles even harder.

"You should have seen your face." By now, she's laughing so hard, her eyes are watering from it. I gag as I burp the sweetness back up.

"How can you drink this shit?" I give her the cup she should've had and take mine back, chugging as much of it as I can to get the sweetness out of my mouth. She's still laughing at me, so I don't expect an answer out of her any time soon. I just continue drinking and glaring at her.

After a few minutes, Nat takes deep breaths trying to calm her breathing down from laughing so hard. She looks over to Savi in the bed, and I see the tears starting to form in her eyes as she watches her little girl, looking so helpless. Just as I'm about to speak up, the nurses come in.

"It's that time. It'll be about an hour before we can get her back up in here, you two should go to the healing garden. Get some fresh air," the nurse tells us as she starts prepping the bed for transport. We don't say anything, just watch as they get everything put up and start wheeling her out of the door.

"Let's go take a walk." I stand up and offer Natalie my hand. She stares at it before looking back over where the bed was. "Come on. They'll be a bit and I promise we'll be back before them. You need to get out of this room. Don't argue with me." She takes a deep breath, puts her hand in mine and we walk out of the room together, hand in hand, stopping at the trash can by the nurses' station to throw out our cups. The minute her hand is in mine, I feel peace. I don't know what's going on with us, if there could even be an us, but holding her hand sends chills through my entire body. I notice the small chills take over her arm and I smile to myself knowing it's my touch that caused them.

# Chapter Seven

NATALIE

Over the course of the past three years, I'd been so consumed by ensuring that Savannah was loved and cared for, that I put myself on the back burner. I didn't think about me in any way, shape, or form. Other than therapy and my photography certification, everything centered around her. Come to think of it, even those were done with her in mind, knowing that they had to be done so she could have a better mother. It was easier to ignore the voices when all my attention was on her instead of me. Only now, the voices remind me of just how frail I am, how weak I've become. The day we arrived in BoothBay Harbor, my life became solely centered on Savannah. The divorce had wrung me dry, emotionally and mentally. Ethan was pissed off because he didn't get his grubby hands on my trust fund, I was annoyed because all he cared about was the money. Through the entire ordeal, not once had he asked about Savannah. When she came up in the proceedings, he signed away his rights, without even blinking. Like she was a business transaction. *He signed off on you too.*

Therapy had helped me calm a lot of the voices I used to

have, but they never really stopped. There are days where it's hard to even get out of bed, let alone take care of another human being. But I do it because I must. Because Savi needs me. I refuse to become my mother, refuse to let my own upbringing cloud the way I parent. My mother only ever cared about moving up the social ladder, and alcohol. My father was absent, always working. I found out at a young age that he was cheating, and my mother would turn a blind eye, as she always put it. But I wouldn't turn into them, I wouldn't allow what they put me through to influence my life in any way.

The past few days had hung me out to dry even more than the divorce had, even more than my childhood. Not knowing if my daughter was going to wake up, not knowing her state when she did wake up. All these accusations are constantly swirling in my head, on repeat. *It's your fault. You shouldn't be working so much.* Tears form in my eyes as the voices continue to hammer away at what little resolve I have left. While waiting on the transfer to this hospital, Madison had gone to my home and put together a bag for me so I wouldn't be stuck in the same clothes every day. I'm running low on clothing to change into and the last thing I want to do is ask the nurses if there's somewhere for me to wash them without leaving Savi's side for too long.

Looking down, I realize my hand is still linked with Lucas as he leads us out of Savi's room and to the nurses' station where we discard our coffee cups. I look at him as we walk down the corridor to the elevator. He has dark circles under his eyes, only solidifying that this has been just as stressful on him. I keep telling him to leave, but he won't. And even though I feel selfish, I'm thankful he keeps telling me that he's not leaving. He's been my rock through all of this. *You don't deserve him.*

"Thank you." I whisper to him as we stop and wait for the elevator to show up. He lets go of my hand and pulls me into his side. He doesn't say anything but simply kisses the top of my head and rubs my back with his hand. I can't help but close my eyes and just take a deep breath. He smells like a mix of cedar and musk. He *smells like home.* I hear the elevator doors open, and he guides me in, keeping me under the crook of his arm.

"There is nowhere else for me, Nat." His soft words cause my eyes to open and look at him. His blue eyes are locked onto mine. It's like time is frozen still in this moment. His eyes are searching mine; I don't know what for, but I can't look away. I lick my lips and I watch as his eyes dart from my eyes to my lips, and I'm wondering what's going through his mind. *Why is he looking at me like this?* But just as he starts to make any sort of move, the doors to the elevators open and the moments gone. He pulls away, clasps my hand in his, and walks us off. *You're going mental, Natalie, he isn't going to kiss you. You're too broken for a man like Lucas.*

We find our way to the little outdoor healing garden area that's reserved for patients and family members. It's like a little grove in here, all crafted and cared for by the retirement home next door. You can see some of the ladies from there watering and caring for some of the flowers. Lucas guides me to the center area, where a Japanese maple is shading a set of benches by a fountain. It's a nice little secluded spot that exudes peace. The nurses have been trying to get me to come here since we arrived, telling me it's a good place to breathe, but I never made my way down on my own. *I don't deserve peace, not until Savi is awake.* I didn't want to leave Savi's side, even when they took her for the tests they do each day. I'm scared I'll miss something important if I leave for even a minute.

As we approach the benches, I'm not sure what to say or

even if anything should be said, so I take a seat and close my eyes. I'm focusing on the sounds of the breeze rustling the leaves of the tree, the fountain water, the birds. It's all so tranquil that I can't help but relax as I settle into the bench. I can feel Lucas sitting beside me. We aren't holding hands anymore, but I can still feel his touch, his presence. I know when he enters a room without even looking up. I can feel him looking at me at this very moment. But I don't know how to handle what's going on between us, if there even is anything going on between us. *There's nothing going on between you. He's your best friend.* I can barely handle what's happening with Savannah and trying to figure this out is taking me for a loop that I wasn't expecting.

"Nat." I hear him whisper. I open my eyes to him watching me. I don't know what to say, but his gaze looks like he is seeing into my head, like he knows what I'm thinking. "I wish I knew how to take away the fear I see in you. I'm so lost on how to help. Tell me how to help."

I lick my lips again, watching again as his eyes dart to my lips with the simple action.

"You just being here is helping me." My voice is barely above a whisper.

"There has to be something I can do." His eyes are on mine again and I can see the pain in them. Lucas has always had extremely expressive eyes. It's probably one of his best features, always has been, even when we were kids.

I take a deep breath and look over to the fountain. I'm just as lost as he is on how anything can help me. The only thing that could possibly help is having my daughter awake, uninjured and safe at home. But I know he can't do that. A tear escapes from my eye as I watch the fountain and I feel his hand cup my cheek, his thumb brushing away the tear and moving my face to where I'm looking at him again.

"I don't like seeing you cry." He's watching me so

intensely. My mouth is dry, and I'm so unsure of what's happening between us. Of what I want to happen between us. He has always been my best friend, even in the years that we didn't speak. He was a constant thought, always there in my head. The minute I saw him again after so many years apart, I knew that I'd be okay. The moment he entered the hospital room, I felt like I wasn't alone anymore. I was able to finally crumble into a million pieces because I knew he'd be there to hold me up. *You'll always be alone, he won't always be there for you. You're not worthy of him.* The voices attack me, but with him right beside me, they don't break through the way they normally do.

"I don't know what's going on here." I admit, my voice is still so low that you'd have to either be great at hearing or near enough to know what I'm saying. His right eyebrow cocks up as he hears my confession. And then before I know what's happening, he's leaning in and kissing me. The kiss is feather soft, like he's unsure of what I want, but sure of what he wants. The minute his lips touch mine, I feel a spark, like a small current of electricity is coursing its way through my body. *Lucas is kissing me.*

He applies a little more pressure to his kiss, not demanding and not expecting, but just enough to make me know that he's there, and that this is happening. In my entire life, I had never been kissed so sweetly, so tenderly. I've never felt so much in a simple kiss than I did in this moment, with him. The hand cupping my cheek moves to where it's now cupping the back of my neck, which provides him the ability to move my face to just the right place for him to take the kiss from simple and soft to deep and exploratory. I feel his tongue gently touching my lips, asking for entrance but not demanding it.

I open my mouth to his request, and instantly his tongue is sliding into my mouth, tenderly, sweetly. This kiss just became the best kiss in my life in a single instant and I can't help but relax into his touch. He's sure of himself and this kiss, applying just the right amount of pressure to elicit a moan from me. The minute the moan releases, I can feel his intensity increase, but he remains gentle, like he's afraid to go too far too fast.

I know he's holding himself back for my benefit, so I cup his cheek and deepen our kiss another level. He groans before clasping the hand I have on his cheek into his own. I hear some footsteps approaching from the entrance to the little cove we went into as he continues to kiss me, his lips marking me as his own. He seems to hear it as well as he pulls back, placing his forehead on mine and breathing in deep breaths. No words are needed as we sit here, our hands clasped as we sit forehead to forehead breathing together. All my thoughts are a hazy mess as I come up from our kiss.

"Mrs. Conaway? Are you down here?" I hear my daughter's nurse asking.

"We're in here." I pull away from Lucas, smiling softly at him, before getting up to go to the nurse. That kiss was unexpected and as much as I'd love to figure it all out, I can't. Right now, I don't have the time to dwell on it. It's time to get back to reality and my daughter.

# Chapter Eight

LUCAS

The minute I see her face, I realize just how stupid I was for doing what I just did. She's here because of Savi, and here I am, kissing her. I'm a stupid dumbass who took advantage of his best friend. The curses running through my head at this moment aren't very friendly at all. *How could I be so freaking stupid? Who does what I just did? Who the fuck do I think I am?* I can't blame it on anyone but myself, but the minute I pulled her into my arms at the elevator, it just felt right. She fit perfectly against me. And then I saw her lick her lips, and I nearly kissed her in the elevator. Her licking her lips again, it was like waving a red flag at a bull, and I was powerless. I knew I couldn't stop myself if I tried. I needed to taste her, to show her I was right here with her. But I took advantage of her and the situation she's in.

Getting up, I follow behind Natalie and the nurse as they make their way back to the elevators inside. The nurse is speaking in hushed tones, so I don't know what's being said. Natalie isn't crying though, so hope blooms in my chest that it's good news. Once we reach the elevator, the nurse turns to me.

"The doctor will be in to speak with you shortly. CT didn't take as long as we expected to take so Savannah's already back in the room." I nod at her and then get into the elevator with Nat. Once the doors close and it's just us again, I turn to her.

"Nat, I'm..." She holds her hands up to stop me.

"Not right now, Lucas. I can only handle one thing at a time. Right now, Savannah's first. We'll talk, soon, but I... can't right now." She takes a deep breath, clearly getting her bearings before speaking again. "I want to talk, I do. Give me a little time." All I can do is nod at her. She gives me a soft smile, puts her hands down and starts wringing them, sure signs she's nervous as to what the doctor's going to say. Dark circles paint the skin under her eyes, lips tight with strain. I'm adding stress to her life that she doesn't need right now, more proof that I'm fucking stupid for crossing the line. I want to pull her in to me, but I don't know where we stand, I don't know what she's thinking, and I don't want to do anything that will only make everything worse.

That kiss changed everything for me. She isn't just my best friend anymore, I want so much more from her than that. I know there's no going back to where we were, at least not for me, but right now, her sole focus is her daughter, and I can't blame her for that. I don't know where she stands on everything, but I'm done denying my feelings for her. As I follow her back into Savi's room, my mind replays the kiss we shared, the intensity of it. As we approach the room, I shove all my thoughts aside, knowing that I'll be what she needs right now, a friend, and I always will be. I can table my own need for answers, but we'll be having this conversation eventually.

Just as we enter the room, my phone starts vibrating in my pocket. I pull it out and growl lightly in my throat as I notice Lauren's name on the screen. Natalie looks over at me, her right eyebrow slightly raised as she looks down at the phone.

*Fuck.* I'm not a cheater, not a playboy. But here I am, wanting to take Natalie and I past the best friend status, and I haven't dealt with my sham of a relationship. *Fuck.*

"I'll be back in a bit." I tell Natalie as I step back into the hallway. She doesn't look at me, but simply nods and goes straight to Savi's side. I wanted to hear what the doctor has to say, but first, I have to handle this. My thoughts consume me as I watch her walk away, eventually turning and heading back to the elevator. *High school, seeing Nat with Ethan, leaving, being introduced to Lauren, falling into a routine with her, becoming comfortable with her.* It all plays into my head like a slow-motion movie as I wait. I don't know if I ever fell in love with Lauren, but just got complacent in the routine of it all. Our relationship started to help both of our careers, and then it became the norm for us.

I don't feel a spark with Lauren, not like I do with Natalie. I don't feel anything for Lauren beyond a mutual respect as co-workers. It's not fair to her to keep doing this. Especially with what just happened in the grove. I don't know what that kiss means for Natalie and me, but I do know that I want to see where it takes us. I wanted Natalie in high school but didn't take the chance when I had it. Now I have a chance, and I'm fucking it all up. Taking a deep breath, I walk out of the hospital to the benches on the other side of the doors and dial the one number I don't want to be.

"Lucas, what the fuck? I've been calling you, texting you, for days. Where the hell are you?"

"Hi Lauren, how are you? Oh me, I'm good, thanks for asking." The annoyance in my tone clear as I answer her. I hear her blowing out a frustrated breath before she responds.

"Seriously, what the fuck, Lucas?" This right here is why I didn't want to deal with her. Her attitude is atrocious. She only thinks about herself, and if it doesn't help her, she doesn't care for it. She wasn't always this way. When we first met, she was sweet and caring, always wanting to help every-one. And then as her fame grew, she let it mold her into this person that only thinks about herself.

"I'm at the hospital with Savannah, Lauren. She got hurt." I say, wishing I was back in that room with my girls instead of out here, dealing with this.

"She isn't your daughter, Lucas," she screams at me. The anger that courses through me fuels me in a way I didn't know was possible. I'm usually a carefree kind of guy but that just took all my patience and blew it out the window.

"Are you serious, Lauren?" I yell back at her. I hear her gasp of surprise, but she doesn't have a chance to get a word in because I'm not done. "I tell you she got hurt and the first thing you throw back at me is that she isn't mine? I know she isn't mine, not biologically. But that little girl means the world to me, always will. She's in a fucking medically induced coma and I'm here for her and for Natalie." She scoffs through the phone, clearly ignoring everything I said.

"Naturally, that's where you are, Lucas. You've been pushing me away ever since that bitch and her bastard child came back into your life. I didn't even know about them, you never told me about Natalie and your past, and then there they are, taking up all of your time, all of your energy. I'm your girlfriend, Lucas, and you pushed me aside for them like I'm nothing." I can hear her attempt to keep herself from crying, but my anger is too intense to care at this point.

"First of all, never ever call them those names again. That's crossing a line I never thought you'd cross. I thought you were better than that. Especially considering the past you had. We weren't even in a real relationship so what the fuck do you expect from me..." My words fail me because I'm so angry. I don't even know what the hell is happening anymore. This isn't the girl I met at the agency when we were both starting our careers. She's so far from it that I don't even know how we are still together.

"What do you mean we aren't in a real relationship? We've been together for years, Lucas. Everyone knows it. You can't deny that we're in a relationship, have been in one. Just because we got together through the agency doesn't mean that none of this wasn't real." She takes a deep breath, continuing before I have a chance to tell her it was all fake. "You didn't show up to the shoot we had scheduled, you didn't even tell me what was going on. Justin told me you canceled all of your jobs, including the ones with me, and then I couldn't get a hold of you. Now, I find out you were with *them* this entire time. These photos show the story loud and clear." *What the hell is she talking about? What photos?* I can hear her breaking down on the other end of the phone, finally exposing some humanity underneath a wall of cold ice.

"I don't know what you want me to say, Lauren. I don't owe you an explanation for anything. As far as I'm concerned, what I do with my time is my business. We may have been in what feels like a real relationship to you, but it wasn't. I have respect for you as a fellow model, but I don't have feelings for you. We never even slept together Lauren. So, tell me, what part of this was real? What part of this was nothing more than a way to get our careers off the ground?" I hear some rustling in the background, and then silence. I pull the phone away to make sure she's still there. In all reality, I hope she hung up on me.

She's crying now, which isn't her norm, I can hear the pain and anguish in her voice. She knows it's her shot of getting to me. Unfortunately for her, I have nothing left. All my emotions are used up. I sigh as I realize what I just said to her. *Did I just break up with her? Is it over?*

"Are you fucking kidding me right now, Lucas? You're breaking up with me? Like this? You'll regret this, you don't have a career without me." I laugh at that. I could care less about my career at this point. I've been questioning everything about it anyways, wanting to take a step back and do something else.

"Bye, Lauren." I hang up on her. I lower my head into my hands as I sit here, not sure what to do next. I don't regret breaking up with her, especially with all that she said.

Looking up to the hospital, I'm lost in my thoughts. I know what I want, but how to get there is where I draw a blank. I know Natalie needs me to be strong for her, that this is the last thing she needs to deal with, but I can't deny this anymore. She's mine. She's always been mine, no matter how long it took me to realize that I can't fight these feelings for her. And when the time's right, I'll stake my claim and show her just how much her and that baby girl of hers mean to me.

I've been outside for over an hour now, sitting on the bench outside the hospital. I watch the cars drive by, not really paying attention to anything as I try to come to terms with what I want. My career as a model gave me a lot of opportunities and I'm grateful for them, especially since they got me away from the expectations my parents put forth for me. Expectations to marry for money and not for love. I hated the world I grew up in, the only light in my life back then was Natalie. Looking back on the past few years, I realize how much it's taken from me at the same time. I'm tired of leaving all the time, flying to wherever I'm needed, hardly ever home. Since Natalie came back into my life, all I want to do is be home with her and Savi.

"Hey man." Looking up, I see Justin standing over me, a smirk on his face. "What're you doing out here?"

"Phone call." That's all I give him as he sits beside me on the bench.

"I take it you didn't see the tabloids this morning?" I look at him confused.

"What the hell are you talking about?" He pulls a copy of *The Daily Hang* out from his bag and hands it my way. The minute I see the cover, the words Lauren said on the phone come back to me. *"These photos show the story loud and clear."* Staring at the picture, I realize it's from the session Natalie did for me. I have her pulled onto my lap after she found out about Savannah. And then I see the caption. *Is top international model Lucas Moreno stepping out on girlfriend for a new girl?* Oh shit. I didn't even realize anyone was around when I did what I did. I was consoling a friend, nothing more. Well, at least until the grove.

"You didn't know?" I look up to see Justin studying me.

"Fuck no, I didn't know. I was consoling her after she found out Savannah was hurt. I didn't want her rushing off and possibly hurting herself." I toss the magazine between us and bury my face into my hands. "There's nothing going on in this photo other than me being a friend."

"You need to get back to work. I smoothed things over with the advertisers and they're making it work without you. But after this," he motions to the magazine between us, "shit is hitting the fan." I watch as he pulls open his calendar on his phone, all the orange marks all over it displaying the work coming my way. *I fucking hate those orange marks.*

"I'm not going back to work, Justin." He drops his phone in his lap and looks at me.

"What the fuck, man?" I start explaining what's going on upstairs with Savi, watching his reaction at the story.

"I'm not leaving until they do. No more jobs. And honestly, I don't think I'll be coming back to modeling at all after this." I eye the tabloid, hating the paparazzi even more than before. I've never been one to care what they say about me because I know better than to believe the lies they spout.

But they pulled Natalie into this mess and that's not something I can ignore. He runs his fingers through his hair, his eye twitching as he tries to come up with some sort of response to what I said. He stands up, his anger clear as he paces in front of me.

"Are you kidding me right now? Not going back will only fuel the flames of this damn story, Lucas. You can't just give it all up. Not after everything you've done."

"I can, and I will. I'm so fucking tired of all this pretentious bullshit. Tired of the vain, self-absorbed people." An image of Lauren flashes through my mind. Even though she hadn't started out that way, she had changed to fit in, and I didn't want that same thing to happen to me. My voice gets quiet as I admit the one thing I want to say. "I'm done."

"So that's it. You're giving it all up? For her?" He stops pacing and stares up at the side of the hospital towards the pediatric floor.

"I'd give everything up for her. For them."

"So, what am I supposed to tell everyone? How am I supposed to clean up all these messes you've left for me?" I can see the temper but there's a sense of anxiety too and... camaraderie.

"Come with me."

# *Chapter Nine*

NATALIE

**I**'m trying to listen to the doctor explain things to me, but all I can think about is that earth-shattering, axis-altering, kiss. I never knew I could be kissed like that. I don't know where we  go from here. *How do you come back from a kiss like that?* And then I saw who was calling him. It was like a shock to the system. I knew he had a girlfriend, and here I was, making out with him like some horny teenager. To make matters worse, my daughter was up here while I was doing that. *I am a freaking fool.* I shake the thoughts out of my head and focus my attention back on the doctor.

"Can you please repeat that, Dr. Johnson?" I look up at him as he smiles at me apologetically.

"Your daughter's brain is stable, which means we should be able to start weaning her off the medicine that's keeping her in this sustained state. By weaning her, we'd need to remove the tubing in her throat and most of these wires. I've talked to the top neurological team here, and we've all agreed that this is the right course for her." I sigh in relief and look back down at my beautiful little girl. I've missed her sweet little voice, her

77

beautiful eyes. Tears form in my eyes as I look back up to the doctor.

"How long after you reduce the drugs will it take for her to wake up?" I ask, almost timidly, afraid of what his answer might be.

"It changes from patient to patient, Ms. Conaway. We won't know until we start the process and can monitor her." I'm trying hard not to cry, but that wasn't the answer I was wanting. "If you have no other questions, I can send the nurse in with the paperwork for you to start the process." I nod at him and he walks out of the room.

The beeping and whooshing of the machines helping my daughter are all I can hear now. I try to focus my thoughts on the good. Savi's brain is healing. They are about to wean her off the meds that are keeping her asleep, removing the tube that is helping her breathe. *Lucas.* I sigh deeply when his name enters my head. *What the hell am I going to do about Lucas?* I know what I want to do, but it goes against the very center of my moral compass. He's in a relationship and has been for quite a while. I can't be that girl. I won't be. *Cheater, home wrecker, skank...* the words swirl through my mind as I replay the kiss with Lucas. *You're no better than Ethan,* the voice chides me as a wave of nausea sinks its hooks into me.

I grab Savi's hand in mine, bringing it up to my mouth for a soft kiss. The nurses have been encouraging us to talk to her more often. I've been singing to her a lot, but I haven't just talked. She's three, so she isn't the best to have regular conversations with. Most of our conversations revolve around her favorite shows, collecting shells, or whatever it is that a three-year-old loves to talk about. Lucas is better at talking with her than I am. He just has a way with her, which is probably why he's her favorite person. Every time he'd come home from a job, they'd become inseparable.

"I miss seeing those beautiful eyes, kiddo. I miss your

spunk, your sass. You're the best part of my life, baby girl. It's you and me, us against the world." I kiss her small hand and then start singing to her. I go through some of our favorite songs from her favorite movies, the tears falling as I do. I want so bad for her to open her eyes, to sing with me. I feel shattered into a million pieces and the only chance I have at being put back together is in a medically induced coma.

It's been hours since the nurse came in to lower the medication keeping Savi asleep, hours since Lucas walked out of the room to take his call. I've tried not thinking about it too much, but the more time that passes, the more my thoughts seem to take over. I knew he had a girlfriend. Granted, she refused to acknowledge my existence, but he still belonged to her. *To her.* I had no right to allow that line to be crossed. I've been the one in her place, the one cheated on and I refused to put anyone in that position. Some people may say that it was only a kiss, but it was still cheating in my eyes. I had taken on that role when I had not stopped Lucas. *The other woman. The one thing you said you'd never be is the one thing you became. Hypocrite. How can you ever look at yourself in the mirror again?*

I grab my phone off the charger, hoping to see a message from Lucas explaining why he's been gone so long, but I'm met with a blank screen. *Why would he text you? He has a girl-friend,* the voice reminds me. No missed calls, no texts. I've already let my clients know what is going on and they've all been so understanding. When I had to take Savi on shoots prior to getting her into daycare, she'd steal the show. The clients adored her. I pull open my contacts, pausing when I come to Lucas' name. I want to talk to him. He's been such a huge help to me, but I don't want him to think I can't handle things on my own. *He left you.* The voice is getting louder the longer I sit here by myself. I scroll past his name and land on Madison. I haven't talked to her much since she left, and I feel like a horrible friend for it. I push the call button and hold my breath as I wait for her to answer.

"Nat? Is everything okay?" She sounds like she's been crying.

"Maddy, everything's ok." I take a deep breath before continuing. "Do you think you could come?"

"Of course, Natalie. I've been wanting to be there for you this entire time, but I didn't know how you felt about me being there. This was all my fault."

"Mad, stop it. I'm not angry at you, I don't blame you. Please come." She sniffles a little.

"I'm on my way. Do you need me to grab anything for you?"

"More clothes. I'm almost out. But really, all I need is for you to be here. Please." My voice breaks knowing that the only reason I'm asking her is because I want to set Lucas free from this responsibility.

"Okay, girlie. I'll see you in a bit." We hang up and I already feel better. With Madison here, Lucas can go back to his life. He doesn't need to keep putting everything on hold for me. *He's probably on his way to Lauren anyways.* Tears are starting to form at the thought of him with her. He's always been my best friend, my confidante. But now, it feels like everything has changed and I can't help but feel like it's all my fault. I swore to myself that I wouldn't ever be the kind of woman who tears a relationship apart, but here I am, the exact thing I said I wouldn't be. The tears are freely falling when Lucas walks in just a minute later, Justin right behind him.

"Nat, what's wrong? What did the doctor say? Is Savannah okay?" He has my hands in his, rubbing his thumb over the back of them. I look from him to Justin. Lucas sees my eyes tracking to the guy behind him.

"Natalie, why are you crying?" Lucas' question draws my eyes back to his face. His face is scrunched up in concern. I look back over to Justin. He's watching the interaction between us like it's something from the Sci-Fi channel on TV. Like he isn't sure what he's watching but can't pull his eyes away from the scene unfolding in front of him. He notices me watching and turns his gaze away, instead looking at the wall.

"I'm fine. Savannah is fine. Madison's on her way." I'm still watching Justin, who's now leaning against the wall by the door. His face flinching when I mention Madison's name, like the sound of it physically attacked him in some way. *Wonder what that's all about?*

"What did she say that has you crying?" My gaze swings to him. *What? Why would Madison make me cry?*

"She didn't say anything. I called and asked her to come. It's time for you to get back to work and get back to your life." He looks like I just handed him a death sentence. His face goes from shocked to upset.

"Why would I leave? Natalie, what's going on?" He looks genuinely surprised at what I told him, like he couldn't imagine me asking him to leave.

"Because I need you to leave." I whisper, just barely loud enough for him to hear, but not loud enough for Justin to hear. The air whooshes out of his lungs like I sucker punched him in the gut.

"I don't understand. Is this because of the picture in the tabloid? It's just a picture, Natalie." *What the hell is he talking about?* My face scrunches in confusion as I try to figure it out.

"What picture?" His eyes go wide at my question, and he realizes I have no idea what he's talking about.

"You haven't seen it then?" I shake my head no. My eyes go

to Justin as he brings a magazine over. I stare down at the cover, reading the caption below it.

"Oh my God. How?" My whispered words have Lucas grabbing the magazine and tossing it to the floor. *I'm the other woman. It's right there in color on the cover of a fucking tabloid. Oh God.* The tears fall from my eyes as I stare at the papers that are now strewn across the floor.

"The paparazzi must've still been in the area. I didn't know. I thought I got rid of them all." His eyes hold so much sorrow in them.

"What do you mean, you thought you got rid of them all?" He tells me how he showed up early because the paparazzi found out what was going on. *This is too much.* I can't handle this on top of everything else.

"You need to go. I can't do this. I won't do this." I push his hands away from me as the thoughts in my head barrel into me, crushing me with accusations. The verbal assault in my head is pulling me back to the darkness I was in before I came to BoothBay Harbor.

"Please, Natalie. Don't push me away."

"I have to." My whisper has him sitting back, his posture defeated. He has tears threatening to spill out of his beautiful eyes. Tears I caused, but I can't think with him so close to me, not after everything that has happened.

"Madison should be here any minute, and then you can go." I turn back to Savi, putting more space between us. I hate doing this, I hate pushing him away, but right now, it's the only chance I have at saving our friendship, if it can be saved. *You're pathetic.* I don't know what will happen from here, but I do know that I can't be his. And if that means we need space to find our way back to where we were as friends, then that's what will happen.

I can tell he's upset. I can feel it coming off him in waves, feel his eyes on me, but I can't look at him. I can't break, because I know if I do, I won't let him leave. And right now, I need him to. For me, for my sanity, for our friendship. I can feel as though he's about to say something to me, but just as he turns to say what he has to say, Madison rushes into the room and stops short at the sight of Justin standing there, dropping the bag she brought in with her in the process. I see the anger brewing behind her eyes, but I have no idea why.

"What the fuck are you doing here?" Justin spits at her. *What the fuck is going on?* Why is he angry at her? How do they know each other? My eyes widening as they stare each other down.

"Do they know each other?" I hear Lucas whisper at me, his eyes trained on the two currently killing each other with their eyes. I shrug my shoulders, unable to tear my eyes away from the scene unfolding in front of us.

"Excuse me, but what the fuck are you doing here?" Madison's eyes are blazing with an anger that I've never seen out of her. It's interesting, and scary, if I'm being honest. One of my favorite things about Madison is that she has so much passion for everything, and she isn't afraid to show it.

"Guys, seriously. Savi is in that bed right now. Cut it out with the screaming and the cursing." Lucas yells at them, not as loud as they were screaming. Madison looks sheepish as she looks over at him.

"Sorry, Lucas." She turns to me. "Hey sweetie, you okay?" She looks down at the papers strewn across the floor, the cover of the tabloid still visible from the mess. I can't pull my eyes away from Justin, who's staring at Madison like she has horns growing out of her head. Madison doesn't even notice him as he crosses his arms, moves to the other side of the room, and continues his glare at the redhead who just busted into the room. I don't know what happened between these two, but they are the last thing on my mind at this moment.

Madison grabs the bag she dropped, steps over the papers

without mentioning what she sees and pulls me closer to Savi's side. She gives me a look, knowing there's a story, but not quite sure what she should say.

"I'm so glad you're here, Mads," she smirks at my nickname for her.

"You have some explaining to do." Her eyes are glinting mischievously as she looks at the papers on the floor, then over at Justin and Lucas, who are having a conversation of their own.

"I can't get into it right now, but I promise to talk soon."

"Tell me about Savi."

"They started weaning her off her meds that are keeping her under. So now, it's just a waiting game." There are tears rolling down my face as I look down at my sweet daughter.

Next thing we know, Justin's storming out of the room and Lucas is left standing there, watching us cautiously. After Justin walks out, Madison visibly relaxes her defenses.

"Natalie, can I talk to you in the hall?" Lucas' words draw my eyes to his. "Please?"

"Go ahead, mama, I got Savi." Madison pushes me towards the door. I give her a dirty look before stepping over the papers. Grabbing his bag from the closet, I take the lead as we head out to the hallway. He goes to take my hand in his, but I pull away. I've never pulled away from him before. *It's better this way.*

"Lucas. I can't do this right now. You need to get back to work. You need to go fix things with Lauren. I know she's seen those pictures. I won't be the other woman." I'm talking low, not low enough to be a whisper, just enough that our conversation is private.

"No, I don't, Nat. I canceled all my shoots until further notice. And I don't give a fuck about fixing things with Lauren." His eyes are full of tears, pleading me to change my mind.

"I don't want you here, Lucas." I hand him his bag, tears fall from my eyes. Tears I can't stop. I know it kills him to see them, I can see the pain in his eyes as he watches my face. He takes the bag and sets it down beside him, reaching again for my hands, but I don't let him grab hold.

"I want to stay." He wrings his hands together in front of him as he stares at me. His eyes are pleading with me to give in, but I need to remain strong.

"You have a girlfriend, Lucas. And I will not be the woman who tears a relationship apart. I was the scorned woman, I won't do it to someone else. You need to leave. I'll text you with updates about Savi, but I don't want you here."

"Baby, you don't understand. Ple..." I stop him before he can even try to explain.

"You do not get to call me that. I'm not your baby, I'm not your anything. As of right now, I don't even know if I can be your friend. I became the other woman today and I don't want any part of that. There is no explanation. No excuse. I don't want you here. Leave, or I will call security and have them escort you out. You're not welcome here right now." I watch his shoulders slump, the air leaving his body.

"Natalie, please, just let me explain." I can see the tears that were in his eyes are now falling and I hate that I'm hurting him, hurting myself.

"No, Lucas. I just want you to go." I hold my head high, push my shoulders back, and walk away from him and back into the room.

"Fuck." I hear him scream into the hallway.

"Holy shit girl, what just happened?" Madison makes her way over to me as I come into the room, pulling me into her arms before taking us across the room.

"I told him to leave." I slump down into the chair beside Savi's bed.

"Girl, what the hell's going on? Why am I here? What's with the papers all over the floor?" She rapid fires her questions at me so fast that my head is spinning. Seeing my face, she backtracks a little. "Don't get me wrong, I'm so glad you called, but you had Lucas. So, to put it simply, I'm not picking up what you're putting down." A laugh bubbles out of my mouth at her word choice.

My voice is a whisper as I make my confession. "We kissed." She leans in, acting like she didn't hear me, searching my face.

"Say that again, 'cause, girl, it sounded like you said you kissed Lucas." A blush creeps up my neck and onto my cheeks. Her eyes are wide when I finally look at her. "Holy shit. You kissed him?"

The blush only gets deeper on my face. "Shhh." Her smile is so wide, and she looks like I told her I won a million dollars, not that I kissed Lucas Moreno.

"Tell me everything."

Another blush creeps up my cheeks and I can't help but feel like a teenager as I start from the beginning and tell her everything.

# *Chapter Ten*

LUCAS

As I walk out of the hospital, my shoulders slump in defeat. I don't know how to fix this, if she even wants to fix it. But I have to give her what she wants, even if that means breaking my own heart in the meantime. Justin's somewhere in the hospital, but I don't want to hear his bullshit right now. He'll figure out that I left eventually. I just need to get out of here before I do something stupid, like rushing back into that room and begging her to hear me out.

Thank goodness my car had been delivered since we got here. I didn't want to deal with waiting to get a cab. Throwing my bag across the seat, I get in and start the car. This is the hardest thing I've ever had to do. It's killing me to walk away, but I have to. Taking a deep breath, I look up at the fifth floor where I know Savi's room is.

"I'm not leaving you, baby girl. I promise I'll be back." I send a whispered message up to my favorite three-year-old. Wiping the tears away, I put my car into gear and pull away.

○

Pulling up to my house feels surreal, and so fucking lonely. Usually when I pull in, Savi's running out of the guest house to greet me. Now, there's nothing. My house is completely dark, only highlighting just how alone I am. Walking inside, I grab a beer out of the fridge, and pop it open. I brace myself on the counter and look over across the yard at the dark house sitting on my property. It's lifeless, empty. *I can't fucking be here. Why the fuck did I come back here?* I take a long pull of the beer and head over to the living room, plopping into the recliner facing the TV.

It's been about three hours, and seven beers, since I got home. I haven't moved off this spot, except to grab a new beer. No TV, no music. Just me, my thoughts, and silence. I look at the beer I'm currently drinking, toying with it in my fingers as the liquid sloshes back and forth. I shouldn't be drinking, I should be in that fucking hospital with my girls. *Fuck.* I throw the beer across the room, causing it to explode against the wall by the TV.

Grabbing my keys, I stumble outside and make my way to the guest house. Nat and I have keys to each other's houses. When she first moved in, I had the keys redone so that she'd be the only one to have one, but she begged me to make a spare for her, saying it made her feel better knowing I had a key just in case. It was just something we did, no pretense, no expectation. Using my spare key, I let myself in. The air's stale in here, much like it was when I first bought this property.

Flipping on the main light, I turn on the AC unit to get some air moving through here. I don't know why I decided to come to her place but being here makes me feel somewhat better. I can smell Natalie's perfume, a light and floral scent that is all her. *Smelling it feels like home.* I stumble my way through the house, stopping short when I notice the living room. Savi's drawings are all over the table. She'd bring me a new one every day that I was home, saving them all up to give them to me if I was away at a job. Seeing those pictures are the final straw to what I thought was me being strong. I grab one of the pictures and fall to my knees. As I stare at the drawing, the last of my defenses fall, and I allow myself to break for the first time since that night in the hospital.

My head's pounding when I wake up, like tiny little construction workers are doing a full remodel of my brain. Without opening my eyes, I feel around me. I'm on the floor, but it doesn't feel like my floor at home. I don't have carpets in my house, and this is soft like one. Barely squinting one of my eyes open, I'm assaulted with the light coming in and I slam my eyes shut again. *Fuck.* I need to not drink so much. Massaging my temples, I try to sit up but the beer I drank last night is threatening to make its way back up if I move too fast. Stopping all movement, I lay back and massage my temples hoping it helps with the pain.

After a few minutes, I attempt to open an eye again. The light's excruciating but I can make out where I am this time. Taking in my surroundings with one eye, I realize I'm on Natalie's floor in her living room, her rug to be exact. I catch sight of the pictures on the floor beside me and memories of last night flood into my brain, only making the headache worse. *Coming home, drinking too many beers, throwing a beer, coming here, the pictures.* Tears are threatening to fall again as I think about the pictures. *I should be there with them, not laying on this floor with a hangover.*

"Well, isn't this a nice sight to behold." I look over to the entrance to see Madison smirking at me as she takes in the sight of me on the floor. *What the hell is she doing here? Why isn't she at the hospital with my girls? Did something happen?*

The questions hammering my brain only make the pain worse, but I can't stop them from coming.

"Not so loud. And why are you here? Who's with Nat?" My throat feels like sandpaper as I struggle to get the words out. She rolls her eyes at me. At this point, I'm cursing my hangover. If it weren't for my drinking, I'd rush out that door and get to the hospital.

"Well, she sent me here to grab some stuff for Savi. They're hopeful that she'll be waking soon, and Nat wanted some things of hers to have there to help when she does wake up." She's looking at me like she has more to say.

"Savi's waking up?" I realize that I didn't know anything about the status, that the doctor had come in while I was talking to Lauren and then all that shit went down. I sit up quickly, hating the decision to move so fast almost immediately. My head is swimming and I feel like I'm about to puke now. Bracing myself against the coffee table, I look up at her. Madison isn't my type at all, and after what I saw yesterday with Justin, I'm pretty sure they have a history.

"They're hopeful." She gives me a small smile before walking into the kitchen. I sit back against the coffee table, praying it won't move with my weight against it, my fingers massaging my temples again. The pounding in my head is relentless as I sit here. *Why the fuck did I drink so much*? I hear the water running, cabinets opening and closing. Then she's back in the living room, kneeling beside me with a bottle of Tylenol and a glass of water.

"How is she, Madison?" I ask, looking up at her. Even with the beer swimming in my belly and my head feeling like it's under a full reconstruction, Natalie is all I can think about. I hate not knowing how she's doing, hate not being there with her.

She looks at me like she's searching my face for some sort of answer. I guess whatever my face says is what she's looking for because she finally answers. "She's confused, Lucas. That woman went through so much more than you could ever imagine. What happened between y'all, it was a catalyst. I can't say much else than that. Just give her the space she's needing, the space she asked for." My eyes dart up to hers. *She knows about the kiss.* She gives me another small smile before setting the glass down on the table allowing her to open the bottle of medicine for me.

"What can I do? I want to be there with her." I feel so fucking lost. I need to be there, but I can't force this, can't force her to listen to me. Natalie has always been the more stubborn out of the two of us and I know trying would end up making everything worse. That's the last thing I want to do.

"I understand, but I'm just as protective of her. So, first of all, clean yourself up, you smell like a fucking brewery." She makes a face at me. Taking a deep breath, I try my best to calm down because that's not the answer I was looking for, and she knew it. "Then, when the time comes, you go back to our girl and you make her listen." That draws my attention back to her as she smiles and winks at me.

"I can't lose her, Madison." Admitting that I can lose her feels like my heart's being torn out of my body.

She pats my arm gently. "You won't. You need to understand her side of things though. Her marriage ended because he chose another woman. Multiple other women." I cover my face with my hands and sigh. *Fuck.* I knew it was stupid to kiss her. Our first kiss shouldn't have been while I was still technically with someone else, it should've been special.

She touches my arm again before standing up to start the process of getting Savi some things together. I finally get myself to the point where I can stand up and take in the scene around me. Grabbing the pills and water she set out for me, I feel a small weight lift off of me. I don't have the answers right now, but that doesn't mean I'm giving up.

"I got this, Lucas. Go home, take a shower, and then put together a plan to get her back." She smiles at me and then gets back to work on what she came here to do.

Knowing that Madison's on my side makes my outlook a lot better than it was before. I don't know how I'm going to do it, but I'm going to get Natalie back. But first, I need to take a fucking shower because Madison's right, I do smell like a brewery. Once my head isn't pounding too badly, I give her a small wave and head out the door and back to my house. The minute I enter my back door, the smell of the beer hits my nostrils causing the nausea I was feeling earlier to come back with a vengeance. Guess I'm cleaning first.

Steeling my stomach, I grab some cleaning tools and get to work on the mess I made last night. There's a stain on the wall from the beer that I threw against it. Nothing I can do about that right now, but I clean up what I can and then get myself moving towards the bathroom. Turning the water to the hottest it will go, I let the steam fill the bathroom before I get undressed.

The cleaning helped clear my head and it finally feels like the pounding is taking a break as I step into the shower and take a minute to just lean into the water. Closing my eyes, my mind instantly takes me back to the kiss, back to before things went stupid. I think of the way she opened up to me, the moan, the feeling of her relaxing into me. All my blood drains south and my cock hardens as the kiss plays itself out in my head. I feel like a jerk for even doing this, but I can't help it. Just knowing how she responded to me has me feeling things I didn't know I could.

Taking myself in my hand, I think of Natalie, of her gasps as I kiss her, how I can keep those sounds coming out of her, of how I can make her moan and writhe under me. I want to give her so much pleasure that she's screaming my name. I feel my cock stiffen even more at the thoughts of her moaning underneath me. That body, those breasts, that ass. *She's fucking perfection.*

Working my cock in my hand with thoughts of Natalie on my mind feels so fucking wrong, but I can't help but keep going. That kiss changed everything for us, and I'm going to get her back. I'll give her pleasure like she's never felt before. I imagine her legs wrapping themselves around me as I pound into her. It's no longer my hand, but her tight pussy gripping my cock. With that thought, I explode onto the shower wall. Turning the water to cold, I finish my shower. *It's time to figure out how I am going to get my girl back.*

After the doctors told me that Savi was completely weaned off the sedation meds, I felt a huge weight lift off my shoulders. I'm still worried because my baby hasn't opened her eyes yet, but the doctors are hopeful, and that's all that I can ask for. They told me they see normal brain activity, which is a very good thing considering all she went through. There's a small possibility that there's damage they aren't seeing, but they can't know anything for sure until she wakes up. As soon as they had finished giving me the news, I sent Madison off to my house to get some stuff for Savi to try and help her be more comfortable when she does wake up.

Sitting in the quiet has given me more time to think. Between Madison and the doctors, I haven't had much of a chance to grasp everything going on around me. Madison's been a trooper since yesterday. Having her here has helped with the loneliness, but she isn't Lucas. She cleaned up the tabloid and threw it in the trash, saying *you don't need to see that*. I hate that I'm missing Lucas so much, even with Madison here. I feel such a divide between us, and I'm the reason for it. I'm the one who pushed him away. *He has a girl-friend, you had no choice but to push him away.*

I did tell him I'd keep him updated, but I also didn't think it'd be this hard to not have him here. I've reached for my phone to text him so many times now, but I couldn't get myself to pull up his contact info. I'm worried that he'd ask for more, for answers that I don't know if I am ready to give him.

Grabbing my phone, I notice I have a text waiting for me.

**Madison:** Just got to the house. Found Lucas on your floor, passed out and smelling like a brewery. I sent him to get himself cleaned up. I'm getting Savi's stuff together and then I'm heading back that way. Do you need me to grab you anything?

Did he get drunk because he felt guilty over cheating on his girlfriend? This is all my fault. *You're a filthy cheating homewrecker.*

**Natalie:** No, I'm good. did he say anything?

**Madison:** He's confused Nat. I think he genuinely doesn't know what to do. He was holding Savi's pictures that she drew. I'm guessing he came in here after he was already drunk and saw them and broke. I didn't ask though.

I don't even know how to handle that response. Could it be guilt? Could it be that I made a harsh assumption? Should I have let him talk before throwing him out? *You kissed him while he was technically with another woman. You're no better than the nanny your husband was fucking.* The voices are relentless today. Kicking him out was the right thing. I did what I believed in my heart was right and that's just all there is to it. Will I let him explain? Eventually, yes.

But right now, the only thing I want to be worrying about is my baby.

The more I think about it, the more I know I owe him an update. I don't know if Madison gave it to him, and she didn't mention if she did or not. Picking my phone back up, I go to his contact info and prepare to message him. I'm going to be the bigger person and do what I told him I'd do.

**Natalie:** They weaned Savi off the sedation meds. They're hopeful she will wake up soon.

**Lucas:** I'm glad to hear that. Thank you for telling me. How are YOU?

I stare at that question for what feels like hours, when it's only a few minutes. I don't know how to respond. I told him I'd update him on Savi's progress, but that doesn't mean I have to talk about me. Closing out the message, I put the phone aside. I can do updates on my daughter, but the rest, I'm not ready for that. *You're nothing but a filthy excuse for a woman.*

Over the next few days, the text messages between Lucas and I are more of the same. I give him an update, he asks how I am, I don't respond. I know I'm probably acting immature about all of this, but I haven't had much time to sit and figure us out. Madison told me everything that happened during her trip. I wish I could just get past this, but my heart and my head are in two different places. And right now, my head is winning the battle. *He has a girlfriend. You're the other woman. The one thing you said you'd never be.*

"When are you going to let him come back, Natalie?" Madison's question interrupts my thoughts. It hurts knowing

I pushed him away, but I needed this time. Granted, I haven't figured anything out since the day he left. If anything, I've only gotten more confused with each day that passed.

"I don't know, Maddy. I don't want to be the other woman and I don't want to lose my best friend." I've been pacing since they took Savi for her latest CT scan. It's been four days since they weaned her off completely and she still isn't awake. My nerves are shot, I haven't slept. Madison does her best to keep me calm, but she isn't who I want here. She's been my rock since everything happened, but it's nowhere near the same.

"I get it, I do. But he loves that little girl so much and I think he needs to be here. I know it's confusing for you, so I won't force anything. But I see you struggling, and I know he could help you more than I ever could." I look over at her. She's wringing her hands together. I wish I could take the blame she places on herself from her. No matter how many times I tell her that it was an accident, she shrugs me off. She carries this on her shoulders.

Just as I'm about to respond, the door crashes open and Justin's standing there.

"Where is he?" he bellows at me, his face contorted in anger as his eye twitches. I step back, away from him. I've seen him be an asshole, but I've never seen this side of him. I don't know him well enough to know if he'd hurt me or not.

"Excuse the fuck out of you. You don't burst into her daughter's room and yell at her." Madison throws down her phone and jumps up to stand in front of me. These two haven't been face-to-face since the first showdown in my room, at least that I know of anyways. I don't leave the room much anymore.

Justin glares at her, but Madison isn't the type to shrink down. If anything, she gets taller as she stands in front of me. Her anger's a match that I don't see lit very often, but on the off chance that I do, it's like dynamite, and I don't want to be around for the explosion. I put my hand on her shoulder, causing her to turn to me, and give her a small nod.

"If you're talking about Lucas, he left a few days ago and hasn't been back." Justin turns his glare to me. But unlike Madison, I shrink down under his scrutiny.

"Then, where the fuck is he? He isn't answering my calls." That's news to me. I've texted him small updates, but otherwise, I don't have any idea where he'd be.

"I'm not his keeper." I go to turn away but am caught by movement in the doorway. My body stiffens as I take in the woman standing there. She's taller than I am, her presence demanding attention as she looks around the room. I instantly recognize her from her shoots with Lucas. Her nose is slightly upturned as she continues looking around, until her eyes collide with mine. Her eyes turn to slits as she looks me up and down, judging me. *You deserve to be judged.*

"What the fuck is she doing here?" Madison points to Lauren in the doorway.

Justin turns and sees her standing there. She shrugs him off as he goes to speak and enters all the way in.

"Where is he?" She's looking down her nose at me, scrutinizing me. Her judgment is well received though. *This is the woman he should be with.* She's perfect with no hair out of place on her head, her manicured hands. She's tall and beautiful. I'm tall, but the beautiful thing, I'm definitively not.

"I just told Justin that he hasn't been here. I don't know where he is. He left a few days ago and I haven't seen him since. Now if you don't mind, my daughter will be back in this room soon and I need you both to leave. You're not welcome here." I turn away from her, maneuver myself around Madison and Justin, who are in their own little stare-off, and walk back to the chair that sits beside where my daughter's bed usually goes.

"I think you do know. I also know that something happened between him and you, while he was dating me. That tabloid only showed the truth. So, you're going to tell me where my boyfriend is and you're going to tell me now." She keeps walking toward me, her eyes glaring daggers at me. *She knows. Oh God, she knows.* I flinch with each dagger her words throw at me, wondering when she's going to hit me.

"I don't know what you're talking about. I don't know where Lucas is, so I don't have anything else to say to you. Now please leave my daughter's room before I call security." She scoffs at me as she looks around the room again.

"I know you know where he is. I don't know what he's doing with a piece of trash like you. He's my boyfriend and I'm here to talk to him." She crosses her arms as she stares down at me.

"Ex-boyfriend." Lucas says from the doorway, causing every single person in the room, including me, to look his way.

*Chapter Twelve*

LUCAS

Walking into the door of the hospital room, I tense as I see Lauren standing over Natalie with a look of smugness all over her face. Justin is standing off to the side, anger rolling off of him in waves. Neither of them noticing me until I speak up.

"Baby, we've been looking for you." Lauren bounds over. I give her a look of straight confusion. *What the fuck?* The minute she spoke, Natalie broke eye contact with me and is now looking everywhere but at us, Madison's glaring daggers at me, even though she was the one who let me know what was going on. I was already on my way here, but the minute I got the text saying Justin was in here yelling at Nat, I pushed my gas pedal down to the floor and broke several laws getting here. Justin's smirking at me, which only pisses me off more. *He's a dead man.* Lauren kisses my cheek and curls up into my side while I try to escape her grasp. Just as I'm about to put her in her place, Natalie turns towards us, throws her phone against the wall, shattering it into pieces.

"All of you, get the fuck out of my daughter's room." She screams at us. Lauren stares at her with wide eyes. Justin stands there shocked at the outburst but starts moving towards me. Madison's smiling at her friend, pride in her eyes. "Madison, go get security. I want them out." Madison goes to make her move out the door, but Lauren's words stop her.

"Don't bother, now that we have Lucas, we'll be on our way." Her remark sends Natalie to shoot daggers directly at her.

"Get the fuck out." Natalie yells again, her voice breaking on the last word. Security barges in, hearing the screaming.

"Ma'am, is there an issue here?" he asks her.

"Yes, these three," she says pointing at us, "need to get out of this room. They aren't allowed back in." He nods at her and turns to look at the three of us, pointing at the door.

"You heard the lady." He ushers us out the door. I look back at Natalie, who's currently watching Lauren. The latter is clasped onto my arm like she's been surgically attached to it. I watch as tears form in Natalie's eyes and my heart breaks at the sight. She won't look at me at all. This shit just got so much more complicated.

Security escorts us all the way down to the front entrance. Once we step outside, I break Lauren's hold on my arm and turn to face her. "What the fuck are you doing here?" I spit at her.

"I talked to Justin about what happened, how it was a big mistake and he told me you were here." I turn to Justin, who holds his hands up in response.

"I'll deal with you in a minute." I turn my gaze back to her. "I told you it was over. I know I didn't stutter, so I'm going to ask you again, what the fuck are you doing here?" My eye is twitching profusely as I struggle to hold onto my emotions. I didn't explain anything to Justin before I left, but he should know me well enough to know I didn't want anything of this nature happening. I wait for her to respond, but she's just standing there, a look of shock on her face. I make a gesture for her to talk.

"What are you even still doing here, Lucas?" She tries to turn the conversation on me, but she isn't getting me that way.

"Are you fucking kidding me? I'm here because my best friend's daughter was hurt, because I want to be here. Last I checked, you aren't in charge of me, let alone where I go and who I hang out with. So, I'm going to ask for the last time, what the fuck are you doing here Lauren?" I see her bottom lip starting to tremble, but I know she won't show weakness, especially with Justin standing here.

"I wanted to be supportive of you, Lucas. I know how much Shannon means to you." I start laughing at her, full-on belly laughter. Even Justin can't contain the small smirk that comes to his face at her obvious mistake of Savi's name. Glaring at him, he holds his hands up defensively, stepping away to give us more privacy.

"Shannon. That's what you're going with?" I raise my eyebrows as I turn back to look at her.

"You know what I meant." She stomps her foot like a toddler, throwing a tantrum. *What did I ever see in this woman?*

Taking a deep breath, giving myself a chance to breathe before I finally end what should have been ended years ago.

"Her name is Savannah. And that right there is one of the biggest reasons why I broke it off. You don't care about anyone but yourself, Lauren. The only reason you came was because you knew you were losing me, and that it'd be bad for your career. The photographers and clients didn't want you until our agents put us together. I knew that and still I went along with it." She looks at me, her eyes shooting daggers at me.

"Fuck you, Lucas. I came here because I love you and I didn't want to lose you. We were put together to help our careers, but we fell in love. Are you telling me after four years of us being together, you don't love me?" Tears have started making their way out of her eyes as she looks at me. Her question hanging in the air.

"Are you listening to yourself, Lauren? Love, seriously? We were nothing more than a way to get more work. Our relationship was as fake as the new nose you're sporting." I hear her sharp intake of breath at my words, her hands coming up to cover the nose job I pointed out. I keep my voice low so as not to gain even more attention than we already have. "I realized I was comfortable with you. And that's all it was. We grew comfortable. We never even had sex. So, tell me, how the hell did you get love out of that? There was no love here, not on my part anyway. Just mutual respect and a career that matched." I feel the slap before I hear it. Her palm hitting me hard on the right side of my face. *Damn, that stings*. But at this point, I don't care, I just want her fucking gone.

She turns with a huff, looking at Justin who's staring at his phone. "I thought you said you'd handle him." She screams at him, the shrill in her voice causing my eye to twitch. I turn to Justin at her words, wondering what the hell she meant by that.

He shrugs her off before turning and walking off in the direction of the parking lot. She stomps her feet again, clearly unhappy with how the situation played out.

"Goodbye, Lauren." I make a shooing motion with my hands towards her. She glares at me for a second before flipping me off and stomping off after Justin, yelling at him to stop and talk to her.

I pull my phone out and call Natalie. When it goes straight to voicemail, I remember that she shattered her phone against the wall. *Fuck*. I scroll my contacts, finding Madison's number. I go to call, but after one ring, I'm sent to voicemail. *Damn it*. Pulling open my messenger, I send her a text.

**Lucas:** I need to talk to her.

**Madison:** not a good time Lucas. I'll text you later.

*Fuck, fuck, fuck.* I sit down on the bench outside of the entrance, the same one I sat at when I ended things with Lauren the first time. My head hangs between my shoulders as I sit here. The guard from earlier is still standing right inside the door, watching me, so I can't just bolt inside and make sure everything's okay. Right now, all I can do is wait for Madison. I also need to have a long conversation with Justin after this clusterfuck. I don't know what he was thinking, bringing her here, but he must be out of his damn mind if he thinks that's what it'd take to get me to leave.

It's been about an hour since all the commotion happened when I feel a weight sit beside me on the bench. The guards still stationed just inside the entrance of the hospital, so I haven't moved. Looking over, I see Justin sitting beside me. He's not looking at me, but across the parking lot that we are facing, a red handprint on the cheek closest to me. He blows out a large breath and then turns to me.

"I didn't realize you'd broken up with her." The usual smirk on his face is gone, instead it's just a hollowness.

"Yea, well I didn't exactly fill you in before I left. But that was still a shit move, and you know it." I shrug my shoulders, my elbows on my knees. I'm still slumped over but instead of looking down, I'm watching his face. He's always been the kind of guy who rarely shows emotion, except anger. You can always tell when he's angry. It's every other emotion that he keeps well-hidden behind his tough outer self. Even being one of my good friends since I entered this business, I rarely see any sense of humanity out of him.

"She called me in hysterics saying she couldn't get a hold of you, that she wanted to be here to support you because she knows how much you love that little girl." He rolls his eyes as he puts his hands behind his head, leaning back into them, closing his eyes as he does. "I'm sorry man."

That small statement takes me by surprise. Justin's never been apologetic. It's what makes him such a good agent. He takes no bullshit and gives no fucks. I lean back, expelling my breath. *I have so many fucking questions.*

"Why did she say you'd handle me?" He opens his eyes to look at me.

"Fuck man, I don't know. She heard what she wanted to hear. When she told me that she wanted to support you, I told her where we were. That was it. I didn't say shit about handling you. Like that's even possible." He laughs at that statement.

"Why would you confront Natalie? Seriously man, what the fuck was that?" His face winces at my question. He knows he messed up.

"I wasn't thinking. I just know you weren't answering my calls, Lauren was blowing up my phone. I have so many reporters calling about the tabloid. It all just kept compounding."

"Still fucked up. Especially since you know everything she's going through."

"Yea. Guess I owe her two apologies now."

Leaning back, we both take a deep breath, our gazes going out to the parking lot.

"So, what's going on between you and Madison?" I break the silence after a few minutes. He sucks his breath in and turns to me.

"That's a story for another day, brother."

# *Chapter Thirteen*

NATALIE

As soon as the guard escorts them out, a scream tears itself out of me as I fall to my knees. Madison tries to catch me, but I hit the floor hard, my knees taking all the impact as I break down. I can feel her rubbing my back as I sob my eyes out. I cry because my daughter's still in a coma and although the doctors seem hopeful, I still haven't seen her beautiful blue eyes. The tears continue to fall over hearing Lucas say ex-boyfriend, yet he let her cling all over him. I feel the tightness of my chest, the pain of it, but the numbness takes over. *You're nothing but a cheating home-wrecker. You caused all of this.* The voices only seem to bring more anguish to my already failing mental warfare.

The nurses enter to wheel Savi's bed in and stop short at the sight of me on the floor. Madison hasn't been able to move me, nor do I want to be moved. I just want to lay here and succumb to all the pain. *Fuck all of this, I don't care anymore.* I can hear Madison speaking to the nurses and doctors, but I'm not paying attention to anything. *You're nothing. You'll never be anything more than a fat, single mother.* Ethan's taunts pull me further into the pain, pushing me further into darkness.

The floor is cold, but at this point, I'm too emotionally exhausted to care. As the darkness starts to take me, I feel myself being lifted and placed onto a bed and a prick in my arm. As the medicine kicks in, the blackness feels more welcoming than anything as I allow it to consume me.

I can hear whispers around me, but I don't care about anything anymore. Shutting out the noise, I allow the darkness to consume me once again. *Cheater.*

I feel the warmth of a hand in mine, the heat of it trying to pull me out of the numbness holding me down. It feels familiar, but I know it can't be who I think it is. Instead of allowing it to wake me, I allow myself to fall deeper. *Homewrecker.*

"It's been two days Madison. Why isn't she awake yet?" I can hear the harshness in his voice, the pain laced into each syllable he utters. My heart's breaking, hearing the pain in his words, but he shouldn't be here. *You're too broken for a man like him.*

"The doctors said it was a panic attack. Her body shut down from all of the stress. When it's time, she'll wake up. There's no damage. This is just her mind protecting her. We have to be patient." The room goes quiet again. I feel his presence beside me, but I'm not ready to wake up yet. I like having him here with me, even if that makes me a horrible woman who destroyed a relationship. I've missed him so much. *He deserves so much better than you.*

"Please wake up, baby." I hear him whisper into my hair before the medicine takes over and I'm lost to the dark all over again. *I'm not your baby.*

Barely opening my eyes, I can tell the room around me is dark. I'm able to make out some shapes, but otherwise, I don't know anything about what's going on around me. Instead of relying on my sight, I start using my other senses to figure things out. I hear a monitor beeping, the smell of disinfectant. *In the hospital.* I feel the bed beneath me, it's not too hard, but definitively a hospital bed, and my right hand is being held tightly. As my eyes adjust to the darkness of the room, I notice there is a body slumped over the right side of the bed. I look over to the chair and see another body slumped there. Then I notice the bed on the other side of the room. *Savi.*

Attempting to sit up is hard when you have a head partially on your leg. I don't want to wake him, but I need to move. My ass is going numb. Shifting slightly to the left, his head falls from my leg and lands. He sits up, his eyes blinking as he wakes. Once he realizes what's going on, his gaze swings to my face.

"Oh, thank God." He breathes out. His voice is barely a whisper. He releases my hand and then moves to sit on the side of the bed, making sure to not mess with the IV they have placed in my arm. Before I know what's happening, both of his hands are cupping my face, forcing me to look at him. "I don't think I've ever been so happy to see those beautiful eyes." He leans his forehead against mine, breathing me in.

I close my eyes and breathe him in as well. This man has the power to destroy me. But, even with that knowledge sitting in the forefront of my mind, I lean into his touch. We sit like this for a few minutes, before I finally pull back from him. *He's not yours. He'll never be yours.*

"How'd you get in?" I ask quietly, searching his eyes. I can tell from the bags under his eyes how exhausted he is, the tear stains on his cheek showing that he's possibly been crying.

"Madison ran out to grab me when you blacked out." He gives me a small smile. "What happened, baby?"

"Please don't call me that, Luc." His eyebrow raises at the nickname I called him back in high school.

"We have a lot to discuss. But before we get into anything, tell me what happened." His hand is caressing my cheek, his eyes refusing to leave mine.

Taking a deep breath, I shake my head silently. "I don't know. It all just became too much."

"I'm so sorry, baby. I'm so fucking sorry." He closes his eyes, allowing a tear to run down his cheek. I catch the tear with my thumb, caressing his cheek as I wipe it away. Before I can go to pull it away, he grasps my hand and keeps it on his cheek. *Why is he tormenting me like this?*

"Lucas, please don't. I can't." I try to pull away, pulling my eyes from his face. Seeing him hurting is killing me.

"Natalie Renee Conaway, stop pulling away from me." His use of my full name pulls my attention straight to him. "I know we have some shit to talk about, but you will not pull away from me again. I let you push me away before and it fucking killed me, so no more, okay?" All I can do is nod at him. I have no idea how to handle what's going on. My eyes dart all around the room before settling on Savi's bed.

"Savi." I whisper.

"She's fine. No damage detected on the last CT. She's been making some small eye movements, but she hasn't woken yet." I look back at him.

"Why won't my baby wake up?" His eyes soften at my question and I know he's asking himself the same thing. He looks to her bed before bringing his eyes back to mine. I know he'd give anything to have her wake up, just like I would.

"Maybe she knew mama was resting and was waiting for you." He gives me a small smile. "It's close to 2am, lay back down and get some rest, morning will be here before you know it." He lays me back down, caressing my cheek with his hand as he watches me. My eyes are back on Savi's bed. I stifle a yawn and hear him chuckle at me. I turn back towards him.

"How long was I out?" I ask as I lay my head back down.

"It's been almost three days." His shoulders slump as he looks back at me, his hand smoothing the hair back from my face.

"I missed you." I admit before allowing myself to close my eyes and rest.

"I missed you too, baby." He says as he leans in and kisses my hair softly. I feel him move back to his chair, not leaving my side, but still making the bed feel empty again. I reach out for him and he clasps my hand into his. "I'm not going anywhere. Rest, baby. I got you." And with that, I fall back to sleep, the thoughts and voices going quiet just by the touch of his hand on mine.

Waking in the morning, I feel more restful than I've felt since all of this happened. I've lost track of the days so I couldn't even say how long we've been in this damn hospital, but it's been too long if you ask me. I look around the room, glad to be able to see more than just shadows and silhouettes. Madison's in the chair beside Savi's bed, slumped over, much like Lucas is with mine. I hear a cough and look to the entrance of the room where Justin's standing.

Immediately, I want to yell and scream at him to get out. But upon seeing my face, he instantly puts his hands up defensively.

"I promise, I'm not here to make a scene. Just wanted to check on you." I raise my eyebrow at his words. "And to apologize for the last time you saw me. And for the first time we met." He looks sheepish, almost apologetic. I don't know him well enough to know if he is being sincere or not, and right now, I don't care to hear anything from this man.

"Justin. What are you doing here?" Lucas asks, pulling my attention away from Justin and to him. I didn't even realize he was awake.

"I just wanted to make sure everyone was doing ok. I'm heading back to the office today, have to clear out my desk."

"What? What are you talking about?" Lucas asks. I can't help but look between them. Lucas looks shocked and Justin just looks careless.

"I quit." Justin shrugs his shoulders and leans against the entryway to the room. Just as Lucas is about to talk again, I hear loud beeping on the other side of the room and a nurse rushes into the room. She notices that I'm awake and smiles at me. Just behind her, I watch Justin discreetly exit.

"Oh sweetie, I'm so glad you're awake. I'll get Barb in to take out that IV. I'm gonna go check and see why Savi's alarm is blaring and then we'll get you taken care of." She moves over to the other bed, and then I hear the words I've been waiting to hear since we got into this damn hospital.

"Mama."

# Chapter Fourteen

LUCAS

The hospital room burst into a flurry of activity the minute we all heard that one word. Grabbing Natalie, I stop her before she can rip her IV out. She glares at me, but right now, the nurses are all surrounding Savi, so she needs to give them a minute.

"Nat, baby, I'm right here, and I promise you'll get to her. Just give them a minute." Her eyes find mine and I can see the tears she's fighting back. I know how badly she needs to be across this room, how desperately she needs to see her baby's eyes. I want the same thing, but I can't allow my girl to hurt herself getting over there, as much as it's killing me to hold her back.

"Mama!" Savi cries again. It takes all the strength I have to keep Natalie in place, causing me to yell for some help. A nurse finally comes over and quickly takes care of the IV in her arm and before I know what's happening, Natalie's out of my arms and across the room. I release the breath I've been holding when the nurses finally part well enough for me to see Savi. Her blue eyes are trained on her mama, tears flowing readily. I can barely hear Natalie whispering to her, trying her best to keep her calm while the nurses do what they need to do.

Walking over to the bed, I come up beside Natalie. I take her free hand in mine and squeeze, letting her know I'm right here with her. She squeezes back, but never takes her eyes off Savi. As I watch my girls together, I sigh in relief. Standing there, watching the two girls I would give my life for, I feel a huge weight lifting off my shoulders.

However, that moment is broken as the doctor comes in. "I need everyone who isn't direct family out of this room please." He says. He has lost his ever-loving mind if he thinks I'm leaving. Not fucking happening. He comes to stand directly across from us. "Sir, you need to step out for now." I remain planted right where I am. I watch as Madison gives me a smile before walking out of the door.

"He can stay." Natalie says, looking at the doctor. The doctor eyes me a bit before nodding and getting to work.

After ten minutes of tests, he tells us that everything looks great, but he'll need a new CT to make sure there's nothing else going on. Natalie's crying again as she nods at the doctor, whether it's happy or sad, I can't tell, but my best guess is they're happy tears.

"Please let me know if she goes unconscious without being woken to stimuli, has difficulty breathing, or you notice she is slurring her words at all." We nod at him again and he leaves the room. Natalie hasn't released my hand, so I make no move to do it for her. If I can, I'll gladly stand by her side every second of every day for the rest of my life. Nothing can pull me from her, I just need to prove to her that we are real.

"Lucy." I look down at the sweet girl who has dubbed me with a girl's name because she couldn't pronounce the hard c in Lucas. She's staring at me with the sweetest blue eyes in the world.

"Hi, sweet girl. I can't tell you how happy it makes me to

see those pretty blues." Savi attempts to smile, but only half of her face is allowing her lips to move. I give Natalie a questioning look, but she's so enamored with Savi being awake, that she doesn't seem to notice. Instead of voicing my concern, I decide to go let a nurse know.

"I'll be right back," I whisper into her hair before kissing it and stepping away. I walk out to the corridor and mention what I saw to the nurse at the desk. She makes a note in the chart before smiling and nodding at me.

"I'm glad you're back. Natalie's so much more relaxed when you're here with her." She whispers to me as I turn away. My heart swells with so much happiness hearing that, but I have some work to do for my girl. I pull out my phone and text Justin.

**Lucas:** Hey man, can you do me a favor?

**Justin:** Whats up? How's the squirt?

**Lucas:** She's good. They are running more tests. I need you to run to the store and get Nat a replacement phone. Then I need you to run to my house and grab me some spare clothing.

**Justin:** What kind of phone did she have? You want me to go all the way to your house? Didn't you pack a bag when you came back?

**Lucas:** Same as us. And yes, but I left it behind on accident.

**Justin:** You're a pain in the ass.

I smile as I type out my response to him.

**Lucas:** Takes one to know one. Take Madison with you so she can grab stuff for Natalie.

**Justin:** You want me to die a gruesome death, don't you?

That message makes me laugh aloud, causing the people in the hallway to look at me funny.

**Lucas:** Fuck. Just get the phone. I'll ask her to grab my bag and stuff for Natalie.

I send off a text to Madison letting her know what I need from her. Luckily, her only response is thumbs-up. I know there's a story there, one I don't know about. But that's the last thing on my mind. First, I need to take care of my girls.

It's been hours since the tests were completed. Hours since all hell broke loose, in the best possible way, and now all we've done is sat here. Natalie refuses to leave Savi's side for even a moment. Looking at her, I can see her struggling as she keeps wiggling around, a clear sign that she needs to use the bathroom. I'm laughing to myself as I walk over to her.

"Baby, let me sit here while you use the bathroom." I know she can see the amusement on my face from watching her struggle the past five minutes. When she glares at me, I can't contain my laughter anymore and I burst out laughing. "You've been doing the pee-pee dance for five minutes. Go use the bathroom." She glares at me even more, but finally nods and passes Savi's hand into mine. I kiss her forehead as she passes.

Taking Nat's position, I gaze down at the sweet girl currently resting after hours of tests. There's no tubes in her nose, no monitors on her head. She could pass for being at home in her own bed, if it weren't for the light bruises on her cheeks and the IVs in her arms. I gently push her hair off her face and smile at her. My movement causes her eyes to open, and her blue eyes take in her surroundings before landing on me.

Her smile lights up the room again, and this time, there is no delay or lack of movement on one side of her face. I smile right back at her. She got so fucking lucky. I have no idea what would've happened if she didn't pull through the way she did. But she's a fighter, she's our fighter. Now we just wait until they let us take her home.

I look up at the door to see Natalie watching us, a smile on her face. My heart bursts at the sight. I'd give anything to keep that look on her face. I grin in return and step aside, motioning for her to take her position back. She walks over and places a kiss on my cheek.

"Thank you." Her voice is a whisper against my skin.

"Always." I take her hand into mine as she goes back to her spot right beside Savi. She's fallen back to sleep, her lashes resting peacefully against her cheeks.

"Why did you come back, Lucas?" Her question startles me, but looking at her, I can see the doubt and fear in her eyes. I hate that she has questions about us, especially given what she has been through. I didn't think she'd be ready to talk so soon. Taking a deep breath, I pull her to the chairs beside the bed, so she isn't too far from Savi.

"Are you sure you want to do this right now?" I see a blush creep up her cheeks at my question, but I need to know. If we're going to talk about this, then I won't be holding back.

"Honestly, I don't know, Lucas. But Savi's awake with no complications, and now I can't help but think about what happened between us." Her blush deepens as she utters the last word.

"I came back because you are, and always have been, every-thing to me. You and that little girl are my everything. And that day, in the garden, the moment my lips touched yours, it was like my world finally made fucking sense." Her eyebrows quirk at my colorful language. I don't normally curse in front of Savi, but she's asleep and my emotions are overflowing. "When we kissed, it was like my brain and my heart got shocked. You went from being my best friend to the woman I knew I'd never be able to live without."

She goes to interrupt me, but I hold my hand up. I'm not done yet. "I know some of what happened with Ethan based on what little I heard from Madison, and it pains me to know that he did that to you, that he stole that piece of you. I know why your head went to where it did. But I had broken up with her. Or I thought I had. I don't know. But she was never on my mind. I hadn't even thought of her at all. And then when you made me leave, it shattered me into a million pieces." I see tears are forming in her eyes, but I can't stop talking. I'm scared of what she's going to say so I want to get everything out before she has the chance to tell me to get lost again. "I can't lose you, Natalie. When I say that I want to see where this goes, I mean that I don't know which way is which anymore. You've been my best friend since we were eight years old, but that kiss changed everything for me."

"Luc, can I say something now?" I look at her. She's biting her bottom lip and all I want to do is pull it out of her mouth with my teeth, but that would probably set us back again. I quickly look away from her mouth and give her a small nod. "I was so confused by all of that, and it compounded because of my past, with what was currently going on."

"I understand..." I start to say, but her hand covers my mouth.

"I wasn't done. I feared losing you, losing our friendship." She takes a deep breath and looks over at Savi. Her hand is still on my mouth, so I can't say anything. "What you said about that kiss." Her voice is so light, I can barely hear her. "I felt the same. The minute you touched your lips to mine, it was like my world finally made sense."

The minute those words reach my ears, it takes all I have to contain the excitement. She felt it. *Holy shit.*

"But, even if you hadn't been thinking of Lauren, or thought you had broken up with her, you were still technically hers when you kissed me." And all the excitement I just felt rushes out of my body and my shoulders slump in defeat. But I'm not giving up. I know that she feels the same based on what she just said, but she's scared.

"I officially ended it that day when you saw that she called. It's been over for a while, if I'm being honest." I look off to the other side of the room, to the bed she was in recently when she had a panic attack because of Lauren. And before I can even think about it, I tell her what I've never told anyone about my relationship that the agency put together. That it was a relationship of convenience for our careers and nothing more, how Justin and her agent got us together to help us because we were both new to the business and Lauren wasn't booking many jobs. I give her details about how she started acting more like a girlfriend only because my best friend, who is a gorgeous woman, showed up with her baby. I explain the amount of jealousy that she had over my relationship with Savi, and how that's when I found myself questioning our relationship, or lack thereof. I admit that I got comfortable in what we had because it was for work, but I never had any feelings beyond that. I tell her how we'd never even slept together. Everything pours out of me, from the moment I was introduced to Lauren to the day Natalie had her panic attack.

When I finish my spiel, I look up to find Natalie staring at me with wide eyes, like she can't believe the words I just uttered. From the corner of my eye, I notice Justin watching us from the doorway. He's holding the bag with her new phone. He's gawking at me with the same expression as Natalie, pure shock written all over his face.

"Wow." I hear Natalie whisper. Just as she's about to say more, Justin interrupts.

"I got the new phone." He walks in and hands her the bag, his eyes never leaving mine. "Mind if I steal Lucas here to go get some coffee?"

"Yea, I need some time to process all of that anyway." She takes the bag and gives me a small smile. Kissing her on the cheek, I stand and walk out with him, looking back to find her watching me.

Grabbing our coffee from the cart, we make our way to a secluded corner of the dining area. There aren't many people in here, lunch having passed a while ago. Sitting across from me, I can see his shoulders deflate as he takes his first sip of his coffee.

"So, you walked out of the agency?" I figure I may as well start off since he hasn't said a word since we left Savi's room.

"The mess you left for me to clean up after walking away, it wasn't pretty." He takes a deep breath, his fingers pinching the bridge of his nose as he tries to figure out his words. I didn't mean to make a mess for him, but once the decision to stop modeling was made, it's like a weight lifted off my shoulders.

"I didn't mean to make such a mess for you." He shrugs me off.

"The agency wasn't happy, especially after the bullshit with Lauren. She's pissed and making a scene. They basically told me to get you back or it's my job." He rolls his neck before meeting my eyes. "Instead of fighting, I walked out." *Fuck.*

"What about all of your clients?"

"They took them." *Double fuck. The last thing I wanted for him was this.* Trying to find the words to say to even try to apologize for the mess I created is interrupted when he keeps speaking. "Listen, I've been thinking since I walked though. I've been doing this shit for as long as you've been modeling. You took me on as an agent because we were both new. I know my shit." I nod my head at his words. His being a new agent made it easier for me to take him as an agent. "I'm thinking we start our own agency, in BoothBay Harbor."

"Uh..." It's like the words are stuck in my throat. "Say that again?" He smirks at me, running another hand through his hair.

"I want to start a new agency, in BoothBay, with you." I feel like that GIF of Nathan Fillion using his hands but being rendered completely speechless.

"I screwed you over by walking," the asshole nods, *fucker*, "the shit with the paparazzi is still haunting me, and you're telling me you want to start an agency together?" He nods again, now smiling.

We sit there a few minutes, staring at each other. If you were an on-looker, you'd think we were a couple lost in the love we share with how intense the moment is. Finally, he breaks and goes to smack me. I manage to lean back just in time for his hand to whoosh in front of my face.

"So, what do you say?" He asks, finishing off his coffee.

"I'm in."

It's been two days of test after test for Savannah as the doctors and nurses work to get us out of here. Two days of Justin hanging out when Madison isn't here. Lucas talked to me about stepping down from modeling and opening the new agency with Justin. It shocked me because I always thought he loved modeling. I'd never ask him to step down, especially not for me. They went downstairs to the cafeteria to discuss more business when the nurses came in to take Savi for a lap around the halls.

I watch as Savi and the nurse walk back into the room. This is the last test we're waiting on and it fills my heart seeing my baby girl standing on her own two feet. The nurse smiles my way as they make their way over to the bed. There are no more IVs, no more tubes.

"I'll go update the doctor and he should be in to speak with you soon." I smile and nod at her as I take over tucking the blankets around my girl.

"You ready to go home, baby?" I kiss her forehead as she nods her head at me, her eyes fighting to stay open. She still tires easily but the doctors said that once she's back home, her energy should start coming back. "Get some rest, baby, it could be a little while before the doctor comes in." She closes her eyes as I grab her hand and sit in the chair beside her bed.

Just as I'm about to close my eyes, I hear a soft knock at the door. Looking up, I'm shocked to see the doctor already standing there.

"Sorry to wake you." He gives a boyish grin as he walks into the room, his voice quieting even more as he notices that Savi is asleep. "I just wanted to give you the good news."

"I wasn't asleep yet." I stand, keeping my hand gripped around Savi's.

"All of her tests came back normal. She has no delays, no muscle deterioration. She's a very lucky girl, considering. I'm giving the orders to start the discharge paperwork so you should be out of here within the next hour or two." He reaches out to shake my hand. Releasing Savi's hand, I give him a quick shake before I put my hand right back where it was.

"Thank you, Dr. Johnson. For everything." He looks from Savi to me before nodding and walking back out of the door. As soon as he exits, the tears start coming. Not because I'm sad, but because I'm so unbelievably happy that I can finally take my baby girl home.

"Natalie, baby, what's wrong?" Lucas runs straight to my side. I didn't even notice him, or Justin come into the room.

"I'll call you later, man." Justin says before exiting, not even waiting for a response. Lucas doesn't take his eyes off me as he brings both of his hands to my cheeks, his thumbs drying my tears.

"Baby, please talk to me." His eyes show so much sincerity as he continues to watch me cry.

"We're going home."

Coming home from the hospital seems surreal. I'm scared to think of what my house looks like, it's been weeks since I've even stepped one foot into my little house. But even with my house in complete disarray, nothing beats knowing my daughter is safe and healthy. After being in a coma for weeks, my sweet baby has no delays at all. It's a miracle, plain and simple.

Lucas hasn't left my side at all. Ever since our talk, it's like he stopped holding himself back. He's constantly touching me in some way, whether it's holding my hand, placing his hand on my thigh, touching my face sweetly, or whatever other way he could find to have his hands on me. Madison kept eyeing me every time she caught him touching me, but he never left us alone long enough for me to talk to her about what's going on. *You're too broken for him.* The voices in my head have only gotten stronger, breaking me down slowly.

I've been off in my own little world since we pulled away from the hospital. Lost in my thoughts about everything that's happened. I have no idea how to handle what he told me. All I could do was nod at him when he finished his little speech about his relationship with Lauren. I was shocked, to say the least. I didn't know much about their relationship. When Lucas was home, she never came with him and he never discussed her. I hadn't even met her until that day in the hospital when she showed up. But to find out that it was all for their work, it was just... I don't even know.

"You okay over there?" I turn to look at Lucas, who's studying me while driving.

"Just thinking." I shrug my shoulders and turn back to the landscape as it passes by.

"I want you and Savi in the house with me." His statement shocks me. The last thing I want to do is move in with him so soon after everything. Sighing, my lips pursing, I turn to look at him.

"That's not going to happen, Lucas. We'll be in the guest house, as always. I need time to come to terms with everything. You have to give me that." My voice is very small, afraid of making him angry.

"I get that, Natalie, but we will explore us, who we are outside of being best friends. I'm not letting you push me away again." I take my bottom lip in my mouth, chewing on it as I take in the words he's saying. Before I know what's happening, his hand on my face and his thumb is pulling my lip out of my mouth.

"If I weren't driving, I'd be using my teeth to pull that lip out of your mouth. The only teeth chewing on that gorgeous lip of yours will be mine." *Holy shit.* He smirks at me and I can feel the blush rushing up my neck and covering my cheeks. I don't even know how to respond to that. His words are eliciting feelings from me down in my core, something I didn't think I'd ever have again. I can feel the butterflies in my stomach taking flight as I roll the words around in my head.

Before I can respond, or even think of a response to what he just said to me, the road turns to gravel and I realize we've arrived at his house. He smiles over at me, grabs my hand, and places a soft kiss to the back of it.

"Madison came over and got your house ready for you to be in there." I give him a confused look. He just said he wanted us in his house, yet he told Madison to make sure mine was ready for me. "I want you in my house, but I figured you wouldn't be ready yet, so I texted her before we left the hospital." This man just can't stop finding ways to make the wall I built up after Ethan to break apart, and I'm not even sure how to feel about it.

He follows me into the house, bringing a sleeping Savi into her room. I look around at the clean house. Madison took care of the dishes, straightened up my living room. I investigate the laundry room and notice the laundry is still piled up. Well at least she left me something.

"So, are we going to talk?" I jump about five feet into the air, holding my chest as I turn around to look at him. He's holding his hands up, like it wasn't his intention to scare the living daylights out of me.

"I need time, Lucas. Please." He gives me a nod, then walks over to me.

"Time is what you will get then." Just as I'm about to thank him, he leans down and kisses me softly on the lips. I'm frozen in place, shocked into position at the feeling of his lips on mine again. His hand caresses my cheek as he pulls his lips from mine. "I just wanted to give you something to think about." He winks at me, and before I know what is happening, he's walking out the door. All I can do is touch my lips, still feeling his lips on mine.

"I want to see Lucy." Savi yells at me for the fourth time since we've been home. When we walked in two hours ago, she was asleep, and Lucas put her in her bed for me. I haven't heard from him since he gave me a kiss as something to think about. The minute she woke up, she asked to see him. At first, I thought it was sweet. Now, I want to pull my hair out in frustration.

"He's not home right now, bug, we'll see him later."

"But I want to see him now." she screams the last word, stomping her foot. Apparently, we have the three-nager present this evening. I roll my neck, popping it a few times before turning to her.

"Savannah Marie, I said he isn't home, so you need to take that little attitude you're sporting and quit." She screams at me, stomping her feet at me and then turning and running back into her room, slamming the door. Putting my head into my hands, I take a deep breath. *I love my child. I love my child. I love my child.* I repeat the mantra in my head as I continue to hear her screaming in her room.

Sighing deeply, I grab my phone. I don't want to give into this tantrum, but I also want to make being home easy on her. She just went through a whole ordeal, and even though she won't remember much, I still feel like I'm stuck between a rock and a hard place when it comes to making her smile right now. Blinking away the tears, I wake up the screen and notice I've missed a couple messages from Madison.

**Madison:** Hey girl, just checking in. Need anything?

**Madison:** I hope you're ignoring me because you're currently lip-locked with Lucas right now.

I face-palm as I read that last message. I should have kept my mouth shut about Lucas when it came to telling Madison about what happened. But she's also a good voice of reason, most of the time. Laughing off her last message, I respond.

**Natalie:** Not lip-locked with anyone. Having a screaming match with a three-year-old.

**Madison:** Well, that's no fun. Want company?

**Natalie:** Yes. Bring wine.

**Madison:** You got it!

The screaming has stopped, so I'm hoping she either tired herself out and fell asleep, or she figured out I wasn't going to give in. Either way, I'm happy with the quiet.

"Ok girl, spill." Madison sips her wine and quirks her eyebrow at me.

"Straight to it huh?" I chuckle as I take a sip of my own wine. She gives me a look like she isn't going to take any of my shit. "Well, um, I don't even know how to make this any clearer than this. His relationship with Lauren was set up by his agency." She spits her drink out.

"First of all, what a waste of fucking wine. Second, what the fuck do you mean?" I start explaining what Lucas told me. By the time I finish, her glass is on the table in front of us, her eyes are wide, and she looks just as shocked as I did when he told me. She picks up her wine, finishes it one gulp and then looks at me again.

"Say something." I whisper.

"I don't even know what to say. Now that I think about it, she's never even visited here. I don't think I've actually ever seen them together." I roll her words around in my head. "Fuck, now it all makes sense." I look at her, wondering what the hell she's talking about.

"Care to elaborate?" I continue sipping my wine.

"Before you moved here, they were never together unless it was for work. If I saw them together, they were with their agents as well. Never actually alone with each other and she never hung around long, always going back to wherever it is that she calls home." I take this information in. I didn't know how it was before I showed up, but hearing Madison tell me this, it's like what Lucas told me clicks into place. *He still technically belonged to her.*

"So, what do I do?" My voice is quiet again. I want to give him a chance, but I'm so scared. I have Savi to think about, and even though I know he loves her with all his heart, I worry about what will change when I let him in. *What happens when we don't work out?* I don't even say if because I know the minute he sees how broken I am, he'll run for the hills.

"What do you want?" She tips her empty glass towards me with her question.

"I'm scared." I shrug, down the rest of my glass of wine and lean back into the couch. After the way Ethan tore me apart, I don't know if I can be the woman Lucas needs. I had a baby, so my body isn't anywhere near where it should be. I'm soft and saggy, not fit and toned. I'm no longer the strong girl he knew in high school. Ethan broke me and I'm not sure if I'll ever be good enough for anyone ever again. All the words my ex ever said flaying me in my head as I sit here. *Fat, single mother that no one could ever want.* The words continue to taunt me, a single tear escaping from my eye as it trails down my cheek.

"I swear, that man needs to be stabbed." I choke on my spit as I look over to Madison, wondering what the hell she's talking about. She looks at me and shrugs. "Not Lucas, dummy, your ex. I can see you over there playing his words in your head. I may not have been there for you when it happened, but my life isn't all cupcakes and rainbows." Her gaze moves to her empty glass as she stops talking. Her words skewer me in place. She'd never mentioned her past to me before, and now I only have more questions.

"I'm here if you need to talk about it." I whisper to her. She smiles and pulls me into a side hug.

"I know you are. But it's not something I'm ready to deal with out loud yet." I nod and relax into her as we lay back into the couch, both of us lost in our own thoughts.

# Chapter Sixteen

NATALIE

Over the next couple of weeks, Lucas makes his presence known, but never pushes for anything. He still gives me a kiss goodbye every day when he leaves. Just a light peck on the lips, never asking for more from me. On one side, it's driving me crazy, and on the other, I'm thankful he's being so understanding. I'm still stuck in my head on everything concerning him to going back to normal around here with Savannah. Her primary care doctor cleared her to go back to daycare tomorrow, and I'm freaking out. I know I can't keep her home with me forever, but just letting her out of my sight again is causing me to panic so badly.

"Hey beautiful, what's going on in that head?" Jesus, I didn't even hear Lucas come into the house. I've been sitting here staring at the same image on my laptop for who knows how long. I look over the computer at him. He's smiling at me, that trademark smile that puts butterflies into my stomach. *Damn that smile.*

I shrug my shoulders and redirect my attention back to what I'm working on. Taking a deep breath, I open a new picture from the unedited folder and start my process of editing it. I can still feel him staring at me, searching my face for answers that I don't have yet.

"Lucy, you're home." I hear Savi run into the room.

"Savi, my sweet girl." He picks her up and spins her around while she giggles. I peek over the top of the computer at them. Her smile's a mile wide and he's looking back at her with a huge smile on his face. This is what scares me the most. Their relationship suffering because we took a shot at being more than just friends. I know he loves her with everything he has and the last thing I want to do is take him away from her. *He deserves better.* I watch for another minute before going back to what I was doing.

I've been awake for hours, my nerves shot. I've paced the entire length of the guest house up and down trying to calm myself down but no matter what I do, I can't shut up the fear that's grabbing hold of me while I wait on Savi to get dressed. She officially goes back to daycare today, and I have my first shoot since everything happened. I'm so lucky that I had such understanding clients. My calendar is booked solid for the next two weeks as I work to get caught up on the shoots I had to reschedule.

"Savi, baby, are you ready?" I call out. I plant myself by the front door, wringing my hands together as I try to get myself calmed down. I'm doing my best to put on a brave face, well as brave as I can considering the circumstances.

"I can't wait to see all of my friends, Mommy. I missed them." I'm trying my best not to freak out about leaving her at daycare, but I already feel my panic setting in. I know she's perfectly healthy, but after what happened, I'm not ready. I smile down at her, swallowing my panic. Nodding my head, I take her hand in mine and we head out.

"How are my two favorite ladies this morning?" Lucas is sitting on his porch, a mug of coffee in his hand.

"I go back to school, Lucy." Her nickname for him pulls the corners of my lips into a small smile. *That will never get old.* Savi pulls her hand from mine and runs to him. He sets his mug down and sweeps her into a giant hug.

"I know, bug. How's your Mommy handling it?" He gives me a knowing look, like he can read my mind. I simply shrug my shoulders.

"Come on, Savi, you don't want to be late." She pouts her lip out, torn between going to see her friends and staying with her favorite person. *My favorite person besides her.* The thought startles me, but instead of dwelling on it, I shrug it off. I'll deal with it later.

"I'll walk with y'all." Lucas situates her onto his hip, grabs his mug, and joins me in the driveway.

"Yay." Savi's smile stretches across her face as her dimples pop. Shaking my head at their antics, I walk off, leading the way to her daycare. I can hear them back there, talking amongst themselves, but I'm stuck in my head again. *What if she gets hurt again? What if this time she doesn't wake up?* Before I even realize it, we are at the daycare and Savi's excitement has caused her to wiggle out of Lucas's arms to get into the building.

"She's excited, isn't she?" he asks, coming up beside me. I pull my bottom lip into my mouth, chewing on it. He eyes my lip, quirking his eyebrow at it. It's then that I remember what he said in the car. A blush creeps up my neck and onto my cheeks, and I release my lip. He gives me a knowing smile before joining Savi at the door. *How could I ever be good enough for a man like him?*

"Come on, Mama!" I take a deep breath, steel my panic, and head into the daycare to drop her off.

"You're awfully quiet." Lucas bumps my shoulder with his as we walk up the driveway.

"I'm scared to death." I admit quietly.

"I couldn't tell." I can feel the sass dripping from his words. "You wouldn't leave until they promised to call you if something happened, multiple times." He's laughing at me. Tears threaten to spill out of my eyes. I didn't realize I had been that bad, I'm just so damn worried about leaving her there.

"Hey, don't cry, baby. I was just joking." He stops us and stands in front of me, forcing me to look at him. "I know you're worried. I am too. Talk to me." His eyes look so soft and honest right now, his eyes searching mine. His thumb reaches up and dries the single tear that managed to escape. He keeps his hand on my face, caressing my cheek as he waits for me to talk.

"I'm just scared something is going to happen. I can't handle it if something else happens." My voice is barely above a whisper. He smiles softly at me. I take a deep breath, averting my eyes from his. He pushes slightly on my cheek, causing me to look back at him. He is searching my eyes. "Lucas." My whisper seems to break the trance he is in and before I know what is happening, his lips are on mine again.

This kiss isn't like his soft ones from the past couple of weeks. It's a searing kiss, the kind of kiss that hits every part of my body. I can feel it all the way down to my toes. He applies more pressure, his tongue asking for entrance. I lean into his kiss and open slightly, giving him the permission that he is looking for. He groans into my mouth as he continues to deepen the kiss. The hand on my cheek is keeping me right where he wants me. *Why does he have to be such a damn good kisser?*

When he pulls away, our breathing is labored and ragged. My eyes stay closed as he leans his forehead into mine. I can feel his body shaking as he fights to control his breathing. Hell, for all I know, it's my body that's shaking. He places a soft kiss to my lips, my cheek, and my forehead before pulling away. Opening my eyes, I find him looking directly at me. Taking my hand, he continues us down the driveway and up to my door.

"I know you want to go slow, baby, but you can't deny our chemistry together. That kiss was just as intense as the first kiss we shared. Please give us a chance." His eyes are pleading with mine, asking for more than I know how to give.

"Promise that when we don't work, you'll still see Savi." I choke on the words as they come out of my mouth. He looks at me in shock as he hears the words I'm saying.

"We will work. There is not a when here, no ifs. It's just us, baby, and I know we *will* work. But I can promise that you'll never have to worry about me turning away from Savi. Is that seriously what's stopping you?" It's one of many things, that being one of the biggest. All I can do is nod at him. "Oh, my sweet Natalie, you have my promise on that."

"Then I think I can try." The smile that graces his face is so damn big, so damn happy. I want to keep making him smile like that for as long as I can. "But, Lucas, I'm so damaged." He puts his fingers on my lips, stopping me from finishing.

"You are not damaged, Natalie. I don't know what Ethan did to make you think that way, but I promise you're the furthest thing from damaged." He removes his fingers and kisses me lightly on my lips. He pulls me in to hug him and I notice a man with a camera at the end of the driveway shooting pictures of us.

"Who is that?" Lucas pulls back and turns around. The minute he does, the man with the camera takes off.

"Fucking paparazzi. Damn it." My body starts shaking,

knowing they found where we live. I didn't think we had to worry about them anymore, but here they are.

"Oh God." I whisper as I pull my arms around my body, shielding myself, even though he's long gone.

"I'll take care of this, don't worry." He kisses me lightly on the lips before opening my door and watching me walk in. He winks and pulls out his phone before walking off.

I go to close the door, but his words stop me just as I go to push it. "Justin, we need to talk."

It's been a few weeks since our kiss, since I saw someone from the paparazzi hanging around the house. I don't know what Lucas did, but they've ghosted. The tabloids are still running stories like crazy but there's no sign of any photographers around.

Since the day I told him we could try, Lucas has done everything in his power to show we can work. He's never pressuring with me, but I can tell he wants more from me. We haven't gone past second base, and every time we stop, I can feel how hard he is for me. I want to give him so much more, but I'm so scared that once he sees my body, he won't feel this way anymore. Where Lauren was fit and tone, I'm flabby. My body isn't beautiful, no matter how badly I wish it were. I have stretch marks that make me cringe. *Fat, unworthy, disgusting.* The words Ethan said to me as I gained weight from the pregnancy play in my head on a loop, tearing me apart.

Grabbing my laptop, I make my way out to the deck to do something besides sit here and judge my misshapen body, a body that I hate but can do nothing to change because I'm a mom now. The weather is beautiful for being outside, and after spending weeks in a hospital, it feels good to just get outside. I finally caught up on all my work that I fell behind on during my time off, so today I'm putting together galleries and sending out confirmations for next week's shoots. I look down at my phone to see if Lucas had texted me recently, but the screen is blank of all notifications. He went out this morning with Justin to get some things handled for the next move in his career.

After a couple of hours of working, I save my progress and head back inside to make some lunch. Lucas sent a text saying he's on his way back. Plugging the laptop in, I set it on my desk, and walk into the kitchen. Pulling out some ham and cheese, bread and butter, I set out to make one of my favorite meals from when we used to hang out in high school. Ethan used to scoff at the childhood meal, telling me I need to grow up. I shrug off the memories of him, not wanting to deal with it today, and start cooking. A few minutes later, I hear my front door open.

"Where you at, beautiful?" I smile and shake my head at the greeting.

"In the kitchen." He comes in, smiling as he walks around the corner, one hand behind his back. I step away from the counter and quirk my eyebrow at him. He smiles at me, pulling a bouquet of lilies out in a vase from behind him.

"I saw these and remembered that you've always loved lilies." I smile at his words, loving that he remembered something that Ethan never did. He only ever got me roses, and even then, it was few and far between.

"Thank you." I grab the vase of flowers from him and kiss him lightly on the mouth. Bringing them to the table, I arrange them to where they are in the center of it. A smile touching my lips as I look at them. "They're beautiful."

"You're beautiful." His words are a whisper in my ear, and I feel him pressed into my back. My breath catches in my throat as I take in his presence surrounding me. Putting his hands on my hips, he turns me around to where I'm facing him. His hand goes to the back of my head and he pulls my hair out of the bun it's in. He's instantly in control as his fingers mark their way through the base of my hair and up into it.

Next thing I know, he's grabbing onto my hair and pulling, causing me to look up at him. His eyes are dark with lust, darting between my eyes and mouth. Before I can even stop anything from happening, his mouth is on mine, his tongue seeking entrance. His kiss commands me, steals my breath, making me weak in the knees. He pulls my hair again, taking even more control of me as his lips trace a path from my mouth to my ear. A jolt of electricity shoots straight to my core as I feel his lips on my ear.

"You're mine," he growls. "Say it. Tell me." This alpha mode isn't one I've seen from him before, but it doesn't scare me. If anything, it excites me.

"I'm yours," I say, my voice hoarse as I struggle to keep up with what he's doing to me and my body. I have no choice but to do what he's asking. Even the voices in my head can't stop this from happening.

With his other hand on my hip, he pulls me in close and I can feel just how hard he is in his jeans. He continues kissing his way down the side of my neck, stealing nibbles as he marks a path down.

"Tell me what you want, Nat" he whispers into the crook of my neck. I lose myself to his touch, his kiss, his presence. I feel like I'm in a dream and I don't want to wake up.

"You." His hand leaves my hair and next thing I know, both hands are cupping my ass and he's lifting me up against him. He's taken full control of my body and at this point, I'm fully willing to relinquish all my control to him.

# *Chapter Seventeen*

## LUCAS

The moment I walked into the house and saw her wearing that tank and skintight jeans, her hair in a messy bun exposing her neck, it was like all the blood drained straight down into my cock. I couldn't think straight anymore. The light kiss she gave me after taking her flowers only drove the blood south faster. In this moment, all I can think about is marking her as mine. Carrying her into the bedroom feels like a dream. I didn't know if we'd ever get here, especially after all we've been through. The past few weeks have been a test on my patience, all the kisses and touches were all I could think about, even when I wasn't with her. I'd taken more cold showers lately than I have in my entire life. But right now, it was all worth it because she's here in my arms. I've been waiting for this moment but never rushing her to get here.

I set her down on the floor by the bed and stand in front of her. She's biting on her bottom lip, a sign of worry on her features. I use my thumb to pull her lip from her mouth, notating the teeth marks that her biting has caused, her eyes to dart up to mine. The alpha in me wants to claim her, possess her in a way she's never felt before. Looking into her eyes, I notice they have a touch of fear in them, stopping me from moving too fast.

"What's going on in that gorgeous head of yours?" She scoffs at my statement before taking a deep breath, it's shaky and I can feel the nerves coming off her. Putting both of my hands on her face, I force her to look at me.

"I don't know if I'm what you want." Her voice is a whisper so I'm barely catching what she's saying. "I'm not in shape, my boobs are saggy..." I don't let her finish her words as my lips seal themselves over hers. She gasps in surprise and I use that as my opportunity to slide my tongue into her mouth, tenderly. She relaxes into my kiss, giving me this piece of her. I pull back, placing tender kisses to her lips, the corner of her lips. I don't know why she thinks she isn't enough. But I'm going to show her that she's more than enough, more than I ever deserved.

"You're beautiful, Natalie. I only see you." Her eyes are searching mine, questioning my words. "Let me see you?" Her tongue darts out and wets her lips. She gives me a slight nod when my hands move to the hem of her shirt.

She allows me to pull her shirt off, hiding herself as best she can as it exposes her soft belly, her beautiful curves, shame shining in her eyes as I take it all in. The girl I grew up with is now a beautiful woman. I want to explore each curve and crevice I can, with my tongue, my lips, my teeth. I'm taking in every detail, from the slope of her breasts covered in a plain cotton bra to the delicate contour of her hips. Grasping her wrists in my hands, I move them away from her body.

"Baby?" She looks into my eyes again, I can see her hesitation, her fear of not being good enough. "Each and every single thing about your body is beautiful." I put my hands on the slope of her waist, sliding them across her beautiful soft stomach. She goes to pull my hands away as I reach her belly button area, but I push her hand away.

"I have a pouch and stretch marks…" Once again, I'm quieting her, this time with a finger on her lips. She gives me a little glare, but I pay her no attention as I start taking her in again. Her body is a fucking symphony of curves, each one more delectable than the next. I haven't even seen her tits yet, but I still feel my cock hardening in my jeans as I take in each part of her that is exposed. My gaze is hungry by the time my eyes make their way back up to hers. She's eyeing me with confusion, like she has never been looked at in such a way before.

"That pouch and those stretch marks are because you carried a life inside you, Nat. They are from that rambunctious little girl you carried. They are marks showing that you are a mom. And that right there, is fucking beautiful." I remove my finger from her lips and kneel in front of her. I hear a sharp intake of breath as I start kissing her stomach, finding each stretch mark, and kissing it tenderly. "Don't ever be ashamed of your body, baby, it's perfect."

When I stand back up, I notice she's looking away, like she's scared to look me in the eyes. Putting both of my hands on her cheeks, I force her to look at me. Her eyes have unshed tears in them, showing all of the nervousness that she's feeling, and I'm going to do everything in my power to prove to her that she has no reason to be nervous with me. I move my hands around her back, making my way to her bra and before she can protest, I snap it open. My fingers are trailing a mark lightly up her back as I make my way to the straps sitting loosely on her shoulders. Knowing that I can't let myself take her the way I long to, has me suppressing the lowest growl as I push her straps down. I know I need to take it slow with her, for her, even if all I want is to hook her hands above her head and mark her in ways that will just show her how much she turns me on.

Slowly, I remove her bra and reveal the most beautiful set

of tits I've ever seen. They aren't too big, just enough to get a good handful. I search her eyes, silently asking for permission to touch her. She's biting her lip again, her eyes looking everywhere but at me. Pulling her lip out of her mouth again, I smirk when she rolls her eyes.

"Look at me, Natalie." Her eyes come to mine. I use the moment to put my hands where I've been wanting them. Holy shit, they are perfect. Round globes that aren't too heavy. Tight, pert nipples with a beautiful shade of pink that matches the blush that covers her neck and cheeks. My mouth's watering, wanting to taste them, taste her. I want to mark her, defile her, show her just how beautiful she is. Her eyes are watching mine, her lips parted as she feels everything I'm doing to her beautiful body. Her breath is shallow, and I feel her heart beating rapidly in her chest.

I move my hands to pinch her nipples, not hard, but just enough pressure to elicit a response from her. The response is everything I'm hoping for as a small moan escapes her parted lips, giving me the perfect opportunity to seal my mouth over hers. I'll never get enough of kissing this woman. Her lips were made for me, her body was made to be a perfect fit against mine. My cock is hard as a rock at this point, straining painfully against the jeans that are holding it back, but he'll have to wait, because right now, I need to show this woman just how radiant I think her body is.

Leading her gently over to the bed, I continue to kiss her as her knees hit the edge causing her lips to break from mine as she sits. I kneel in front of her, my arms going around her back to pull her to the edge, closer to me. Her lips are swollen, her eyes hazy with lust, but still showing a mark of uncertainty. I want to take that unease away, show her just how good it can be with us.

"Nat?" Her eyes find their way to mine again. "Do you trust me?" My words are barely above a whisper against her stomach, my hands holding her hips possessively.

"Always, Luc." I smirk at the nickname. Only she's allowed that courtesy, no one else. I hate the shortened version of my name, except when it's her saying it. She could call me a dickhead and I'd probably feel the same, as long as she's talking to me. I smile as I start the process of standing, using my hands to gently lay her back on the bed, hovering over her. Her trust shatters me because she doesn't know just how badly I needed to hear her say it. My own sense of control is on the edge wanting, no needing, to take her.

"Close your eyes." My voice has gotten husky, desire coating every word I'm uttering. I want her to feel everything that I'm feeling, to feel the desire that I have for her. I want to show her just how much her body turns me on. Her eyes search mine for a moment, a soft smile touching her lips, and then she closes them. "I need you to relax and feel. Can you do that for me?"

"Uh huh." I watch as she relaxes into the bed. Her face shows no sign of distrust, no signs of running the moment she has an opportunity. Letting my eyes roam over all her curves, my mouth waters again. The bottom half of her body is still covered by her jeans, but I will get to that point soon enough. The top half needs some love first. I lick my lips, kiss her lips lightly and then make a trail to her right ear, nibbling on the lobe a bit.

"You are breathtaking. Every inch of you is perfection. I'm about to show you just how perfect you are. Feel, Natalie, feel just how fucking amazing I know your body is." I hear her breathe in deeply, the shakiness apparent. She nods her head and relaxes even more as I take my time nibbling my way around her ear. I can feel her shaking, I don't know if it's from nerves or desire, but the only way to find out is to keep going. I trail my lips up her cheek, noticing that she's chewing on her lip again. I pull it from her mouth with my teeth.

"How many times do I have to tell you that the only teeth nibbling on this lip are mine, baby?" Her eyes dilate as she looks at me. I kiss her nose, her cheeks and then finishing lightly on her mouth. "This mouth, this body. It's all mine, Natalie. I'm going to show you just how desirable you are." My voice growing huskier with desire with each peck. Her breath is coming heavier now, her eyes closing as I make my way down the crook of her neck.

While in the kitchen, I noticed it was one of her pleasure spots. I take my time, sucking lightly on her skin there. I can feel her heart pulsing rapidly in her throat, her breathing getting heavier with each movement I make. Her hips have started moving slightly and as I lift myself up, I can see that her perfect nipples are now both erect. I smile down at this sight. My woman's feeling, and it feels so good to know that I'm eliciting all of this from her.

Lightly, I trail my fingers up her sides, which causes her to giggle lightly. I mentally notate that she's ticklish but continue my perusal of her body. My fingers make their way up her shoulders and then follow the curve down the slope of her breast. I don't stop at the nipple, but instead trail my fingers all around her beautiful tits. The top, the sides, the bottom. Each movement of my finger by her nipple causes her to move slightly. I know what she wants, but I'm enjoying myself too much to just take, even with my cock throbbing in my pants. The animal in me is barely holding back, but I need to do this for Natalie. I don't know how she doesn't realize just how beautiful she is, and it's my job to show her.

I'm watching her face as I finally roll her nipples between my fingers. She takes a deep breath in, and then a slow low moan comes out. *Holy fuck, that was hot.* My cock thickens even more at the sounds she makes, straining against the zipper in my jeans. I smirk as I continue rolling her nipples, her hips are moving, legs are rubbing together like she is trying to find some friction. I can't take it anymore, I need to taste more of her. I descend my mouth down and take her right nipple into my mouth, sucking it gently, rolling her nipple around with my tongue.

"Oh God." She yells out, causing me to smile while her nipple is in my mouth. I stop sucking, letting my tongue do the caressing instead.

"Ah ah ah, baby, the name is Lucas." Without letting her respond, I glide my tongue across the valley between her breasts and then take her other nipple into my mouth, this time using my teeth to pinch. I hear a sharp intake of breath from her as she pushes her chest up, like she's trying to keep her nipple in my mouth permanently, as though she's welcoming the pain with the pleasure. All her reactions are turning me on even more than I already was.

I let go of her nipple with a pop and then make my way back up to her mouth. I kiss it gently at first, and then I feel both of her hands on the sides of my face as she pushes her tongue into my mouth. I push back with my tongue, marking her mouth as mine, only mine. This girl's setting me on fire. I need her more than I need a glass of water. Pulling away, I kiss her lips lightly. She opens her eyes to look at me, her eyes are dark pools of lust and desire.

"I'm going to keep going now. Every part of you will be tasted by me. Every single inch will be kissed, licked, sucked." Each word I say has her body flinching, as her eyes drift close and she rests her head on my shoulder. "There will be no place on you that will be left untouched. I want to own all of this delectable, sinful body." I hear her gasp, and then she nods into my shoulder. My mouth starts salivating. I haven't wanted to taste anything as much as I want to taste her.

My lips and tongue trail their way between the valley of her breasts, down her beautiful soft stomach. I stop and kiss each stretch mark I come across. Making my way to her jeans, I look up to find her watching me, her body leaning back on her elbows. Her eyes are filled with lust as she licks her lips, watching me. I put my hands on the button, watching for her reaction. I lift my eyebrow to her as she watches my face. She nods slightly, her eyes going back to my hands.

Slowly I unbutton the jeans, pull down the zipper. She lifts her hips for me, so I can pull them down. I don't know what I was expecting but seeing the bright red triangle on a nearly bare pussy is making my mouth water even more. I bite my bottom lip as I continue pulling her pants down, my eyes not leaving that bright red strip of fabric. She's still watching me as I finish pulling her jeans off. I start at her right ankle and kiss it, letting my tongue slip out to taste her skin.

I trail my tongue up her calf, stopping to suck lightly on the back of her knee. I continue my path up her thigh, getting closer to that red fabric. She pulls her bottom lip into her mouth, her teeth making an indent the closer I get to it.

"What did I say about that lip and those teeth, baby?" My voice is filled with a huskiness I don't recognize, but then again, I'm not the same man I was before this moment. She releases her lip from her teeth, raising her eyebrow at me, daring me to continue. I smirk before looking back down. The red fabric is wet from the desire I pulled out of her. Taking a deep breath, I smell her musk, her body. It fills my senses as my mouth waters. I want to stop here, but I know I can't, not yet. I pull myself away and I hear the protest as she breathes out. Lifting her left leg up, I do the same thing to this leg that I did the other, her eyes watching every movement I make.

Once again, I reach the red fabric. The last piece of fabric on her body. My fingers hook into the sides of the underwear, and I tear my gaze from her pussy and look up to find her eyes watching me. I'm seeking permission again, not wanting to do anything without her telling me I can. Her eyes are still on my hands and the moment they stop moving, her eyes dart up to mine. She licks her lips as she nods. *Fuck yes.* She lifts her hips for me again, and I take my time pulling the fabric down her legs, not being able to take my eyes off what they revealed to me. I toss them over my shoulder, not caring where they land.

Her pussy's fucking perfect. Not totally bare, but not taken over completely by hair. I can see the lips are glistening, wet with her arousal. I lick my lips in anticipation, knowing that once I take my first taste, I may not want to stop. Her smell alone is an aphrodisiac to me, I can only imagine what her taste will do to me. I glide my hands up her thighs and though I don't want to look away, the need to see her face is greater than my need to dive right in and feast on her.

Her eyes are hooded, her breath shallow and quick. She's gripping the sheets like she's trying to anchor herself to the bed. She's watching me, mainly my mouth, with such intensity. Her look alone has my cock jumping in my pants. I have never been so fucking hard in my life, my cock pulsating in time with my heart, like all the blood drained and my heart now resides in the lower half of my body.

"You have such a pretty pussy, baby." Her eyes dart up to mine in shock, my dirty talk causing her eyes to darken even more. "I can't wait to taste you. You smell like heaven, so I can only imagine how you taste. Are you ready for me to taste you?"

"I've never..." she stops herself from saying what she was about to. My eyebrows shoot up at what she doesn't need to say. *Her fucking ex is an idiot.* I lick my lips and trail a finger around the lips of her pussy, stopping to gather some of her wetness, spreading it around her lips, lightly touching her clit.

The moans coming out of her have the bottom half of my body grinding against the bed, trying to get some sort of friction.

"No one's ever tasted this perfect pussy, baby?" She shakes her head no, looking away from me. "Do you know how happy that makes me? I get to be the first and only man to taste you." Her shocked eyes find mine again and she watches as I start kissing the inside of her thighs, the area right beside her lips. Her smell has me so fucking high on her. I lick my lips in anticipation as I use my fingers to spread her lips open.

I keep my eyes on hers as I take my first lick, groaning as I taste her. She's sweet, but not overly sweet, just enough to make my mouth water. She gasps as I continue lightly licking her clit. I suck it into my mouth, feeling it harden as her arousal becomes more evident. Her head falls back between her shoulders as she moans loudly. Her sounds, her taste, her smell, it all goes straight to my cock, and I can feel the pre-cum coating the inside of my jeans as I continue grinding against the edge of the mattress. The more noises she makes, the harder I grind, wishing like hell her pussy was enveloping me and not my damn jeans.

"Fuck, you taste like heaven, baby. I could savor you for breakfast, lunch, dinner and every meal in between and still not get enough of you." My voice is just loud enough for her to hear me. She shivers at my words, her moaning increasing. I continue my assault on her clit with my tongue, sliding it down to enter her with it. She's so fucking wet, so close to getting off. I want her to come on my tongue, on my finger, on my cock. I want all her orgasms.

Taking my right hand, I replace my tongue with my finger and slowly penetrate her. She's so fucking tight, and I know she's going to hug my cock when we finally get to that part. My cock's twitching as I feel how warm and velvety soft she is. This woman might just be the death of me. There's no part of her that isn't sheer perfection. Licking her clit softly, I can feel her on the cusp of an orgasm. I apply a little more pressure with my tongue on her clit, crooking my finger to find the spot that I know will detonate her. As I feel her getting closer, I feel my hips gyrating against the bed even harder, my cock wanting to be where my finger is.

Her orgasm hits and her hips are flying, her hands are pushing and pulling on my head, fingers tangled in my hair as she screams my name. I'm not stopping though. I won't waste a drop of this nectar flowing from her. I'm sucking and licking, taking everything she has to give me. I can feel her legs shaking as she comes down from it, putting a smile on my face knowing that I did this to her.

# *Chapter Eighteen*

NATALIE

Stars explode in my vision as the orgasm rocks through my body. My heart's beating rapidly in my chest, like it wants to explode as well. I'm catching my breath as I go through everything he just did to me in my mind. Never have I had my body worshipped the way he just did. No one has ever done the things he did to me, talked to me the way he did. Even my own husband hated the sight of my body after our daughter was born. Before I know what is happening, I'm thrust into a memory I don't want to have, not right now.

*I'd have to wear a shirt for Ethan because the stretch marks and pouch disgusted him. He wouldn't even touch my chest anymore. There was one night that had been marked in my head, stemming almost all my insecurities. I put on one of my favorite negligees to bed, hoping we would recapture us again. The moment he walked into the room and saw what I was wearing, his face fell into a look of disgust as his eyes perused my body. Tears escape my eyes as I remember his words. "Jesus Christ, put a fucking shirt on, Natalie. Your body is nowhere near what it used to be. You can't expect me to get it up if I have to look at that during."*

I shake the memory from my head, not wanting to lose the moment I'm in now, with Lucas. I feel him lightly kiss the inside of my thigh before he gets up and lays beside me.

"Why are you crying, baby?" I can hear the concern in his voice as I look over to him.

"No one has ever done that before." He smirks causing a blush to creep up my cheeks when I realize I didn't clarify what I meant. "Calm down that ego, I'm not just talking about that, but I also meant with my stretch marks." A light smile plays on his lips.

"So why the tears?" He caresses my cheek with his hand, drying my tears with his thumb.

"I remembered something." That's all I need to say before he jumps up and is straddling me, hovering over my body.

"Oh, baby. Don't do that to yourself, don't give him that power over you. You're fucking perfect, and the fact that he didn't see that just shows how big of a moron he was. He didn't appreciate what was right in front of him, and I'll be damned if you play his words in your head. Not anymore." He places a light kiss on my lips before maneuvering himself to where he's lying beside me again, turning onto his side so he can look at me.

"I just never thought it could be like this." I'm chewing on my bottom lip again. At this point, it's a reflex I didn't realize was happening until Lucas pointed it out. His eyes are staring straight at my lips and I release it before he has a chance to do it himself. He doesn't say anything, but instead pulls me close, laying my head on his chest.

All my emotions catch up to me as I lay here in his arms. I've never felt so worshipped in my life, but based on what I just remembered, I'm not as healed as I thought I was. Lucas says all the right words, but when your mind has been broken by another, it's hard to repair the damage that was done. I want to let him in all the way, to show him I'm all in, but I'm scared that I might just be too broken to give this man all of me in return.

"Mama." Savi runs and jumps into my arms the minute she notices me, fastening her little arms around my neck before looking around. "Where's my Lucy?"

"He had some stuff to get done, bug." She loosens her grip and grabs my face with her hands, giving me a serious look.

"He was 'posed to pick me up, he promised." Her bottom lip pokes out, tears starting to shine in her little eyes. When I left earlier to pick her up, I told him that I needed a little space. I knew it hurt him when I said that, but I couldn't get past the memory that flooded my head. Those words, the look of disgust on Ethan's face, it's all there in my head and no matter what Lucas says, it's not easy to forget how much my ex destroyed me. *You are disgusting. Nothing but a fat single mother. Who would want someone like you?*

"I'm sure he'll come see you later." It's all I can say to her because I don't know how to explain any of this to her, how to even figure it out for myself. She doesn't respond to me, just buries herself deeper into the crook of my neck. The last thing I want is for any of this to affect their relationship, but I also know that I'm dealing with demons in my head that won't let me be happy.

When we arrive back at the house, Savi rushes off from me, still not saying a word. I don't know if she blames me for Lucas not being here or what, but she's playing the silent game. Sitting at the table, I stare at the flowers he brought me, thinking of what transpired after he walked in the door. He's always been in my head, even when we didn't talk for years. Somehow, I always knew I could count on him. And when I needed him most, he was there. All this time, he's only ever shown me that he's here for me. So why am I holding back so much? Why can't I just leap in without looking back? Why can't this just be easy? *Because you are too broken for a man like him.*

Grabbing my phone, I send a message to the therapist I saw a couple years ago after my divorce. I stopped seeing her because I thought I had finally moved past it all. I wasn't completely healed, but I had learned some techniques that helped keep the voices at bay. But the more I let Lucas in, the more these voices are destroying me. Once I get the message off, I lean back in the chair, the way the sun is hitting the flowers capturing my attention. The longer I sit here, the more I wish that I had the answers for what's happening.

I must have been staring at the flowers for longer than I thought because the next thing I know, there's limited light in the house with the sun setting outside, the flowers no longer illuminating like they were before. Shaking all the thoughts from my head, I stand and take a deep breath in.

"Mama, Lucy's home. Can I go say hi?" Savi runs into the dining room, a smile lighting her beautiful face.

"Of course, you can, bug." The smile on her face gets even bigger as she takes off out the door. I watch from the window as she barrels her way into him. He's laughing as he pulls her in and swings her around in a circle before setting her back down and planting a wet kiss on her cheek. I can hear her laugh from where I stand at the window. As I'm watching, Lucas looks up and we lock eyes. He winks at me before turning his attention back to her.

It's been a couple of days since Lucas and I were together and yet, I find that I'm still stuck in my head regarding it all. From my shit show of a marriage to what happened in my bed with Lucas, it's all running in my head, slowly making me crazy. Pulling up into a parking space, I take a deep breath as I gaze at the door with my therapist's name on it.

Grabbing my stuff, I get out of the car and head in. I'm not even sure why I'm here. *You're here because you're worthless and pathetic.* Shaking the voice off, I hold my head high and walk into the office with the knowledge that I need to do this if I want a future with Lucas.

"Good morning, how may I help you?" I smile at the receptionist.

"I'm here to see Dr. Hart. I have an appointment at 10." She clicks on the computer in front of her, while I take in the office. Dr. Hart made quite a few changes since the last time I was in here. There's some floral displays and a new set of sofas in the waiting area that weren't here before.

"You're all set. Take a seat and she'll be out in a few to get you." I nod and make my way to the sofa across the room, as close as possible to the door so I won't have far to go.

*You're so pathetic. This isn't going to help you.* The tears are forming the longer I sit here.

"Natalie, I'm ready for you." I look up to see Dr. Hart watching me with a smile in her eyes. While I didn't believe in therapy when I first started it, I know that it helped me and that's exactly what I need..

We walk back into her office. She takes the small recliner while I take the full couch. We make small talk as she preps for our session together. She asks about Savi and my work. As I settle myself on the couch, I breathe in deeply. I hate that I'm so broken, that I've had to resort to coming back to therapy just because I want to take things to the next level with Lucas.

I don't know why I can't get over it. Hell, I thought I was over it and here I am, sitting in this room again.

"So, what brings you in today?" Her words pull me out of my thoughts as I look over to her. She doesn't pull out her notebook, just sits with her hands clasped into her lap.

"I don't know where to start." I lean into the pillows she has on the couch. Her office smells like jasmine and lavender. A smoothing mix that has me relaxing even more.

"Well, it's been a couple years since I've seen you. The last time we spoke, we discussed your marriage and all that it entailed. The divorce had been finalized and you were doing your best to move on. What's been happening recently that has you coming in?"

"Do you remember Lucas?" She nods, giving me a small smile at the mention of my best friend. When I first started seeing her, Lucas was my starting point. I wasn't ready to dive into everything that happened with Ethan yet, so talking about him was my safety net. She knows everything about him, from our friendship as kids all the way through to when he talked me into coming to this town. "Things have been progressing in a new direction with him and I'm not sure what to do."

"What do you want to do?"

Her question takes me by surprise, not because I didn't expect it, I just didn't expect it so soon. Taking a deep breath, I look over to her. She's still sitting the same way, her hands clasped in her lap. She's not pushing me to answer as she patiently waits for me to come to what she asked on my own.

"I want to make it work." Her smile gets bigger as she nods and leans forward, her elbows meeting her knees as she holds her hands out in front of her.

"What's holding you back from doing that?" I move the pillow from beside me to into my lap, holding it tightly against my body as I reflect on what she's asking. My memories are holding me back. My life prior to BoothBay being a huge red mark on my file of life, making me feel like I'm not worthy enough of his love.

"He doesn't know." She takes a deep breath, but doesn't say anything, allowing me to continue. "He knows some of what's happened with Ethan, but he doesn't know the extent of the damage."

"I see. And what's stopping you from telling him everything that happened during your marriage?" My breath catches as I listen to the question. I know exactly what I'm afraid of. I'm afraid he'll walk away again. He's done it before, and while we weren't dating at the time, just watching him walk out of the graduation party the way he did, broke me. My father had just announced my engagement to Ethan in front of everyone. I was in shock and as I looked out to the crowd, I watched as he hung his head, turned around, and walked away. The minute he walked out was the day everything changed in my life. I no longer had my best friend in my life, and that hurt more than I could ever say.

"He's going to walk away. I'm too broken." I say quietly, my voice breaking on the last word.

"You're not broken, you're healing. There's a big difference in that. No one said this was going to be an easy process, especially with all you went through. I remember you talking to me about how it felt to watch him walk away, and what it did to you. Did you ever talk to him about that?"

"What if he does walk away?" I ignore her question and return one of my own, scared to know what she's going to say in return.

"I'm going to pretend you didn't ignore the question I asked and instead are thinking about it. And I have a question in return for you. What if he doesn't?" She retorts as she sits back, her eyebrow lifting as she takes me in. My shoulders deflate and I pull the pillow in tighter. My eyes fall to the floor as I think about everything. If he were to walk away again, I don't think I'd survive it.

"I'm scared."

"Fear is natural, considering all you went through, but Natalie, look at me." I pull my gaze back up to her. "Lucas isn't Ethan. You have to give him that chance to prove himself to you. I can't say what'll happen because that's beyond my expertise, but you'll never know unless you try. You also need to open yourself up to him, all the way. Not just with what happened with your ex, but also with how you felt when he walked away the first time."

Her words hit hard. I've been living behind the fear that Lucas will be another Ethan, but I should know better than that, having known him almost my entire life. He's never given that kind of impression. And even though he did walk away that one time, he hasn't done it since. I've been the one pushing him away.

"Thank you." I lift my lips in a small smile. She smiles back and leans forward.

"I'm always here if you need me. I know you ended your sessions before because you felt you didn't need them anymore, but I'm so glad you reached out to me." For the first time, I realize that maybe I don't have to be completely healed to let Lucas in. "This is a huge step and I'm proud of you, Natalie."

We talk for a few more minutes about Savi and everything that's been going on before the hour ends and we're both standing. She shows me out to the reception area and gives me a small smile before heading back to her office.

Walking out, I feel a renewed sense of peace. Grabbing my phone out of my pocket, I send Madison a text asking her if she can pick up Savi for me, explaining what's going on. She sends me several heart emojis and a thumbs-up. It's time to tell Lucas everything.

# Chapter Nineteen

LUCAS

The past couple days have been complete shit. I've been busy as fuck setting things up with Justin as we prep to open a new agency here. I know for a fact Natalie's avoiding me. When she asked for space, it gutted me, but I knew there were things still holding her back. I just wish she'd talk to me instead of running from me. I don't know how to get her to do that though. Grabbing my phone, I head down the path behind my house that leads me past her window and straight to the beach for a run. The lights inside are off, a clear indicator she isn't done avoiding me yet.

Reaching my starting point, I get some stretches in before taking off. I've always preferred to run on the beach here than anywhere else. Every time I was at another location for a photo shoot, I'd end up in a gym. Nothing feels more like home than the feeling of sand beneath my feet. The sounds of the waves crashing onto the shore, the blue skies, the smell of salt water; it all helps me center myself as I find my pace. I can see a few families in the distance playing, but otherwise the beach is empty.

As I run, I think of everything I know about Natalie's

marriage. I took off right after graduation, not sticking around once her father made the engagement announcement, so I don't know much. It's not that I didn't want to stick around, it was that I couldn't. I couldn't watch her marry a man that wasn't me, a man that her father groomed to take over his business. Mr. Conaway never liked me and barely tolerated me being around his family, but since my father was higher on the social ladder than him, he sucked it up. I wanted nothing to do with that world, and I knew Natalie had felt the same. The day her father announced her engagement, I felt my heart splinter into a thousand pieces. It was too late for me and her.

Shaking my thoughts, I try to think about what my mother would say when I'd do my check ins. I didn't hate my parents. They were good people, just stuck in a world where money ruled everything. Mother didn't mentioned Natalie much, and I never directly asked. I know about the cheating, based on how she reacted to the whole Lauren thing and what Madison shared with me. I can tell he hurt her in other ways, I just don't know how. I want her to talk to me, but I can't just come out and ask her either. I know her well enough that the minute I ask, she'll build that wall again, and that's the last thing I want her to do.

The more I run, the clearer the answer gets to me. I can't force her to talk to me, but I can show her that I'm not going anywhere, no matter what she thinks. I won't walk away now that I know what she tastes like, what she feels like in my arms. A plan starts to formulate as I reach my turnaround point and start making my way back to the house. The moment I see the house in the distance, a smile forms on my face because I know exactly what I'm going to do.

I take an extra few minutes to cool down with a walk once I reach the beach directly behind the guest house. Based on the amount of sweat I feel dripping down my back and into my shorts, the first thing I need to do is take a shower. I feel my phone vibrating in my pocket, but the sight on my back porch has me stopping right where I am, jaw almost dropping in shock as I take it in. Natalie's sitting on the steps on my back porch, her head resting on the banister behind her. Her shoulders look as though she is carrying the weight of the world on them. She hasn't noticed me yet, but the way she's wringing her hands together in her lap, I can tell her nerves are eating at her. She's also chewing on her bottom lip again. The thought of pulling it out with my teeth has me cracking a small smile.

"Hey there, beautiful." My voice pulls her from whatever trance she's in. Her eyes are wide as she looks over at me. "What did I tell you about that lip?" I'm eyeing the lip she's chewing on, but instead of releasing it, she quirks an eyebrow at me, almost like she's daring me to go through with my statement. She holds her ground as I step even closer to her.

"Last chance, Natalie." There's a smile playing on her face, her eyes are twinkling with mischief, and she continues to hold that lip between her teeth. I search her eyes for any hesitation and when I don't see any, I grab her by the back of her head and bring her face to mine. Pulling her lip out with my teeth, I feel her smile and then my lips are on hers, consuming her. Before I can get too deep into the kiss, I feel her pull back from me. The hesitation I didn't see before is now sitting in her eyes, but otherwise, the twinkle that I finally started seeing again is still there.

"You're all sweaty. Where'd you go?" She laughs as she takes in the sweat trailing down my face.

"A run on the beach." She nods at my statement, her eyes roving down my body. The shorts aren't hiding much, as the sweat has plastered them to my body. I watch her as her gaze finds my already hardening cock. Her eyes widen even more, and a blush creeps up her neck and onto her cheeks. If she only knew just how hard she's always made me.

"I can come back later, if you need to go shower." Her eyes

are on mine again, the hesitancy I see in them making me wish I hadn't taken a run.

"If you can handle me being a sweaty mess, I'm good with waiting." I offer her a small smile. She pauses for just a second before returning it with one of her own.

"You kinda stink, Luc. Go shower and then come over when you're done. There's some things we need to talk about."

"I'll be over in ten." I kiss her lightly on the cheek and then rush inside and jump into the shower to take care of my hard-on before it's even had a chance to warm up. I don't know what she wants to talk about, but I'm hopeful. *She came to me.*

# Chapter Twenty

## NATALIE

Walking inside, I grab a bottle of water and sit at the table. My eyes are on his back door, waiting for him to come out. With each minute that passes, I'm doing my best to calm my nerves. They're frayed at this point. When I showed up and he wasn't home, I was worried that I missed my chance to talk to him. The moment I saw him, it was like part of me felt whole. I was playful with him, not wanting to ruin the moment with my ugly truth. And then he kissed me. That kiss only solidified that I need to do this. But now that I know the moment's arriving, all I want to do is run. *He will be once he hears what you have to say.*

I must have missed him walking out of his door because the knock on my door is pulling me from my thoughts. Taking a deep breath, I walk over and let him in. The second he passes by, all I smell is him. The musk that I've come to know fills my senses, seeming to calm my frayed nerves.

"I'm scared." My whispered words stop him from walking past me. He pulls me into him, holding me tightly. The security I feel in his arms is nothing like I've ever felt before. It fortifies my decision that he needs to know. I can feel his breath on my neck as he holds me, gently rubbing my back but not easing up on his grip.

"I'm right here, baby. Please let me in." His voice is soft in my ear. Closing my eyes, I nod. Grabbing my hand, he leads us to the couch and sits beside me. I look over to him as he watches me. His patience with me is probably the best part of him, other than his relationship with Savi, anyways. He never pushes, never forces. His eyes are soft, filled with questions only I can answer. Taking a deep breath, I turn towards him, pulling my hand from his, I bring my knees into my chest as I relax into the couch.

"The only thing I ask of you is that you don't interrupt. I have to get this out, so all I need is for you to listen. Can you do that?" He grabs my hand back into his and nods, telling me he'll listen. I can already feel the tears threatening to spill out of my eyes, but I can't let them out yet. Not until I get these words out. I try to pull my hand back, but his grip tightens on it, refusing to let it go. Taking a deep breath, I start at the beginning.

"So, I know you remember the day Ethan came to school, and all of it up until we started dating, right?" He nods his head, keeping his word that he won't interrupt. "I was so naïve, Lucas, so damn naïve. What I thought was undivided attention was manipulation and control. Nothing huge, but looking back, I can see it all so clearly now. He would isolate me from my friends, even you, mostly you." My voice breaks a little as the emotions filter through me, threatening to release. He squeezes my hand. In return, I give him a small smile, letting him know I'm okay.

"I didn't even realize it at the time, but that was the start of it all. We didn't hang out much anymore and then graduation happened, and by then, I was already in so damn deep. I didn't know about the engagement until that night at the party that you walked out of." My voice catches here, and I see him wince at my statement. "My father surprised me with it. Surprised everyone, except Ethan and my mother, who were in on it. I don't know why I didn't see the manipulation, but I was so captivated by him, by the falsities, to see anything except the picture he painted for us. Watching you walk away that day broke me. I didn't even realize how much until I saw you again. You were my best friend and then you were gone. Nothing made sense anymore." The tears start to spill over my lids, no matter how much I try to keep them back. I see Lucas fighting his own set of emotions as he watches me. I know my words hurt him, but they need to be said. "After we got married, he got even closer with my dad than he already was, working at his firm, alongside him. I didn't think anything of it because that was Ethan's dream, and all I wanted was for him to be happy.

"He started cheating on me, like my dad does to my mom. I turned a blind eye because my mother told me *that's just what you do*." I scoff at that statement, hating the words as they spill out of my mouth. "The perfume scent on his shirt, the hickeys on his chest, the late nights at work. My marriage had become exactly like my parents." I squeeze my eyes shut as I recall the smell of the perfume on his shirts. I'm lost in the memories of the past as they sweep through, one by one, taunting me with their words. *Why did I think I was strong enough to do this?* Lucas squeezes my hand again, bringing me back into reality. My eyes find his and it shocks me to see tears in them. I hate that this is hurting him.

"When I got pregnant with Savannah, things started going back to before we got married. He was the guy from high school again, always a loving word for me. He'd tell me how happy he was about the baby, constantly kissing my belly and just being there for me. He was even smiling again. We were happy. It was the marriage I wanted it to be. Ethan was coming home on time every night, we would eat, and everything felt normal. And then my parents visited." I stop here, hating how manipulative my entire family is. Taking a deep breath in, I continue, "I was probably three or four months along by this point. My father took Ethan into the study to 'toast' the news." Rolling my eyes, I focus on the picture across the room from me. It's of Savannah on the day she was born. Seeing that picture and feeling Lucas holding my hand gives me some sort of renewed strength to get through the rest.

"I don't know what happened in the study, I never asked, but Ethan went back to his old ways after that night, but he started drinking more. Every night he'd come home, there was something new for him to pick at. My weight gain was his biggest thing to go after." Tears fall even more as I recall all the harsh words he said to me. I can see Lucas fighting his emotions as well, his other hand tightening into a fist as I bare my soul. "I won't say what he used to say, but it was so bad that I became so self-conscious over it. I started watching my weight, even though I was pregnant."

I see him open his mouth before clenching it shut again, jaw ticking but keeping the promise to let me get this out. It's just one more thing that makes the difference between Ethan and Lucas so apparent. Where Ethan loved to hear himself talk, Lucas is willing to listen to what I have to say. I squeeze his hand, drawing his eyes to mine. I can see the anger reflecting in them, not at me, but at what I went through.

"When Savannah was born, he refused to be in the delivery room with me, preferring to be at work. My parents couldn't be bothered to show up for me, but I expected that. My mom too drunk to care, my father, well he was with Ethan. I was alone in that hospital room, with the nurses and the doctors as I labored through the delivery. I'd never felt more alone in my life." The tears are streaming steadily down my face at this point. I see Lucas through the haze as he reaches to the table behind him to grab the tissues without releasing the hand he's holding. I grab a tissue with my free hand and use it to dry what I can, but the tears aren't stopping so I know it's pretty much useless.

"After she was born, I did my best to shed the weight, but you could clearly tell I had a baby." I raise my head and look to the ceiling, knowing that this next part is probably where he'll get the angriest. "One night, after I'd been cleared by the doctors, I found an old lingerie set that Ethan used to love." I can see his eye twitching, his jaw getting tighter as I say the words I am saying. "So, I put it on and waited for him to get home."

Closing my eyes, I relive that moment again for the second time in less than a week, only this time, I'm saying the words out loud. "I was hoping we would finally find us again. When he saw what I was wearing, he scrunched up his face in total disgust at the sight of me." My words come out broken as I utter them. *"Jesus Christ, put a fucking shirt on, Natalie. Your body is nowhere near what it used to be. You can't expect me to get it up if I have to look at that during."*

The minute the words leave my mouth, Lucas releases my hands, gets up, and starts pacing the room. *This is it. This is when he walks away from me.* But he doesn't, he simply walks back and forth. He's balling both of his fists, shaking with rage. There's more that he needs to hear, I'm not even finished yet. I don't know if I should continue or let him calm down before I go on. I wait for him to either finish pacing or give me some sort of sign to continue. When a few minutes have passed, he looks over to me and nods, letting me know it's okay to go on. Dragging my hand back in from where he was holding it, I pull my legs even closer to my chest as I prepare to tell him the rest.

"The words of love he used to speak were words coated in disdain and ridicule. He found ways to tear me down with his words, chosen so carefully that you wouldn't believe they were abusive." Sighing deeply, I rub my hands up and down my legs. I'm watching as he paces, watching the anger radiate from him as he tries his best not to unleash all the words I know he wants to say.

"I gave up after that. All I cared about was Savannah. My spirit was broken. I started taking online classes for photography." The tears aren't as heavy now, knowing that the story is coming to an end. "The day I left, I found him in the master bathroom with our nanny while Savannah screamed in her crib down the hall." He stops pacing and turns to me, his eyes wide with shock. "That was the final straw. I packed up our shit and left. It's the day I called and you convinced me to come here."

All my breath comes rushing out as I finish. I close my eyes and lay my head on my knees, emotionally spent in every possible way. I don't even flinch when I feel Lucas sit back down beside me. I feel his arm come around me and then I'm pulled into his lap, his arms engulfing me as he shelters me in his arms, holding me as I silently cry.

# Chapter Twenty-One

## LUCAS

Holding her in my arms right now, the anger coursing in my blood at the man who should've held her high is tempered, but only slightly. I'm mad at myself too. Hearing how badly I hurt her when I walked away was like a knife to the heart. When I walked, I thought I was protecting myself, but I was causing more pain than ever. I can't help but look down at her. Her eyes are still squeezed tight, the tears still falling. Every now and then she takes a breath, but otherwise, it's just the sound of her silent cries that tear my heart in two. I can understand why she never told me the whole story, as much as it kills me inside to know she's held this pain so deeply in her heart.

We sit on her couch for another fifteen minutes before I realize that she's fallen asleep. I look down at her face, the tear marks on her cheeks, the puffiness in her eyes and make a promise that I'll never be the reason for her tears, that I'll never walk away from her again. I kiss the top of her head before slowly maneuvering us to where she's laying on the couch. I grab my phone and pull up Madison's contact info.

**Lucas:** Are you getting Savi?

**Madison:** Um, yea, I got her. Did she tell you?

**Lucas:** Yes.

**Madison:** Good. Take care of our girl. Let me know if I need to keep her overnight.

**Lucas:** I will.

Smiling, I set the phone aside, glad that Natalie has someone like Madison in her life. Growing up, Natalie was popular, but she didn't act like she was above anyone else. She never had close friends though, except for me. Until Ethan came into the picture, she barely talked to anyone. Then he showed up and suddenly she was a socialite, living up to what he wanted her to be. Slipping out from underneath her, I pull the blanket off the back of the couch and cover her up before I sit on the chair across the room. My anger isn't completely gone, and I'd love nothing more than to find Ethan and rip his head from his body. As much as I want to do it, I can't. I need to take care of my girl.

A couple hours later, Natalie starts to stir on the couch. I move over to where she is and watch as her eyes open. They're bloodshot and rimmed with red from all the crying she did, but all I see is the beautiful blue eyes I've come to love.

"Hey." Her voice is soft, almost a whisper. She won't look me in the face as her eyes trail around the room. "What time is it?"

"Almost 4." She sits up quickly, panic crossing her face as she realizes just how late in the afternoon it is. "Madison has Savi. I knew you needed the rest and we still need to talk." She pulls her legs into herself again, shielding herself.

"Oh." Her eyes squeeze shut again, the tears threatening to spill over.

"No, baby, nothing like that." I grab her hands and pull her to where I have her back in my lap again. "This time I'm going to do the talking." She only nods into my chest in response.

"What you went through," her body tightens against me, so I soften my words and kiss her on the forehead before continuing, "you shouldn't have gone through that, ever. I wish you could see yourself through my eyes, Natalie. What you've been told is..." My words catch in my throat as the emotion threatens to spill over. She shifts so she's looking at me.

"You should have never been told any of those words. I should have never walked away from you." I smile at her, moving my hand so it's cradling her face. "You're so fucking strong, Natalie." She leans into my caress, and I want to kiss her so badly, but not yet. Not until I get all the words out that I need to say to her.

"The way he treated you was... the things he said..." It's like the words can't form on my tongue because looking at her, all I can think about is how much I love her. The thought stops me in my tracks. I'm completely and irrevocably in love with her. "The Natalie I see in front of me is beautiful, capable, resilient, breathtaking. I'm so sorry I walked away, baby." There are silent tears trailing on her cheeks as she looks at me. Drying what I can with my thumb, I lean in and kiss her softly.

I can feel her soften to me as my lips touch hers. I taste the salt from her tears on her lips, but it's still her taste. I deepen the kiss, only slightly, wanting her to open to me, needing her to. I can feel her hesitance, so I pull back slightly, wanting to search her eyes, but her eyes remain closed.

"What's going on in that beautiful head of yours?" I whisper. The question causes her eyes to open and find mine. She doesn't answer, just swallows and takes a deep breath. "Talk to me, baby."

"Is Madison keeping Savi for the night?" I know that isn't the question she wanted to ask, but instead of pushing her, I let her have this moment.

"Do you want her to?" She shrugs me off, looking around the room as she thinks about what she wants to say. "She told me to let her know if she is keeping her for the night or bringing her home later. It's up to you though. I'm here no matter what you decide."

She curls up into me, getting comfortable. "Is it okay if she comes home?"

"Baby, you don't ever have to ask me that. She's part of you and I love that little girl so much." She smiles at me, the first real smile I've seen since this morning before she opened up to me.

"Thank you," she whispers.

We sit in silence on the couch, comfortable as we are, holding each other. Having her in my arms is all I could ever ask for. I'll give anything to keep her right here with me. After a few minutes, her phone starts ringing so she ends up getting off my lap. I hear her talking to Madison as she walks into the other room.

"Madison's feeding her dinner and then she'll bring her by." I smile at her as I open my arms, ready for her to get back in my arms.

"You want me to get us something to eat?" She shakes her head as she lays back in my arms. I smile as I look down at her, her eyes have the twinkle back in them. I lean down and kiss her lightly. "You want me to go home so you can have some time with her?" She looks at me in shock, like I just told her I'm leaving and not coming back.

"I want you here." The words make me smile at her as I

pull her in for another kiss. Holding her face in my hands, I lick her lips lightly, hoping she will open for me this time and when she does, the fire in my belly becomes an inferno. It doesn't matter how many times we've kissed, they all light me up in a way I've never felt before. I hear a light moan from her as I continue to kiss her, making me wish we had more time before Savi comes home. Pulling away, I kiss her lightly on the lips and then on the nose before smiling at her.

"You didn't walk away." Her whispered words reach my ears, and it breaks my heart knowing that she was scared I would. Considering I walked away after the engagement was announced, it makes sense that she was. But I'll never walk away again, not if I can help it.

"I'll never walk away from you again, Natalie." I feel her smile into my chest as I hold her tightly against me.

This moment right here is going down as one of my favorites. Her eyes are twinkling, there's a soft smile playing on her lips and she's laying against my chest.

"Mama." Savi runs into the door and straight into Natalie's arms. The sight of them together takes my breath away. *They're my girls, my everything.* I see Madison at the door, and she gives me a light wave. I wave back and then turn my eyes back to my favorite sight. They hug a few more minutes before Savi realizes I'm standing there too. "Lucy." She jumps straight into my arms and I can't stop the biggest smile from forming on my face as I hold her close to me.

Madison gives Natalie a hug and whispers something in her ear that causes her to blush before giving a quick wave and disappearing out the door again. I raise my eyebrows at Natalie, wondering what she said, and it only deepens the blush on her cheeks. Guess I'll have to find out later.

"Can I go play before bath time, Mama?" Savi asks as she escapes my grasp.

"Of course, bug, go ahead." Savi runs off in the direction of her room and I immediately step up to Natalie as soon as she is out of sight.

"What was the whispering about?" I whisper into her ear. The blush returns to her cheeks, making me snicker.

"I'm not telling you," she whispers back before retreating from me and going into the living room to straighten up.

"Oh, but you will." She rolls her eyes as I smirk at her.

Once everything is where it's supposed to be, I pull her back into the couch to sit beside me. She relaxes into the couch as I hold her hand, never wanting to let her go. I don't even realize I'm staring at her until she breaks me out of my trance of thoughts.

"What?" A blush creeps up her cheeks as she looks away, trying to get me to break eye contact with her.

"Let me take you out on a date." She looks to me, confusion on her face. "I want a date, Natalie. Just say yes." She visibly swallows and looks me in the eyes and searches them. I give her a small smile and cup her cheek, wanting her to see just how sincere I am.

"Ok." Her whisper reaches my ear, only making the smile on my face get wider. I pull her into my arms, feeling her relax into my embrace. Just as we are getting settled, Savi runs back into the room and stops short when she sees us.

"I want cuddles, too." She stomps her feet, drawing giggles from myself and Natalie. We open our arms, inviting her to join us. She smiles big and jumps into our arms. Sitting here, I can't help but look down at the two girls in my embrace and feel like everything is just as it should be.

The days are a blur of activity as I work with Justin on getting the new agency up and running, while also trying to plan my first official date with Natalie. Each night after finishing our work for the day, we end up on the couch together. Our make-out sessions are hot and heavy, but it doesn't move past that. I haven't pushed past second base with her again, but it's killing me. Each night when I return home, the shower feels the brunt of my pent-up frustration and passion. I'll never pressure her for more, but I also can't wait for the day I can fully claim her, body and soul.

As I work on the plans for our date, I think back to everything Natalie and I discussed when it came to Ethan. From what she told me, the asshole didn't treasure his time with her. Hell, he didn't treasure her as a person. Knowing that, it only makes me want this date to be perfect for her, to show her just how beautiful I know she is. Grabbing my phone, I reach out to Madison in hopes she can help me.

**Lucas:** I need your help.

**Madison:** What's up?

**Lucas:** I'm taking Natalie on a date.

**Madison:** It's about damn time.

I chuckle at her response.

**Lucas:** I want to set her up with a spa day before I take her out. you're going to be the one to get her there.

**Madison:** Free spa day, hell yes.

Rolling my eyes, I contemplate my common sense in

asking Madison for help. This is either the best idea I had or it's going to blow up in my face. Only time will tell.

**Lucas:** Ok, I'll set it up and send you the details. And then I need you to take Savi for the night.

**Madison:** I'm gonna venture a guess that the spa day is my payment for taking Sav?

**Lucas:** Please.

She sends me thumbs-up and I get to work on planning the day for my girl. After sending her the confirmation for the spa and all the information she needs, I get started on the rest of my plans for the night.

# Chapter Twenty-Two

NATALIE

The past few days since telling Lucas everything has been a dream. We haven't moved past second base, he's never pressuring for more, which only makes me fall for him more. His patience with me means so much. Granted, the hot and heavy make-out sessions are making me tingle all over but being pushed to do more is something I know that Lucas would never do. Being able to trust a man again has crumbled my walls to nearly nothing. *Are you sure you can trust that he won't walk away again?* The voices try their best to pull me back in, but now that I've faced all my demons, I've found they don't have power over me like they used to.

Grabbing my phone, I see a text from Lucas waiting for me.

**Lucas:** Madison will be picking you up for a spa day. I'll see you tonight baby.

When I see the next message come in, I laugh out loud,

wondering how I ever got so lucky to have the friends that I do.

**Madison:** You better be ready when I get there. Spa days are my love language.

Smiling to myself, I grab my purse and head outside to wait on her. Wouldn't want to keep Madison waiting. Lord knows she's impatient already, the last thing I need is to get in the way of her *love language*.

As soon as we arrive at the spa, we're whisked away to our first stop of the day; a full body, deep tissue massage. I've never received a massage in my life, so I was a bit self-conscious when they told me to undress all the way and lay on the table. Shaking the negative thoughts out of my head, I focus on Lucas's words. *"That pouch and those stretch marks are because you carried a life inside you, Nat. They are from that rambunctious little girl that you carried. They are marks that you are a mom. And that is beautiful."*

The massage is perfection. I've never felt so relaxed in all of my life. As we lay on the tables, I hear Madison grunting as her masseuse works out the knots in her back and shoulders.

"You okay over there?" I manage to get out, trying not to giggle.

"Y-y-yep." She groans as more pressure is applied. I know the stress of everything has been getting to her, with Justin and all, but she won't talk to me. I'm hoping she talks to me soon, but I won't force the issue. She'll come to me when she's ready.

Facials, manicures, and pedicures are all done in the same room. We're set up in a small room that looks like a little oasis.

It brings me back to the little garden at the hospital where Lucas first kissed me. A blush creeps up my cheeks as I remember the moment. Madison gives me a knowing smirk as she settles into her chair.

Once masks are applied, I feel myself relax as the aroma of honey and oatmeal surrounds me. Closing my eyes, they apply the cucumbers. I think back to all the spa trips I took with my mother growing up. I never liked going to the spa, but then again, it was about being *seen* and not about relaxation. I was to be seen and not heard, relegated to the corner with a book so that she could gossip with her friends. I shake off the memories and put myself back in the moment.

Once the face masks are rinsed, the manicurist comes in. I haven't had my nails tended to since I moved, and you can clearly tell. The manicurist gives my nails a once over and then moves to her station to gather everything she will need. The more she grabs, the more I feel even worse about the state I let my nails get in.

"Relax. You act like she's never seen bad nails." Madison huffs as I pull my hands in tight and examine every cuticle. I wave her off, continuing my examination.

"Friend right honey. I see worse." The manicurist smiles at me.

She sets us up with the pedicure first, letting our feet soak in a delicious smelling soap that I know will have my skin feeling soft as ever. I've never been a huge fan of pedicures since my feet are ticklish, so I will be sure to warn her before she touches me. I've been known to kick out when my feet are touched.

"So, I know we don't have it on the plan, but what do you think about a wax?" Madison asks as she settles into her own chair.

"Uh, yea, I don't think so." I laugh her off. I don't want to go into tonight with expectations. I know my bottom half might be ready to climb Lucas and have my way with him, but my heart and head both need to catch up.

"Oh, come on." She needles me. I shake her off again. A blush is forming on my neck and I can feel it climbing up onto my cheeks.

"This first wax?" the manicurist asks as she sets about getting my hands in the soaking bin.

I turn to her and nod, still embarrassed that the conversation has shifted to this.

"You go on date?" I nod again. "First wax, no sex. Wait three days after wax for special sexy time." She says it so bluntly that I feel the blush on my face deepen even more. *Oh my God*.

Groaning, I turn to glare at Madison. She laughs even harder once she sees just how deep the blush on my face is. *Bitch*.

"So, have you decided what you'll be wearing?" Madison asks as our feet and hands are soaking. I shrug my shoulders. I haven't been out on a real date in so long, and since Savannah was the center of my universe, my closet severely lacked anything nice when it comes to getting dressed up. "What do you mean you don't know?"

"I don't have anything except my work clothes, which is mainly comfortable clothes since I do pictures, and my lounging clothes, which is the same thing. I have no idea at all." She sends me a sly smile, winking at me as she lays back and relaxes. I tune her out as she hums a tune and close my eyes, doing my best to relax.

An hour later, our nails are buffed and polished. I was going to go with a clear coat, but Madison insisted on a gorgeous teal color that I just couldn't say no to. She sent me small smiles throughout the rest of the time we were there, almost like she knew something I didn't. Instead of indulging, I let her keep her little secrets.

"Ready to go?" Madison comes up to me, linking her arm in mine as she walks us back to her car.

"Am I ready for this?" I ask quietly. My nerves are setting in, not because of Lucas, but because what this means for us.

"Stop that shit right now. You're doing this and you're going to have an amazing time. I'm going to drop you off and then go get Savi from school." I nod my head at her, rolling her words around in my head.

Kissing my cheek, she whispers me luck as I get out of the car back at the house. I take a deep breath and prepare myself to try and find something in my closet to go out with Lucas in. I do have a few pairs of nice jeans, but all my nice stuff was left behind. I haven't had a reason to dress up in so long that I can't even remember the last time I did. *Before you had the baby, when Ethan didn't have a reason to keep you home.* Pushing the thoughts out of my head and turn towards my room.

Walking into my room, I stop short at the gift box on my bed. It's a beautiful white box with a shimmery gold bow wrapped around and a small card tucked in. Walking over to it slowly, I lift the card and feel tears come as I read the words.

*You are beautiful, my Natalie.*
*Wear this for our date tonight.*
*Love, Lucas*

I wipe the tears that managed to fall and set the card down beside the box. Gently pulling on the bow, I unravel it and slowly open it. A small gasp leaves my mouth as I see what's inside. *The dress matches my nail color almost perfectly.* I know Madison had something to do with this but knowing that he took the time to find me something that fits *me* has my eyes tearing up even more as I take in the dress. I lift it up and notice the details I couldn't see when it was laying in the box.

It's a mini dress, with one shoulder. There is a beautiful floral sheen ruffle across the chest area that goes around to the back. A sheer lace follows the dress down with a beautiful solid teal slip underneath. The attached belt is a gorgeous brown buckle that brings the whole look together perfectly. I get giddy with excitement over the dress he picked out for me, especially when I think about the boots I can pair with it to finish off the look.

Laying the dress on the bed, I go to the closet and get the booties out. Sitting them beside the dress, I let out a small squeal of excitement as I see the whole outfit together. Letting out a few more girly squeals, I temper my excitement and start the process of doing my hair and makeup.

I style my hair in soft curls, leaving it down because Lucas prefers it that way. He's always playing with my hair in some way when he's here and it makes my heart beat a little faster at the thought of him playing with my hair tonight. My makeup is soft and light, not too much as I want the attention to be on the dress.

Looking through my underwear drawer, I grab my newest additions. A small gift from Madison after I told her about what happened with Lucas. Giggling, I pull out the beautiful lace boy-short underwear that she gave me. Luckily, the matching bra can be strapless since the dress only has one shoulder. I make the adjustments and pull them on. Glancing over into the mirror, I flush at the sight of me in something so risqué. Before the thoughts can even take residence in my head and ruin my mood, I look away.

I slip on the dress and sigh at the feel of the silkiness of the slip against my skin. It feels like butter gliding onto me as it falls into place. It hits about mid-thigh, making it the shortest dress I've ever owned. Clasping the belt, I run my hands down the outside, smoothing it as I do. The sheer overlay is just as smooth as the slip underneath, feeling silky. As I turn towards the mirror, I notice it gives off just a hint of a shimmer as it catches the light, throwing off different shades as I turn to check it out from the back.

The dress isn't too tight, which allows me to be comfortable with the weight I put on from having a kid, but still shows my curves since the belt sits just right. I bend over to make sure I won't be flashing anyone my underwear. Happy that it sits low enough that I won't be showing anything off, I grab the booties and head out to the living room. As I finish buckling the last one, the knock comes.

# Chapter Twenty-Three

## LUCAS

The moment she opens the door, every single word I was about to say leaves as I take in the sight before me. The dress I picked out for her hugs her curves, highlighting them in a way that makes my mouth water. Her hair is down, softly curled, and framing her face, making me want to run my hands through it the way I know that she loves. I love that she didn't wear too much makeup, allowing her natural beauty to truly shine through. As I trail my eyes down her body again, taking in every detail I can, I feel all the blood in my head rushing straight to my groin and I'm doing everything in my power to stop myself from backing her up into the house and refusing to let her leave.

"Wow." I hear her whisper. My eyebrows shoot up as I look to her face. She realizes she spoke out loud and the blush I love so much creeps up her neck and stains her cheeks a light pink. "Oh my God, did I say that out loud?" She whispers again.

"You stole the words right out of my mouth, beautiful." I give her a smile and step up to the door, closer to her. The blush has deepened, turning the light pink to a deep pink. I kiss her lightly and her smell fills my nose as I breathe her in. The overbearing need to walk her back into the house is killing me, but I refuse to give in. I step back and hold out my hand to her. "You ready?"

Giving me a soft smile and a nod, she closes the door before placing her hand in mine. I walk her down the driveway to my car, being sure to open hers for her. She watches me with raised eyebrows, and I begin to wonder if Ethan never did this kind of shit for her. No matter what it takes, I'm going to show her what it's like to be valued and loved. Going around the car, I start the car and put it into reverse. Before we even start moving, I sense her nerves in the passenger seat as she plays with the hem of her dress. Grabbing her hand, I kiss the back of it and then link our fingers together.

When I originally planned our night out, I knew that I was going for the opposite of everything she ever knew when it came to her parents or Ethan. Her parents were always pretentious and snobby, but I knew Natalie wasn't like that. She hated the country clubs, the restaurants that had wait lists and all the showy bullshit that came along with having money. Pulling up to the little hole in the wall restaurant on the beachfront, I see the smile light up her face as she takes in the sign.

"This is absolutely perfect. I've been dying to try this place." Her excitement's so palpable that I could almost touch it. Madison had told me about how Natalie would gush about this place, always saying how she wished she had the opportunity to try it out. Giving her a smile in return, I kiss the back of her hand again.

"Stay put." I slide out and run around the car, open her door, and hold out my hand to help her. Once she is fully out of the car, I pull her into my side, loving the way her body feels against mine.

Guiding her towards the entrance, I hold her close to my side, not wanting to break contact with her. Once we reach the door, I place my hand on the small of her back as she walks through ahead of me. I see the goosebumps that litter her skin at my touch and smile to myself knowing I caused them. We're guided to a table by the window, allowing us to see the waves crashing in on the sand. The sound of her sigh as she watches the waves hits me right in my groin again, causing my cock to jump in response. *Keep control man.* I pull her chair out for her, allowing her to sit and get comfortable before taking my own seat beside her.

Once the waiter takes our order, I take the time to watch her as she stares out the window. The bags that were once under her eyes are now gone, and the twinkle that was once missing from her eyes is back where it belongs. It fills my heart to know that I helped her get it back.

"What's on your mind?" She turns to me and smiles, causing my stomach to flutter at the sheer beauty of her in front of me.

"I'm just happy I'm here. How are things coming with Justin?" I grab her hand from across the table and link our fingers together.

"It's good. We got Justin set up with a new place in town and now we're working on finding a location for the agency." I smile at her. She returns my smile and just nods. I look out the window as a large wave crashes in. "I'm hoping that once we get it situated, things will slow down." Her giggle throws me off, pulling my attention back to her.

"It's a new business, Lucas. It won't slow down." My eyebrows furrow at her statement, causing her to backtrack. "I mean, I know how it feels to want things to slow down, but with businesses, especially new ones, it takes a while to get to the point where things feel right."

"I know what you meant. I just didn't like thinking about things only getting crazier. I don't want to miss a moment with you." Pulling her hand up to my mouth, I kiss the back of it lightly. A light blush forms on her cheeks at my statement, making me wish we were in private so I could watch as it deepened.

"I live in your backyard, Lucas, it's not like we don't see each other." She chuckles. Just as I'm about to respond to her, the waiter brings out our food and our conversation is shelved for later.

Watching her take that first bite of her food, the moans coming out at the taste has all of the blood rushing back to my groin again. I flex my hands in and out of fists under the table praying I can keep it together long enough. Each bite she takes has me wanting to take her right back home, pulling those sounds out in a different way. Adjusting my cock, I dig into my own food and do my best to ignore the noises that continue to make their way out of her mouth as she continues eating.

By the time we are finished eating, there is no blood left anywhere but my cock. I can feel it straining against the zipper of my dress pants and no matter how much I adjust it, there's no relief to be found. *Thank God I'm not wearing jeans.* I can't stop watching her mouth as she takes each bite, making me wish I was the fork. My thoughts have me picturing her lips wrapped around me, moaning as she takes me in. And with that, my cock pulses angrily in my pants, anxious and ready for the thoughts to become reality.

She notices me watching her and the blush returns to her neck, rising into her cheeks. I pull her hand back into mine, linking our fingers together. The waiter drops the check at the table after we both decide we have no room for dessert.

Without releasing her hand, I grab my wallet and place my card down.

Instead of heading back to the car, I put my hand on the small of her back and guide us down the small boardwalk in front of the restaurant and towards the beach area. Once we get to the sand, she removes her shoes. Sinking her toes into the sand, I watch as she closes her eyes and just takes in the moment around her. The sun is setting so the glow on her is breathtaking, almost ethereal. I pull out my phone and discreetly take a picture of her. As I'm shoving my phone into my pocket, she turns and looks to me.

"So," she twists her hands in front of her as she prepares to say whatever it is on her mind, "what's next on the agenda?"

"A walk on the beach." The smile that fills her face makes my stomach do somersaults and I know I'll do everything in my power to keep that smile on her face. Grabbing her hand, I pull her into me, molding her to my side once again as I rest my hand on the curve of her hip. I watch as the goosebumps make another appearance at my touch. She rests her head in the crook of my shoulder as we walk, completely content in our silence as we take in the beautiful sunset on the water. BoothBay's known for its stunning sunrises and its even more stunning sunsets.

Being on the east coast, it's rare to see a sunset on the water, but since we're a tiny island just off the mainland, we get the privilege of seeing both. You can make out the land on the west side of the island, but even with it there, there's nothing like watching the sun's glow reflect off the water between the island and the mainland. We find a little area on the beach that isn't wet from the incoming waves. I sit first and then pull her down between my legs, making it so she has to lean into me as we watch the sun make its descent.

"Thank you for letting me take you out." My breath is a whisper in her ear as she turns her head slightly to look at me.

"Thank you." She gives me a small smile and the last of my resolve disappears as I lean in and kiss her like I've wanted to all night. My hand cups her cheek and then moves to behind her neck, holding her in place as I deepen the kiss. My tongue darts out, begging to be let into her perfect mouth. When she does open, it's with a moan that sends shocks straight to my cock and I feel it hardening all over again. Applying a little more pressure, I massage her tongue with mine, keeping the pressure just right.

The small sounds coming from her are killing me as I continue to kiss her and if I thought I was hard as a rock before, well, that was nothing compared to the diamond hardness I'm sporting now. Her hands fist into my shirt, holding me right where I am, which is perfectly fine with me. I don't want to move from this spot, from this moment. I move my other hand to the small of her back, pushing her to turn her body more towards mine. She breaks the kiss to move herself, but before she can even form a coherent thought, my lips are back on hers.

Her kiss, her taste... it all consumes me. The small fire that started in my belly when my lips first touched hers is now a burning inferno taking over my entire body. I burn for her in ways I never thought I could burn for a woman. I could spend the rest of my life kissing this woman and it would never be enough.

# Chapter Twenty-Four

NATALIE

This kiss is searing my soul, marking me as only his. I could kiss him every day for the rest of my life and still feel as though it could never be enough. From the moment the door opened, and I saw him standing there, I knew that tonight would wreck me in the very best way. Throughout dinner, I'd catch him watching me as I ate, his eyes tracking the fork, focusing on my mouth. I'd watch as he attempted to readjust himself with each bite I took. Knowing that I had that effect on him only made me keep going with it.

He pulls away from our kiss, resting his forehead against mine. His eyes are closed, as he breathes in deep. I can feel how hard he is against my hip and it excites me. I know he's letting me take the lead here, letting me decide when we make the next step in our relationship. I'm not scared anymore, how could I be when all he's ever shown me is the patience and kindness I'd been missing out on my entire life.

"I could kiss you for the rest of my life, and still feel like it's never enough." His voice is gritty, like he's fighting against the urges he feels to keep going.

"I was just thinking the same thing." His eyes open at my

statement, staring deep into mine. The usual lightness of his eyes is flooded with desire as he stares at me. "Everything about tonight was perfect, Lucas." He smiles at that, giving me another light kiss before making a move to stand up. He offers me his hand, helping me stand beside him. He pulls me into him, holding me tightly against him.

"How about we head back?" he asks as we make our way back to his car.

"Perfect." I give him a smile as we reach the car. He opens my door for me, allowing me to get inside before he closes it and rushes around to get in on his side. As much as I don't want to think about my ex and his shitty behavior, I can say he never once did that for me, even at the beginning. Just the simple act of Lucas being a gentleman speaks to my soul and has me falling for him even more than I already have. He holds my hand the entire drive back to the house.

As we walk up the driveway, he grabs my hand and pulls me to his house. I give him a confused look but all he does is smirk at me as he goes to unlock his front door. His hand is still holding mine tightly as he wrestles with the keys, growling at them for not working fast enough.

The minute the door is open, he pulls me in and shuts it behind me, caging me in with his arms. His eyes are hooded, lust filling them as he stares me down. He licks his lips as his eyes trail my face. His eyes stop at my lips, my bottom lip pulled into my mouth. He growls again, leaning in to capture my lip with his teeth, pulling it into his mouth as he nibbles on it. He licks it softly before releasing it, pulling back to look me in the eyes again.

"Do you know what you do to me, Nat?" I shake my head. "Every single moan you made during dinner, the chewing on your lip. Do you know just how crazy you drive me?" Again, I shake my head in response. His voice is low, and husky and I can see his arms shaking as he tries his best to remain in control. I lick my lips gently and watch as his eyes dart straight to my mouth, watching me.

"What do I do to you, Lucas?" I raise an eyebrow as I watch him fight the control he's trying so desperately to keep in check. "Show me." My words cause him to snap and he dives in and molds his mouth to mine. The minute his lips touch mine, I can feel the difference in the kiss. This isn't one of his soft and gentle ones, it's so much more. His body pushes into mine, flattening me against the door as his mouth continues to consume me. I can feel the hardness of him through his pants as he leans into me. Every single nerve ending is firing at once and I can feel everything that he's doing to my body.

His hands move from the sides of my head and cup my ass, pulling my bottom half into him as he grinds his hardness on me. Moisture pools at my center, wanting him more than I ever thought possible.

Pushing back into the kiss, the need to show him what he does to me consumes me. I don't know if he realizes just how badly I need him. I can't help but put every ounce of that desire into our kiss. My response fuels him as he boosts me higher, my legs naturally finding their way around his waist. The sensation of his cock pressed more intimately against my center forces a moan between us. His lips break from my mouth, nibbling along my jaw and neck as his fingers flex where they grip my ass, keeping me anchored to him.

I don't even realize we are moving until I'm being lowered down his body, my knees grazing the foot of his bed, my purse falling to the floor where I'm standing. As soon as I realize where we are, my body tenses. *Is this where....* I can't even finish the thought before his voice interrupts me.

"No one's ever been here. Just me and my hand." His eyebrow quirks up at me as I find his eyes, wondering how the hell he's able to read my mind so easily. He kisses me lightly and slowly lowers me onto the bed. A shiver runs through me as his eyes take me in, the thrill of him staring at me like this overtaking all my senses. He licks his lips as his eyes continue their journey. "I've dreamed of this moment, seeing you here in my bed." His voice is laced with desire increasing my own need for him.

The moonlight pours through the window, turning his eyes from dark blue to a beautiful pale blue. In this moment, right here, I realize that I may be his dream, but he's mine too. He's completely in control as he starts at my feet, pulling off my shoes before tracing lightly up my legs. The feeling is almost ticklish, like little bolts of electricity shooting through my body with every touch of his hands. I look down, seeing the way his dick presses against the fabric of his khakis and my mouth waters. I've never felt this way before, but I know what I want to do. Before I have the chance to lose my nerve, I sit up. Lucas stands fully, backing up like he expects me to stop. I hook a finger in his belt loop and pull him closer to me. As I start working his button on his pants, I feel his hands cover mine.

"Nat?" I look up at him, his face confused. Licking my lips, I go back to the task at hand. Unbuttoning his pants, I push them down his hips. His boxers barely contain his hardness behind them and my mouth waters even more. "What are you doing, baby?"

I don't answer, instead I slowly remove his boxers, allowing his cock to spring free. It's not too large, but not small either. The sight of him like this thrills me, sending shockwaves down my body to pulse between my legs. Taking my hand, I trail my finger from the base to the tip, watching as it jumps at my touch. Lucas hisses, his hips involuntarily moving forward as I continue my feather touches all over. I look up to his face, his eyes are watching me intently. Without breaking eye contact, I move forward and slowly lick the tip of him, the salty taste mixing with the wine I had earlier with dinner. Before he can stop me, I use my tongue to lick from the base up to the tip, wrapping my lips around him fully.

"Holy shit, Natalie." His hands weave into my hair as his eyes stay locked with mine. Having never done this before, I have no idea what I'm doing, but the way he is gripping my hair and the moans coming from him, I must be doing something right. "Baby, I'm not gonna last long and there is no way in hell I'm finishing before you." He grits out, only making me feel more empowered over the moment.

Before I can go too much further, he pulls me back, my lips releasing him with a pop. He leans down and kisses me hard. Goosebumps form everywhere he touches. His lips release mine and he nibbles his way to my ear, sucking the lobe into his mouth.

"I need you so damn bad, Nat. Tell me you feel the same." His whispered words take me by surprise. *I've never been needed before, not like this.* Before I can respond, his hand finds its way to the zipper on the back of my dress. Slowly, he unzips and pulls it off, pooling it at my waist. Pulling my strapless bra down, he pinches and teases my nipple with his fingers. Reaching around, he unclasps the bra and flings it across the room before returning his attention back to my breasts. My body instantly pushes into his hand, wanting more. My eyes close as I feel every single thing he's doing to me with his mouth, his hand. His hips are pushing into me, his cock is somehow harder than it was before as I feel it dig into my covered core.

His mouth finds mine again, his tongue pushing into my mouth. Taking my hands, I cup his cheeks as I pour myself into this kiss before he breaks it and leans his forehead into mine. Opening my eyes, I find him watching me. I move my hands to his shirt, wanting it off of him. Pulling it up, he removes his hand from my nipples and helps me get it off. His chest is a work of art, a tattoo of a wolf paw print with a wolf inside of it howling on his right pec that I haven't seen before. The makeup artists must cover it for the ads he models for. I trace the outline of it, my movements slow as I take in the details of it.

Moving on, my eyes move down to his stomach. His abs are firm, tight, as they come into a V leading right to his very hard cock that is nestled between my legs, pushing at me as his hips move. Leaning up, his hands find their way to the dress bunched at my waist. His eyes come to mine, seeking permission. I nod at him, knowing that I want this just as badly as he does. Seeing my confirmation, I lift my hips as I help him push the dress off my body, taking my underwear with it. Laying back, completely naked, I watch as his eyes take every part of me in. His eyes stay on mine as he toes off his shoes and takes off the rest of his clothes.

"You're absolutely perfect." His words calm the nerves that were starting to form in my belly at the thought of being completely naked and exposed to him again. He leans into me, his arms on both sides of my head, kissing me as his legs part mine. "Do I need to grab a condom? I promise I'm clean, I've never gone without before. But I don't want anything between us."

"I have an implant, I'm covered." I motion to my arm. He nods as he settles between my legs, his breath coming heavy. I can feel him pulsing against me as he starts nibbling my jawline, working his way to my lips. Lining himself up, he slowly pushes in as he kisses me, his tongue seeking entrance while he continues moving deeper inside of me. The minute he's fully seated inside of me, our kiss breaks and we both sigh at the feeling of being completely joined.

His eyes open as mine do and we stare at each other as he starts moving, slowly pulling himself out before thrusting himself back in. His arms are shaking as he holds his weight above me, his need to go slow keeping him in full control, but I see the desire to take it farther behind his eyes. A moan pulls from me as he continues his slow and torturous movements. It's never felt like this before. With my ex, it was usually rushed, and I never got off. Ethan was a very selfish lover, but Lucas is so much more.

"Jesus, Natalie, you feel so fucking good." His words are hoarse as he drives himself in and out slowly. Every sensation pools together in my belly as I feel everything. The feeling of his body joined with mine, the fullness of him inside of me, the way he kisses me; it all comes together in a symphonic harmony as it builds within my core. His eyes dart to where we're joined together, his movements slow and purposeful. "Oh fuck, baby, please tell me you're close." I can feel it building, that same feeling from before when it was his lips and tongue driving the orgasm.

"I-I." My fingers clench around his biceps as he pushes even deeper, my hips meeting every thrust. His mouth drops, sucking a nipple between his lips, his teeth gently nipping at them. The sensations inside me tighten and I can feel the shimmer at the edges. "Oh God."

"Nat, baby, I need you to come for me." His groan is whispered against my breast and it's as if his words are the permission I've been waiting for. He starts pounding into me, no longer holding himself back and my world crashes into a technicolor light show as the orgasm takes a hold of me and consumes my entire being. He growls out his own release, the pulsing of his cock inside of me sparking another orgasm to roll through my body.

He kisses me gently before pulling out of me. He heads into the bathroom and I can hear the water running and shutting off before he comes back to me. Cleaning me gently between my legs, he tosses the rag off to the side and lays beside me. Pulling me into him, I lay my head on his chest, tracing my finger over his tattoo, his hand caressing my back, our breathing still erratic. Ethan never took the time to clean me or even cuddle with me afterwards, always going into the bathroom to clean off and then turning his back to me before passing out. Laying here like this, in Lucas' arms, feels right. I sigh deeply before falling asleep to his caress, his heart beating in my ear.

My phone wakes me, the tone I have set playing loudly from my purse on the floor by the bed where I dropped it when we came in. Pulling myself from his arms, I roll over to find the phone, trying my best not to wake him while I do. Grabbing the phone, I don't even check the caller ID before answering.

"Is this Natalie Peterson?" My breath hitches at the use of the last name I no longer wear.

"Uh, I'm sorry, you have the wrong number." I attempt to hang up, but his pleading has me bringing the phone back up to my ear.

"Wait, please. I didn't realize you changed your name back to your maiden after the divorce. This is Natalie Conaway, correct?" Breathing deep, I wonder what the fuck's going on.

"Who is this?" I ask, unsure if I even want to know.

"This is Mr. Lederman. I'm the estate manager for Ethan Peterson." *What the fuck? Why is he calling me?* Before I can even attempt to respond, he continues. "I apologize for springing this on you, but I need to speak with you about your daughter, Savannah Peterson."

I pull myself out of the bed, my chest getting tighter as I do my best to breathe. It's like all my deepest fears are coming true. *Is he coming after her? Can he come after her even though he signed away all of his rights to her?* The questions swirl through my brain, attacking me with such precision. I walk into the bathroom and grab the robe, pulling it on in a daze. Sitting on the toilet, I hold the phone to my ear.

"Ms. Conaway, are you still there?" The bathroom door opening pulls my attention from what's happening on the phone as I look over to see Lucas coming in. Seeing the state I'm in, he immediately drops everything he's holding and rushes over to me. He grabs the phone and puts it on speaker.

"This is Lucas Moreno. May I ask who's speaking right now?"

"Yes sir, this is Mr. Lederman. As I told Ms. Conaway, I'm the estate manager for Ethan Peterson. I called because I need to speak with her about her daughter, Savannah Peterson." Lucas looks to me, his eyes wide. The tears are freely falling from my eyes as I battle the demons in my head. *He's trying to take her from me.* He sits on the edge of the tub, pulling my hand into his as he holds the phone with the other. Just this small moment is giving me strength for whatever the hell this phone call means for me.

"Okay. May I ask what this is regarding?" The man takes a deep breath, clearly unsure if he should speak candidly with someone other than myself on the phone.

"Unfortunately, this matter needs to be discussed with Ms. Conaway as she's the legal guardian of the child in question."

"I'm still here." My voice is hoarse as I force the words out of my mouth. It's all I can do not to hang up on the man and run as far away as possible.

"Ms. Conaway, I'm calling in regards to a Mr. Ethan Peterson's will." The words stop my breath. *His will? What?*

"Did you just say his will?" I hear his breath catch as he realizes that I have no idea what he's talking about.

"Oh my, you don't know?"

"Know what?" Lucas asks, rubbing the back of my hand gently with his thumb. He pulls it to his mouth, kissing it before turning his attention back to the phone.

"Ah, well, it seems that Mr. Ethan Peterson was involved in an accident over the weekend with his partner. I'm sorry to say that they didn't make it." The words hit me like a ton of bricks falling from a collapsing building. *He's dead?*

"Um…" the words are stuck in my throat, the questions no longer swirling asking if he's coming back to take my daughter.

"I'm so sorry to bring you this news, Ms. Conaway. I figured you may have heard from your parents."

"I haven't spoken to them recently. Are you saying that Ethan's dead?"

"Yes, ma'am." Oh my God. My daughter's father is dead. He wasn't father of the year, hell, he wasn't even husband of the year, but he was still her father.

"Why are you calling me?"

"It seems as though Ethan left Savannah on his will after the divorce."

"But he signed away all of his rights, how's this possible?" It's like my entire universe has shifted and I don't know which way's up or down anymore.

"The will hasn't been updated since the divorce, ma'am." The words feel foreign. Lucas sits there quietly, offering his strength as all of this plays out.

"So, he forgot?" My statement is full of sarcasm, but all I can wonder is what the hell's happening right now. "Is that what you're telling me? That my ex-husband, who is a lawyer, forgot to update his will after we got divorced?"

"Well, not exactly ma'am. He did have you removed and added his partner onto it after the divorce. However, he never removed Savannah."

"I'm really confused. He signed away his rights for her during the divorce, but he left her on the will?" *That's not the Ethan I know, well, knew. Why would he leave her on the will?*

"I wish I could tell you the reasons, Ms. Conaway,

however, I don't know them. I'm simply calling because there are some things that Ethan left for his daughter— Savannah. Would it be possible for you to come to my office to discuss?"

"I no longer live in that area so I don't think that will be happening." My voice is resigned, my brain firing on all cylinders.

"It's very prudent that you come in to see me, Ms. Conaway, as soon as possible to get this taken care of. As of right now, your parents are trying to fight the will." *Of course, they are.*

"Can I call you back?"

"Yes ma'am."

I push the end button on the phone. My entire body is numb as I sit here and replay the words in my head repeatedly. *Ethan is dead.* The father of my daughter is dead. I'm not sad that he's dead but knowing that he'll never get the opportunity to know his daughter hurts more than I can say.

## *Chapter Twenty-Five*

LUCAS

Placing the phone on the counter, I turn and grab Natalie. I lift her into my arms, cradling her against me and move us back into the bedroom. Sitting us on the edge of the bed, I pull her as close to me as I can.

"Natalie, baby, talk to me."

"He's dead. I can't believe it. How did this happen?" Her words are whispered into my chest. I'm powerless in this moment. I don't know how to help her through this. She starts crying uncontrollably, her sobs taking over her body as she shakes in my arms.

I have so many questions about what's going on. *Why is she so upset about this? Is she still in love with him?*

A few minutes later, she calms down. Her sob is now a quiet whimper as she pulls herself together. She's still gripping me like I'm her only lifeline.

"I need to go." She pulls away. Her eyes are bloodshot, and the tears are still steadily falling down her cheeks.

"Stay, Natalie. Don't run. Talk to me, please."

"No, I can't. I'm fine. I'll be fine." She kisses me on the cheek, gathers her clothing and walks into the bathroom. I

203

listen as the door locks. A few minutes later, she emerges. She doesn't look at me, just picks up her purse and walks out the door.

Getting up, I walk out after her.

"Natalie, please, talk to me."

"I need time, Lucas. That phone call just turned my world upside down all over again and I don't know how to handle it." She gives me a small smile before opening the front door and walking out of it, shutting it softly as she does.

*What the fuck just happened?*

It's been an hour since she walked out. She hasn't come home like I expected. I've been watching through my kitchen for her to show up, for us to talk. I know she's confused but I thought we were together on this. *Why would she run away from me now?* I'm not understanding what the hell's going on. Why would Ethan dying have such a big effect on her?

My phone ringing pulls me out of the trance of watching her house like some sort of stalker.

"Hello."

"Lucas?" Justin's voice sounds strained, more so than usual.

"What's up?"

"I take it you haven't seen the latest tabloid?"

"No. You know I don't pay attention to that shit." I growl as I push away from the kitchen counter and head into the living room.

"You at home?"

"Yep." I pop the 'p'.

"Stay put." He hangs up before I have a chance to respond. *What the fuck's going on now?*

Twenty minutes later, he comes in the door. I notice that

his defenses are up like they were when the whole thing with Lauren went down. He tosses the tabloid into my lap. The minute I look down at it, I realize why he's freaking out.

Natalie takes majority of the cover. She's standing in front of a building in downtown. I bring the magazine closer, trying to make out the name on the building. *Dr. Donna Hart Psychodynamic Therapist*. And then I see the headline. And in the bottom corner, a picture of Lauren looking distraught. *FUCK.*

## Lucas Moreno's new girlfriend in therapy for abuse.
*Ex-girlfriend Lauren tells all in this exclusive look.*

"Did you know she was going to therapy for abuse?" Justin's words pull me from the words I just read.

"I didn't know she was still going. She went after she left her ex-husband. At least, I thought she did." I almost tell him the reason she was in therapy and then stop myself. It's not my story to tell. *Why would she go back after all this time? Why did she hide it from me?* Lauren did this type of shit all the time and I'd always let it go. But seeing Natalie on the cover of this magazine pisses me off. She hid it from me.

"They're painting you as the abuser." The magazine falls from my hand as I try to get my head around the words that came out of his mouth.

"I've never..." He puts his hand up to stops me.

"Lauren told them you're mentally abusive, Lucas." I drop my head into my hands as I take in what he says.

"What the fuck, man? You know me better than that." He nods his head as he sits beside me.

"Lauren is twisting the narrative, Lucas. You need to talk to Natalie and find out what's going on." I look up at him.

"She hasn't come back since she left this morning."

"She's with Madison. I saw them go into the coffee shop

together when I left to come here." The thought that she could turn to Madison and not me only pisses me off more.

"Thanks." Grabbing my phone and the tabloid from the floor, I walk out the door.

Walking into the coffee shop, the anger is simmering just below the surface. The entire drive here, I question everything about our relationship. All the secrets she kept. *Therapy. Her entire marriage.* Natalie faces the window, watching as the cars go by. Madison's talking quietly to her. I approach slowly, not wanting to interrupt their moment but needing answers.

"Natalie, can I speak with you?" My voice scares her, and she jumps slightly before turning to look at me.

"Sure. Madison, do you mind?" Her voice is quiet, subdued. Madison gives her a small nod before turning to me. Her eyes are holding questions as she watches me. I grab Nat's hand, pulling her outside with me.

"Lucas, what's wrong?" she asks as we come to a stop outside.

"Why didn't you tell me you're still in therapy?" Her eyes widen at my question.

"Because it's my business, Lucas," she says back, holding her ground. Her eyes have tears welling in them. I don't like seeing the tears but I'm past the point of return now. Everything feels like a lie, a big giant lie.

"Yea, well, if I had known, maybe I'd have been better prepared for this shit." I toss the tabloid at her. She barely catches it. She takes in the picture on the front, her free hand coming up to cover her mouth.

"Why would they do this?" she whispers, her eyes never leaving the cover.

"Why would you do that to me? You should have told me." I roar at her, not caring that others can hear me.

"I..."

"You know what? Forget it." I don't want to hear her answers, her excuses. I turn to walk off. *Fuck this shit.*

"I went because I was falling for you and I was scared." Her whispered words reach me.

"Bullshit." I spit back at her. "You were still in love with him, weren't you? That's why you broke this morning when you found out he was dead, why you went back to therapy. Why you walked away and didn't come back."

The tears are falling more steadily now but I have no fucks left to give. She goes to talk but I hold my hand up to her.

"I don't want to hear your excuses anymore, Natalie. I thought we were past all the fucking secrets between us." I turn and walk away. The sounds of her crying reach me as I get into my car. I don't look back as I put the car in gear and drive away.

# *Chapter Twenty-Six*

NATALIE

Madison rushes out the coffee shop as I fall to the bench seat just outside. *He walked away again.* He told me he'd never walk away from me.

"Natalie, what the hell just happened?" I hand over the tabloid as she sits beside me. Her eyes read over the headline and the picture before coming up to mine. "Holy shit."

"He walked away from me, Madison." I whisper, the tears falling from my eyes as I stare at the spot his car was in.

"Natalie, honey, what's going on?"

"He says I'm still in love with Ethan, that I'm back in therapy for that. Told me I should've told him I was going to therapy again. But I only went the one time, because I feared taking the next step with him." Her eyes soften as I talk. She pats the back of my hand.

"I'm going to stab that man." My lips twitch as a smile tries to break through.

"I need to get Savi. I have to go back."

"Back where?"

"Galveston."

"What's in Galveston?" I'd barely had any time to tell her

what happened on the phone this morning before Lucas walked in. I was lost in my thoughts as she told me about what happened with Justin while Lucas and I were on our date.

"Ethan's estate lawyer. He's dead, Madison." Her eyes widen as I tell her about the phone call. "I have to go take care of that. I can't stay in that house tonight. Oh God, Madison. He walked away from me again." I wail as the emotions pile against me. Watching him walk away the first time hurt, but this time is a whole new ball game. My heart shattered the minute he drove off, like I was nothing to him.

"I'll go get Savi from school. Why don't you go pack and then you can stay over at my house?"

"Yea, I can do that." She stands and then pulls me up to stand with her.

"It's going to be okay, Natalie." She pulls me in for a hug. All I can do is nod before turning to walk back to the guest house.

His car isn't here when I walk up the driveway. Tears fall as I look away from his house and make my way to my porch and unlock the door. Taking a deep breath to steady myself, I go in and start the process of packing everything we'll need for our trip.

"How long do you think you'll be gone?" Madison asks as she braids Savi's hair later that evening.

"Depends on how long it takes to get the will settled." I don't go into much detail. I haven't told Savannah what's going on, not sure how to approach the subject with her.

"Time for bed, bug." Madison says as she finishes the last braid. Savi jumps up and hugs her before coming over to me for one. Pulling her in tight, I close my eyes and breathe in deep and kiss her on the head.

"Goodnight, Mommy." She kisses my cheek and then goes down the hall into the room that Madison made up for her.

"You okay?" Madison asks as she sits beside me on the couch. I'm still nursing the same glass of wine from when I walked in the house earlier. The bags we need for the trip are in the trunk, the rest of my stuff is in Madison's spare room. I didn't have much since the guest house was fully furnished. I have some odds and ends I left behind because I was in a rush, trying to get out of there before he came home and found me there.

"Yes. No. Maybe." Honestly, I don't know if I'm okay. I wasn't in love with Ethan anymore, but this was the very last thing I was expecting.

"It's okay to not be okay."

"I haven't been in love with Ethan in a long time, Madison. But he was Savannah's father, whether he signed away those rights or not. And now he's gone. There's no chance for him to ever decide he was wrong, for him to wake up and realize that he wanted a relationship with our daughter." The tears start falling again as I think of Savi. My heart breaks for my daughter. She never really asks about him, and I'm thankful for that but I knew one day she would, and now he's dead. *How do I even begin to explain any of this to her?*

"I should kick his ass." She downs the rest of her wine before setting the glass on the table.

"He's dead." I say, taking a small sip from my own glass.

"Not Ethan. Lucas. He didn't even give you an opportunity to explain."

"It doesn't matter anymore, Maddy. He walked away. He told me he wouldn't walk away again."

"So, what now?"

"Now, I go to Galveston. Get this shit settled. Then I'll come back and find somewhere else to stay." Saying those words break my heart, but I can't continue living in his guest house, not after everything that happened.

"What time is your flight?"

"Ten in the morning." She nods her head before turning the TV on and finding a sappy romantic comedy. I don't pay attention to it as it plays. Instead, the scene from earlier today plays in a loop in my head. *He walked away.*

I hold my head high as I walk into Mr. Lederman's office, Savi holding my hand beside me. Looking around, I take in the small waiting area and receptionist's desk. His office looks nothing like my father's, or Ethan's.

"Natalie? Is that you?" My breath catches as I see my mother stand from the other side of the room.

"Hello, Mother." Savi shrinks behind me. I've never known her to be shy, so this isn't something I'm used to.

"What are you doing here?" My father asks as he stands beside her. He's looking down his nose at me. The day I left my ex, they wrote me off and I hadn't spoken to either of them since.

"Mr. Lederman called." I move Savi and myself around them and across the room to the receptionist. She smiles and takes down my info.

"He'll be with you shortly." I smile. My parents are still standing when I turn back to the reception area. Both are staring at Savi as she continues to try to hide behind me.

"Is that Savannah?" My mother asks.

"Yes. This is Savi."

"What kind of name is that?" She scoffs as she tries to peer around me.

"It's a nickname, Mother." Her eyes snap to mine.

"Well, bring her around, let me see her." She makes a move to grab Savannah and I move to block her.

"No, Mother."

"Natalie Renee, that is our grandchild." I feel Savi tense behind me, her body shaking as she continues to hide.

"She's nothing to you. Same as I am. We haven't been anything to you since I left Ethan. You made sure to make that known to me. You haven't contacted us once since we left." For the first time in my life, I'm standing up to them. My voice raises with each word that pours out of me. "Now, if you don't mind, I'm here to see Mr. Lederman." I move around them and sit us across the room. Savi crawls into my lap and hides herself as she curls into me. My mother scoffs as she sits facing me, watching every move that I make. My father glares daggers at me as he sits. I didn't expect them to be here, but the lawyer did say that they were fighting against the will.

"Ms. Conaway, I'm ready for you." Mr. Lederman interrupts our staring match. I stand, hoisting Savi into my arms so she doesn't have to walk and make my way over to him. He turns to my parents. "Mr. and Mrs. Conaway, there's nothing else I can help you with. Ethan was very clear in his will." My father's face turns red as he stands.

"That boy was my son and you're telling me he left us nothing?" I roll my eyes at my father's choice of words. *Of course, he'd say Ethan's his son.*

"I'm sorry Mr. Conaway." Mr. Lederman opens the door and leads us through.

"This is bullshit. He signed away rights to that child. She shouldn't get a single cent of his inheritance. I gave him that inheritance." My father's voice roars as we continue down the hall.

"I apologize for that, Ms. Conaway."

"Please, call me Natalie, Mr. Lederman."

"Alright, Natalie. Please call me Frances. I hate that you

found out about your ex-husband's untimely death through me. I'll try to make this as easy as possible." I nod my head as he pulls paperwork out of his briefcase.

"What was my father talking about?" I watch as he takes a steadying breath, his hands shaking as he finishes pulling everything that he needs out.

"Your father wasn't too happy that Ethan came to me with his final will." I nod my head, waiting for him to continue. "As you know, your father runs a very successful law firm. When he found out that Ethan's final will and testament wasn't done through his firm, he hunted me down and demanded to know why."

"My father doesn't like being caught off guard." He nods his head in response.

"Mama, I want Lucy." Savi whispers from the crook of my neck, pulling me from my conversation. Hearing his nickname hurts me. She doesn't see me flinch, doesn't know what happened. All she knows is that she loves him, and he makes her feel safe.

"Just a little longer, Savi bug. Want to color?" Redirecting her attention, I watch as she smiles and nods at me. Setting her down, I grab her stuff out of my travel bag. Once she's set up with everything she needs, I turn back to the lawyer.

"Suffice it to say, your parents only had a small part in his final will. The inheritance your father was yelling about, it was left to Savannah." I roll my lips inward, trying my best not to laugh at how my father took the news.

"I'm still not sure why though?"

"Ethan never discussed much with me. I didn't handle the divorce, that was your father's firm." I already know my father helped with the divorce, recognizing the man who represented my ex during the entire proceeding. "Over the course of the past couple of years, he's only changed his will once. That was after the divorce when he removed you and added his new partner to the paperwork. He never said anything to me about why when we updated everything. It wasn't my place to ask and I wish I had more answers for you."

Over the next two hours, Frances goes over everything in the will with me.

"Why would he leave this for her?" I don't understand this at all. My ex-husband was calculating, and although he never physically hurt me, I never expected this. Especially considering he signed away all of his rights to her. The money he left is going into an interest savings account that Savi will receive on her twenty-first birthday.

"I don't know, Natalie. He never discussed it with me. We will finalize everything over the next couple of days, and then once that's all said and done, you can head home." Seeing the amount has my mind reeling even more than before. He left every single penny to her.

After shaking his hand, I turn to pack up Savi's stuff. My brain is firing at a million miles per hour, wondering why Ethan would do something like this for Savi. Walking into the lobby, I don't even notice my mother stand up until she's moving in front of me.

"You shouldn't have left him, Natalie. This would've never happened had you stayed." She spits at me. Savi cowers behind my legs the moment she starts talking, the venom in her words scaring my baby girl.

Squaring my shoulders, I look her in the eyes. "He cheated on me, Mother, countless times."

"We turn a blind eye, it's what we do, Natalie. I told you this." The words are dripping with disdain only solidified the knowledge that my parents are toxic, always have been and always will be.

"No, Mother. That's what you do. And all it's done is turn you into a callous, pretentious snob who cares for nothing except where to find the next drink." I hear her sharp intake of breath, but I don't let her get a word in, my need to get every-thing out forcing the words from my mouth. "I turned the blind eye mother. And it destroyed me."

"This is no way to talk to your mother. That mouth of yours is probably the reason he strayed as much as he did." I laugh at her, but it's a lifeless and empty laugh. I don't really care for this conversation anymore.

"You're not my mother, you haven't been for quite a while. You wrote Savi and I off the day we left. And honestly, it's been the best thing you ever did for me, for us." I shrug her off and go to move around her, Savi's hand tightening in my own as she continues to hide. She moves to step in my way again.

"You're a disgrace to this family, Natalie. I don't know what we did to have you turn out this way. And what kind of name is Savi? Her name is Savannah."

"You want to know what you did, Mother? Take a good long look in the mirror and you might just find the answer. You did nothing but drink my entire childhood. Every recital, every time I had something, you were drunk. It was never about being a mother with you, it was about being seen, about notoriety. Life is so much bigger than a bank account, Mother."

Her mouth drops open in shock at my words. Before she can even get a word out of her mouth, I walk around her, my head held high as we exit the office.

"Is it time to go home now, Mommy? I made Lucy a new picture and I have to give it to him." I look down at Savi. Her eyes still hold some fear from the confrontation with my mother, but otherwise, her eyes are sparkling. Hearing her talk about Lucas breaks my heart. Knowing that his walking away means I need to break Savi's heart in the process too. I don't know how I'm going to handle seeing him when we get back to BoothBay. The island is so small that I know we'll probably run into him. As much as it kills me, I can't leave that place. It's become my home. I didn't want any of this when we got together. He promised me it wouldn't happen. *He also said he wouldn't walk away.* Tears fill my eyes as I kneel and pull Savi into my arms, hugging her tightly to me.

"Not yet, baby. We have a couple more things to take care of before we can go back." Her bottom lip quivers as she looks at me.

"I miss Lucy," she whispers quietly.

"I know, baby." I rub her back before standing and taking her hand. "How about some dinner and then we can find some ice cream?" She nods her head at me as we make our way down the street towards the hotel I set us up in.

Chapter Twenty-Seven

LUCAS

The minute I drove away, all my anger dissipated. The sound of her crying haunts me, but it's not enough to make me turn around. I pull onto the highway that takes me to the south side of the beach knowing I can't go home, can't see the guest house. *Not right now.*

I'm on my second beer when my phone rings. Part of me hopes it's Natalie asking if I'm coming home, but my hopes are dashed when I see Justin's name on my screen.

"What do you want?" I answer.

"I'm at your house and no one's here. Where the hell are you?" He asks. *What does he mean no one's there?*

"I'm at the bar in South Beach. Natalie's not there?"

"No one's here, man." His words hit hard. I thought she'd be home by now. It's why I drove all the way down here. I run through all the places she may have gone in my head as Justin continues to talk in the background. "Lucas, are you listening to me?"

"Sorry, what'd you say?" I ask, putting my head on the table in front of me.

"How drunk are you?"

"Not as drunk as I wish I could be." He sighs deeply on the other end of the line.

"I was saying that I contacted Lauren's agency and told them that we're suing for slander."

"You did what?" I yell into the phone, drawing attention my way. "What happened?"

"She recanted the story. Said she wanted to ruin your relationship. Did you talk to Natalie?"

"Uh, sorta." The entire scene replays in my head. Every ugly word I said to her.

"What did you do, Lucas?" I tell him everything that happened. It feels like it happened days ago, but it was only a few hours ago.

"You didn't give her a chance to explain?" he asks. Thinking back on it, I realize I did most of the talking, my anger making me disinterested in hearing anything she had to tell me. And it's not anger at her, more frustration than anything else. The anger is deeper, held over from years ago and the shadows that like to grip me with their fingers, reminding me that I wasn't the one she chose before.

"Why would I? She withheld information from me, Justin." Saying it out loud kills me. She didn't trust me enough to tell me that she went back to Dr. Hart. Her claim that she was falling for me whispers in my ears, her admittance that she was scared.

"You knew about her therapy," he tells me. I'm the one who encouraged her to go, even without the knowledge of everything she went through. But I could see the depression, the self-doubt. I knew she needed it. But then she stopped going, saying she was better.

"She didn't tell me she was going back to therapy." I say, downing the rest of my beer before flagging the bartender for my bill.

"You think she did this on purpose?" His words cause my chest to tighten as I think about what he's saying. Natalie wouldn't do something like that. She's never been that kind of person, even through her childhood, when her parents tried grooming her to act a certain way. Her quiet strength was one of my favorite things about her. Closing my eyes, I hear her crying as I walked away echoing in my head. And then it hits me. *I fucking walked away.*

"I think I fucked up."

"You think or you know?" *I know I fucked up.*

"I'm on my way."

"I'll be here." I grab my keys and head to my car wondering where the hell Natalie went.

Pulling up to an empty house hurts more than I want to admit. When I drove away, I expected her to come back here and hide away. *Why would she come here after you treated her the way you did*? Shaking the thoughts out of my head, I head into the house and walk into the living room. Justin's sitting on the couch scrolling on his phone. He nods his head in greeting at me as I walk in. Instead of sitting with him, I walk back out and go into my bedroom.

Her perfume hits my nose the minute I walk in, enveloping me in the light fragrance that makes my heart hurt. I plug in my phone on the table before grabbing the pillow she used last night. I lay in the bed over the covers as I think about everything that happened since last night.

Morning comes and the first thing I do is pull the pillow Natalie slept on closer to me. Her scent is still as strong as it was last night. I bury my nose into it, wishing like hell it was her body laying here next to me. After a few minutes, I roll over and sit up, planting my feet on the floor as my head falls into my hands. I don't know how to fix things. I don't even know where she ended up last night. Lifting my head, I look at the clock. *10:07 a.m.* Pulling myself out of bed, I go into the bathroom and brush my teeth as I stare at my reflection in the mirror. I have bags under my eyes from tossing and turning all night.

Heading back into the room, I grab my phone, hoping like hell she contacted me. I get a blank screen showing no missed notifications, only souring my mood even further. *Where is she?* Unlocking the phone, I'm greeted by the photo I took of her on the beach when she wasn't paying attention. Tears form in my eyes as I take it in. *I have to fix this.*

I pocket my phone and head to the guest house. The minute I enter, the breath is sucked out of my lungs as I look around. There are a few personal things here and there, but otherwise it looks as though no one lives here. I rush into her bedroom and tear open her closet door and the near emptiness consumes me. I look around the entire room. Other than a few pictures and some random items, it's like no one has lived here. I cross the hall to Savi's room and it's the same as the other. *She left me.*

I open my contacts and tap Natalie's name, praying she'll answer this time. The call goes straight to voicemail. *Fuck.* I close the call and open my texts. I type out message after message, only to delete them again and again. I don't want to do this through text, she deserves more than that. But I have no idea where she could've gone. I close out my messages with her and my eyes move over the other messages in my queue. *Justin. Madison.* Holy shit. Madison.

**Lucas:** Madison, is she with you?

**Madison:** Fuck off

**Lucas:** Madison, please. Tell me she's safe

**Madison:** Not that you deserve any information at all asshole but she's fine.

**Lucas:** Where is she?

**Madison:** It's not your concern. You weren't willing to listen to her when she needed you to.

Taking a deep breath, I realize I not only have to grovel to Natalie, but I'm gonna have to get on my hands and knees for Madison to forgive me too.

**Lucas:** I fucked up. Please, just tell me where she is.

**Madison:** You have a lot of fucking nerve. You don't deserve her.

**Lucas:** Trust me, I know I don't. But I'm worried about her.

**Madison:** Sucks to be you.

Part of me knew that Madison wouldn't tell me, especially if Natalie stayed with her last night. I fucked up big. I don't even know if Natalie will even talk to me after how I treated her.

**Lucas:** I know what I did was wrong. She's my everything, her and Savi both. I just want a chance to make things right. That's all I'm asking.

A few minutes pass and there's no response. *I really fucked this up.* Just as I'm about to give up hope, a response comes in.

**Madison:** Fuck up again, and I'll stab you. She's in Galveston

Switching from texting to the internet, I book the next flight out. I broke my promise by walking way, but this time, I'm not going to let it take as long as it did for us to see each other again.

The plane touches down and I release a harsh breath. The entire way here I fought with myself on how I'm going to handle this. I don't even know where she's staying, let alone where the law office is. I've called almost every hotel within the damn city and no one can tell me anything due to privacy reasons. Pulling my cap lower, I grab my shades from my pocket, prepping to don them as soon as I'm able to. I don't think I'll be recognized, but I don't want to take any chances, especially with the paparazzi focused on me the way they are.

I didn't pack much, just a carry on, so I bypass baggage claim and head straight to the rental place to snag a car to get me around the city. I'm grasping at straws, but I'm going to start with the law offices closest to her parents and working my way out. I have no idea if she's even met with the lawyers yet. All Madison would tell me is that she's here and she's staying until everything's resolved. *I don't even know what everything entails.*

"Lucas?" The voice startles me, pulling me from my thoughts. Looking over, I take in the sight before me.

"Levi? Is that you?" My best friend from high school, other than Natalie, stares at me from the check-in counter.

"Holy shit! What's up man?" He drops his bag and approaches me, pulling me into a one-armed hug.

"What the hell are you doing here?" Last I heard, he'd left this place and never looked back.

"Grandma passed."

"Damn man, I'm sorry." He shrugs his shoulders, his eyes following mine to the rental office entrance.

"They're out of rental cars by the way." He nods his head towards the door just beyond us.

"Fuck." He grabs his keys out of his pockets.

"I got you. Where you heading to?"

"Trying to find Natalie." His eyebrows raise as he looks me over.

"Natalie's back? Shit man, I had no idea. I know her ex died, but I didn't think that would bring Natalie back into town."

"Yea, she's dealing with the lawyers or some shit."

"Ah, I know where to go. I used the same lawyer as Ethan." Hearing his name has my eye twitching, but I keep my mouth shut. I don't know how much Levi knows about what went down after I left, especially since he left around the same time I did.

"Thanks man." He gives me a chin lift before grabbing his discarded bag and heading towards the exit.

"How'd you get a car?" I ask.

"My parents wanted to make sure I got to the damn funeral. No excuses." He rolls his eyes as he unlocks the four-door Audi.

We show up to the lawyer's office and watch as a lady locks the front door and make her way to her car. There's no sign of

Natalie or Savannah anywhere. My body deflates as I watch the woman get into her car and drive away.

"Sorry man." Levi says as the car pulls off.

"It's okay." I grab my bag with one hand, the handle of the door with the other. "I appreciate your help. You got my number, hit me up." He lifts his chin as I get out of the vehicle. He pulls off and I shoulder my bag, looking up and down the street. *Where are you, baby?*

# Chapter Twenty-Eight

## NATALIE

We've been in Galveston for two days now and I'm growing tired of the hotel. Savi is just as restless as I am, consistently asking for *Lucy*. Every time she brings him up, another piece of my heart shatters into pieces. I still haven't spoken to him since I left, and Madison hasn't mentioned him to me at all, at my request.

"Mama?" I look down at the sweet girl holding my hand as we walk down Main Street towards the lawyer's office. The voice pulling me from my thoughts of him and everything that's happened.

"What is it, bug?" She scrunches her nose before looking up at me.

"Is the mean lady and man going to be there today?" My eye twitches as I listen to her question. My parents have been there every time I've shown up, throwing their weight around. The will's cut and dry, and as much as my father would enjoy having his say, there's no way he can fight this one.

"I don't know, baby." I stop walking to squat down beside her, pulling her into my arms. "But, if they are, we'll ignore them."

"They say mean things to you, Mommy." Her words hurt me, not because she's wrong, but because she shouldn't be subjected to their toxicity.

"I'm okay, baby. They can't hurt me anymore." She sniffles into my neck as I pick her up, carrying her the rest of the way.

I'm hoping today finalizes everything, so we can be on our way back to BoothBay tomorrow. I've already decided to move out of the guest house when we return. I can't be that close to him, not after everything that's happened. Madison offered to let us stay with her until I can find a place for us.

Before I know it, we're walking into the lawyer's office, the tiny arms tightening around my neck as we cross the threshold and I'm verbally attacked.

"Jesus Christ, Natalie, at least make her fucking walk." My father rolls his eyes as he watches us enter, his eyes flashing with impatience and anger. Rolling his words off, I squeeze Savi a little tighter to me as her body starts to shake.

"Natalie, he's ready for you. Go on back." The receptionist smiles at me, buzzing the door to the left so I can get out of the reception area quickly.

"She doesn't deserve that fucking money." My father yells as the door shuts behind me. I fight the tears that want to fall, pinching my eyes shut as I take deep breaths.

Once everything is signed, Frances shakes my hand and leads me to the exit on the side of the building.

"I'd rather not see this little girl shaken up by them anymore than she already is." He nods his head down to her when I raise my eyebrow at the direction he takes us. My lips lift into a small smile as he opens the door.

"Thank you for everything Frances." He shakes my hand one more time before I walk out onto the sidewalk on the side of the building. Savi waves to him, a smile on her face. For our meeting today, he had cookies and coloring books for her, to help her pass the time while we finalized everything. The meeting took just over an hour to get through the paperwork, but Savi was sitting quietly with cookies and coloring books. She tore quite a few pages out, shoving them into my bag as she finished.

We make our way to the corner, walking slow enough to allow the afternoon air to warm us after spending so much time in the cooled office. Just as I'm about to turn to head for our hotel to pack, Savi takes off running down the sidewalk.

"Savannah." I yell as I run after her. She's never done something like this before, except when it came to her favorite person, Lucas. I stop short as I watch her barrel her way into him, his eyes never leaving mine as he pulls her in to his chest. My heart stops as he kisses her on the cheek, whispering to her. *What is he doing here?*

"Natalie." His voice is thick with emotions as he watches me make my way closer to them.

"What are you doing here?" I ask, my voice breaking as I watch him hold my daughter like she's his lifeline.

"I came for you, for Savi." His voice reaches me, his words hurting me more than he knows. I can hear Savi sniffling, her body shaking with the emotions I wish I could feel. I have no idea how to even respond to him, to what he's saying. I wasn't mentally prepared to see him yet, my heart still reeling from the blow he dealt when he walked away.

"I can't do this, Lucas." He sets Savi on the ground, her hand clasping his tightly as she moves to stand beside him. "Come on, Savi. We need to go now. You can see Lucy later." She doesn't move.

"Please, baby, just talk to me." He pleads with me.

"Don't call me that. You have no right to call me that, not after you walked away from me again. Ethan may have broken me, but that was nothing compared to the way you shattered me." His face falls at my words, the impact of them hitting directly as I intended. "Savannah, come along now." He squats down to whisper something to her. I watch as she nods her head, tears steadily falling down her cheeks. He kisses her lightly on the forehead before turning her to me, standing as he guides her to make her way back to my side.

Grabbing her hand, I smile down at her. She doesn't look at me, just keeps her eyes on the ground as she stands beside me.

"Please, don't walk away. I'm begging you, Natalie." Tears form as I look back at him.

"That's the thing, Lucas. You've walked away from me twice now. It's my turn." Turning on my heel, I walk away from the man who still owns my heart. The same heart he left bleeding outside my favorite coffee shop.

We've been back in BoothBay for a week and other than answering my questions, Savi hasn't spoken to me. The minute we walked away from Lucas, she pulled into herself and away from me. It's killing me that all of this is happening, and I can't fix it for her. I don't want to keep her from Lucas, but seeing him hurts me deeply, shattering my heart more and more. I'm a coward that uses her best friend as the go between while I hide. I left my key behind with Madison, opting to have her go through and pack the rest of our belongings so I wouldn't have to. There wasn't much since the guest house was already furnished when we got here. I've been living with Madison until I can find a place of my own.

"Hey, sweetie." Madison plops onto the couch beside me, a glass of wine in each hand. I give her a small smile as I take the glass and drink it all in one gulp. Her eyes watch me as I finish the glass. "Lucas is picking up Savi today and then I'll grab her from him in a couple hours." I nod my head, tears threatening to fall at the sound of his name.

"Thank you." My hollowness of my voice doesn't sound familiar to me.

"Talk to me. I know he went there to find you and then you came home and moved in with me." Her gaze is soft and warm. I swallow the knot in my throat as I try to process the words she wants to hear.

"I walked away from him, Maddy. I had just finished settling everything with Ethan's will. Savi ran from me and I was so scared, because she's never done anything like that before. And then there he was, holding her to him like she was his lifeline." A sob escapes me as I remember the look on his face as he held her to him, as he whispered to her before she walked back over to me. "I couldn't handle it. He shattered me when he walked away, I couldn't go through it again.

"So, you protected yourself by walking away." She finishes my thoughts for me. I nod, eyeing my empty wineglass and wishing like hell I had more wine. "He looks like shit, by the way." My head turns towards her as she lifts her own glass and takes a sip.

"Ethan broke me, Madison." I wipe away the tear that escapes. "But what he did was nothing compared to just how shattered I feel right now." She sets her glass down and pulls me into her as the tears start falling freely.

I slowly get back into working as the weeks go by. Savi has opened up to me more, but I can still feel the wall she's erected. She doesn't even know that we were dating, doesn't know that he broke my heart in ways that she won't understand until she's much older. All she sees is that her favorite person isn't always around like before, that I'm no longer around him, that everything's changed.

Walking into the coffee shop, I take a deep breath as I wait in line. Once I reach the counter, the girl smiles and inputs my order without me having to say anything. I go to hand her my card, but she shakes her head.

"It's already been taken care of." Frowning, I look around the coffee shop to the limited people sitting, but there are no familiar faces. I figure it's a one off, maybe the person in front of me bought mine and now I've thrown everything out of whack because I stood here like a dumbass instead of keeping it going.

"Natalie." The barista calls my name, handing me a cup of coffee. Walking to the corner of the shop, I find my usual table and sit. Closing my eyes, I take a deep breath. I have a session in an hour, so I'm taking some time to relax before I'll be rolling around in the sands on the beach trying to get the perfect shot.

Taking a sip of the still hot coffee, I open my eyes and let them drift around. This coffee shop isn't a chain, but their coffee is the best I've ever had. The décor is a little dated, but you can see some minor updates here and there as the owners work on things as they can. Looking down at my cup, I tilt my head. There are words on my cup, and not just my name, but an actual message. Setting it down, I remove my hand and uncover the words written. *You're an amazing mom.*

I turn the cup and find more messages, each one of them written all over the cup. *You're strong. You're the sun in the sky. You're brave.* Each new message brings tears to my eyes as I slowly turn the cup to read them. When I get to the last one, my breath catches, and the tears escape, rolling down my cheeks steadily. *Hoping your day is as remarkable as you.*

"May I sit?" I jump at the voice that pulls me from my thoughts. Looking up, I see Justin standing by my table, a coffee in his hand. I gesture to the seat across from me and he sits, holding onto his coffee with both hands as he looks at me. Looking around, I try to see if Lucas is with him. "He's not here. Doesn't even know I'm here right now." My eyes move to his, a small smile playing on his lips. Using my sleeve, I wipe the tear marks that are sure to be seen on my cheeks.

"Why are you here?" My voice is broken. Seeing Justin only makes me think of Lucas, of how much I miss him.

"I have a job for you." My eyebrows scrunch in confusion. *What the hell is he talking about?* "I need a photographer to take shots for the new agency." He makes the statement and takes a sip of his coffee, his eyes never wavering from my own.

"I can't." I can't be around Lucas right now. My heart is still shattered into a million pieces and seeing him will only make the pain worse.

"Please, Natalie." He sets his coffee down but keeps his hands on the cup. "I know I wasn't in your corner before, and even with my apology, you have no reason to listen, but I need you. You're the best photographer I've seen in a long time, and that's saying something."

"Justin, I appreciate that but..." he holds his hand up, effectively stopping me from talking anymore.

"He doesn't know I'm doing this, has no idea. This wasn't his idea, it was mine. I looked at your website, Natalie. Your work blew me away. The way you capture every moment, even the candid ones, is breathtaking. I don't want anyone except for you. I have a contract with me." My eyebrows raise at his statement.

"I have to think about it, Justin." He nods and pulls paperwork out of a messenger bag. I didn't even notice the bag when he sat down. He slides the packet over to me. His eyes catch mine again.

"Look it over. My number is on there, so you can let me know what you decide. I don't want anyone else but you, though." With that, he gives me a smile before grabbing his coffee again and standing up. "I hope you do it, Natalie. You're an amazing photographer and I'd be fucking lucky as hell to have you as the one who takes the shots for the agency."

After he leaves, I stare at the packet of papers sitting in front of me for what feels like hours, going over everything he said before he left. Pulling them closer, I start sifting through, looking at each page. I get to the last page and gasp, my hand covering my mouth as I stare at the amount he wants to pay me.

*Chapter Twenty-Nine*

LUCAS

The past few weeks have felt like my heart has been ripped out of my chest. I got the recant from Lauren's agent, as well as a heartfelt apology at the backlash it caused, including losing the last few campaigns I had on my calendar this year. Justin was pissed, saying that I should fight it, but I'm done fighting. I want out of modeling and this fast-tracked the whole thing.

I play with the watch on my wrist as I sit in my new office at the agency, my thoughts on Natalie. It's close to ten in the morning and I can't help but wonder what she's doing, how her day has been, if she's gotten the coffees? The door opening barely catches my attention, but then it's followed by a laugh. *I know that laugh.* Walking out of my office, I head to the reception area and stop short. Natalie is standing with Justin, talking. Natalie is smiling, but I can see from here that the joy isn't reaching her eyes.

I stay still, not wanting to spook her. This is the closest I've been to her since she walked away. I don't blame her for walking, I broke my word, hurting her. It pains me to know that I caused pain in her life. Her eyes come up and that's when she notices me, and she stops, standing still. The smile fades, her eyes watering with tears that I know I'm causing. She's gorgeous, even now. Justin realizes she stopped moving and turns to face me. He steps around Natalie as she hides herself behind him. It kills me that she's hiding from me.

"Hey, man." He says, but I don't take my eyes off where I know she's standing. I give him a chin lift, so he knows I'm listening. "Natalie is here to do our agency shoot." With that, my face scrunches in confusion. *Agency shoot, what the fuck is he talking about?* I watch as he turns to whisper something to her before she moves to the other end of the reception area, as far from me as she can get.

"What agency shoot are you talking about?" I whisper when Justin gets close enough.

"We needed pictures for our opening. She's the best in the area. I wanted the best." I haven't taken my eyes from Natalie. She's emptying her photo bag, adjusting her lens. "Please, man, just do the shoot. Leave her be." My eyes come back to his. He's pleading with me, knowing full well how hard this is going to be. Not just for me, but for her.

"Did she know I'd be here?"

"Yea, she knew. But I promised that you'd be a professional. It was the only way she'd agree." I hang my head, hating that he had to make that promise. "I know you two need to talk things out, but not today. I'm begging you man." I nod my head, refusing to lift it from my chest.

"Who are we wanting to start with?" Natalie's question drags me out of my thoughts. I've been standing on the opposite side of the room from her. She's spent the past twenty minutes talking with Justin about what the session is for.

"What do you think, Lucas?" Justin asks, his arms crossed as he leans against the wall. I shrug my shoulders. It fucking hurts knowing that she won't even acknowledge me.

"Do you want business partner photos together or just individuals?" We both look to Natalie, her camera in her hand as she plays with the settings on the back.

"Both." Justin says. Natalie nods her head at him and then motions me to where I'm standing by the door. She shows me the pose before backing up just enough. I watch as her mind works through each shot she takes. "Loosen up, man." Justin's whispered words reach me, and I try to shake out whatever's going on. I start acting silly, making the session more fun. I watch as she shakes her head, a smile pulling at her lips. My chest inflates at that small gesture. *We're not over yet. I just need to bide my time.* She motions for Justin to get into the shot with me.

"Ok, let's grab a couple with the two of you together by the door." Justin winks at her before pulling me into him and hugging on me like we're a couple. At this point, Natalie is laughing at our shenanigans. Justin winks at me as he continues playing around. Her laugh is the balm on my soul. I didn't realize just how much I missed the sound of it until I wasn't hearing it every day.

"What about outside?" Justin mentions, pulling her back into the moment. She looks up from her camera. The smile is still on her face, but it's still not reaching her eyes.

"Let me grab my other lens and I'll meet you outside." She turns away from us as she heads for her equipment on the table across the room. Watching her walk away from me, even if it's just to the other side of the room hurts more than I can put into words. Justin forces me out the front door.

"Listen man, I know this is hard." His words draw my eyes up to his. I can see pain in them, but I have no idea what pain he could possibly be holding onto. "You two aren't done yet."

I scoff at his words. He doesn't see the brokenness in her that I do.

Natalie comes outside and sets us up in front of the building, our door now showing off the custom logo that was designed for us. She works us through several poses in front of the door, the building. She pulls us into the middle of the street, using the buildings on the sides as part of the scenery.

By the time we are finished, it's close to two in the afternoon. Justin has made sure Natalie's been laughing the entire time we've been working, even when she sneaks and looks my way. She doesn't think I notice, but I do. I notice everything about her. I haven't approached her, haven't attempted to talk to her again, which has opened her up a little more as we worked today. I can tell she feared being so close to me, especially since we haven't spoken since Texas.

"Natalie." I watch as my girl tenses to the point that the camera in her hand looks as though it's about to be smashed. I turn to find the source of her tension and find her parents standing off to the side. Her father has a look of absolute disgust on his face as he looks at his daughter. Her mother has her lip turned up in a sneer as she takes in everything around her. Turning back to Natalie, I see her take a deep breath in before she turns towards them.

"Mother. Father." She doesn't take any steps, staying exactly where she is. Justin makes his way over to me slowly.

"What the fuck?" He whispers as he watches her parents move towards her.

"This isn't good." I move away from him, my steps taking me closer to Natalie, not wanting her to have to face them on her own.

"We're here to discuss this bullshit with the will. Savannah is not entitled to that money." *Are they fucking serious right now?* Natalie's shoulders tense as she turns and hands me her camera, her eyes pleading with mine to take it and be quiet. She turns back to them, her spine straight, her head held high. I've never been prouder of her than I am right now.

"There's nothing to discuss. Now, if you'll excuse me..." His father grabs her roughly by the arm and I watch as Natalie's eyes go wide at the sudden movement.

"That bastard does not deserve a penny. I earned him that money, it is mine." Justin walks up beside me, his fists clenched to his side and I push the camera into his hands before he does anything stupid. Without taking my eyes off Natalie, I move to where I'm standing beside her.

"Get your hands off of her." My words are harsh, just as I intended them to be. He ignores me, continuing his hold on her. "I'm not going to say it again. Get your fucking hands off her." This time, his eyes come to mine, and I watch as the spark of recognition enters.

"Well, well, well." He sneers. "If it isn't Lucas. So, Natalie is out here being your whore while her daughter is where exactly?" *Oh, hell fucking no.* Without thinking about it, I throw a punch, my fist landing on his nose.

"Watch what you fucking say. Natalie isn't a whore, but you wouldn't know a damn thing about the woman you raised because all you have concern with is the money lining your pocket, and the women who aren't your wife warming your desk and hotel beds. You're nothing but a money hungry asshole." His wife gasps as her husband crumples, his hands covering his bloody nose as he stares at me.

"That's assault. I'm calling the fucking cops." Justin walks up, pulling Natalie behind him.

"I didn't see a thing." He says, a smirk planted firmly on his face. Natalie's mom is glaring at us as she attempts to help her husband stand.

"I want that fucking money, Natalie. Savannah didn't earn a penny of that money," he yells at her.

"Take it up with Ethan's lawyer." She says, her hand massaging the spot that he grabbed. She turns and walks back to the agency, her body shaking.

"Natalie, get back here and discuss this like an adult." Her mother yells at her. She stops and turns, looking directly at her mother.

"The day you two start acting like adults is the day hell freezes over. I have nothing more to discuss with you. If you have a problem with the will that Ethan had made, then you need to bring it up with the lawyer who made it." She takes a few steps back towards them before stopping right in front of them. "I don't know why he left that money for her, and now that he's gone, I'll never know. But I will say, I'm glad he didn't give it to you."

Turning back towards Justin and myself, she gives us a small smile before walking back down towards the agency.

"This isn't over." Her father sneers at me. "You assaulted me. I have witnesses."

"What I saw was you harassing Natalie. I watched as she tried to walk away and instead of letting her, you physically assaulted her, grabbing hold of her arm and forcing her to stay where you wanted her to. I watched as Lucas told you to let her go. And then I heard you demean Natalie with your words." Justin has an evil smile on his face as he goes through his own recollection of what happened. "Lucas defended her, and when you didn't let her go, he used physical means to make sure that you did. And according to the camera on the corner of that building there." He points to a pedestrian camera that's pointing at where we're standing. "That's exactly what that will show."

Her father's face reddens as Justin stands there with his arms crossed on his chest as he waits for her dad to reply.

When no reply comes, he smirks and lifts his chin at me before turning and heading after Natalie.

"Stay away from her. She can absolutely press charges for the bruises on her arm today." I give them both a wink before I turn and follow Justin.

# Chapter Thirty

NATALIE

My steps are shaky as I walk away from my parents. My arm is throbbing from where my father grabbed me. *Father.* The tears I held back through the confrontation push through, streaming down my face and dripping off my chin. Reaching the agency, I go to pull the door open, but it's locked. Laying my head on the glass, I try to rein in my emotions, but the longer I stand out here, the less power I have over containing them.

"Natalie." Justin's voice causes me to jump. I didn't even realize he had followed behind me. I move aside, allowing him to unlock the door. He goes to pull me in his arms, but I can't be touched right now, not after that. He sees my reaction and immediately puts his arms by his side. "Let's get you inside." He pulls the door open, allowing me to enter before him.

I head straight for my equipment and start packing away everything I brought with me. *Where is my camera?* I remember handing it to Lucas, and then everything happened in a blur. *Where is it?* I turn to Justin, who is holding it out to me. Sighing out in relief, I grab it and put it into my bag. *What the hell just happened?*

"Natalie." Hearing Lucas both calms me and alarms me. I grab the arm my father held in his grasp, the pain radiating from the pressure I'm putting on it. He punched my father, laid him out on the ground. *Is he going to be arrested?* Turning, I watch as Lucas approaches me slowly, trying not to scare me. "Can I see your arm?" He motions to where my dad grabbed me. Up until this point, I've been ignoring the pain, my only thought was to get my shit and get out, get to Madison's. I remove my hand from the spot, refusing to look down at it.

Lucas steps directly in front of me. I close my eyes, not wanting to see his face, my eyes. This is the closest I've been to him since I got the call from Ethan's lawyer. His cologne fills my nose and I do everything I can not to wrap my arms around him and bury myself into his chest. I can feel him gently lifting my arm, checking it. I force my eyes to stay closed as he continues his perusal.

"You're probably going to bruise, but it won't be too bad. Are you okay?" His question disarms me. The words breaking as the tears escape my clenched eyes and run down my face. He pulls me into him, and I have no choice but to succumb to it. His arms feel safe and warm, his scent overpowering my senses.

"I'll give you two a minute." I hear Justin say before a door closes and silence envelopes us.

"Seeing him grab you like that, fuck, Natalie." His voice is breaking, holding so much emotion within it. I hate that he had to see that, had to do what he did.

"My dad isn't going to let that go." I whisper.

"Justin took care of that. Don't worry about me. He should have never put his hands on you." My body is shaking as his words penetrate my head, taking hold of my psyche and making me wish that everything was okay between us.

"I need to go get Savi." I push away from him, my eyes finally opening. He releases me but doesn't step away. I look down at the hand that punched my father. It's bloody, but I'm pretty sure that is my father's and not his own.

"Natalie." Hearing the pain in his voice shatters me. I pinch my lips together, trying to hold back the sob from escaping. *I can't do this right now.* I turn from him and grab my bag from the table.

"I can't, Lucas. Not right now. Just give me some time." He nods his head at me and lets me pass him without reaching out for me again.

It's been a week since everything went down with my parents. I haven't heard from them, but I can't help but be nervous. It's like I'm waiting for the other shoe to drop. Lucas hasn't been arrested, so I don't think my father pressed charges, but like the coward I am, I haven't reached out to him.

"Mama." I smile at Savi as she runs up to me from her class. She hugs my legs tightly.

"How was your day, baby?"

"It was good. I have something for you." She lets go of my legs and pulls her tiny backpack off her back. She rummages for a minute before pulling out a small, folded note with a single red rose. My brain tries to figure out if there's an important holiday today that I'm forgetting, but it comes up empty. "It's for you."

"Thank you, baby." I take the note and rose, holding them in one hand while I wait for her to be done putting her bag back together. She grasps my open hand, and we start the process of walking to Madison's apartment.

We get to Madison's and she instantly takes off to our shared room to put her stuff away. I sit at the island and set the rose down before gently opening the little note that came with it.

> *Natalie, I know you asked for time, but*
> *I just wanted to let you know that*
> *I'm not walking away this time. I'm here*
> *and I'm waiting for you to be ready.*
> *If it takes a lifetime, then that's*
> *how long I'll wait.*
> *Until then, Lucas*

Tears roll down my cheeks and I wonder how he was even able to get this to Savi to give to me. It's been getting harder and harder to ignore the pull I feel for him. Ever since he stood up for me and punched my father, it's like my feelings only got stronger.

"Why are you crying, Mama?" I look down to Savi, her face wrought with concern at the tears falling down my face.

"No reason, bug." I fold the note and place it by the rose before scooping her into my arms. She's still not completely on my side, but her compassion for my tears has me feeling as though everything's going to be okay.

Every day that I get a coffee, it's been paid for. The cup I get is full of sweet little notes, just for me. No other patron has these notes decorating their cup. As each day passes, I realize that it's Lucas who's doing this. He's deteriorating the walls I put up after he walked away again, but there's still a part of me that's completely terrified of reaching out. It took me walking away from him to realize that I was desperately in love with him, but the fear is holding me back.

I leave the coffee shop with my small, decorated cup and head to the empty building next door. When added together with what remained of my own small inheritance from my grandparents, the payment from working with Justin was enough to put down a full deposit for a new studio location. I've been eyeing this place for months, knowing it'd be perfect for those sessions that couldn't be done outdoors. I finally signed all the paperwork yesterday, officially making it mine, or as mine as it can be since I'll be making payments.

Unlocking the door, I take a deep breath as I push inside. The inside is dark and dreary, but with a coat of paint and some love, this front area will be perfect for a reception area. There's three small offices and a bathroom down the hallway to the left, and then to the right is a large open area with large windows that look out to the beach just beyond Main Street.

My focus today is to figure out exactly what I want for each room. I know for sure that I will be converting one of the small offices to a dark room and the other will become my showroom, with my office being the last one. The front portion is a client waiting area. I've always dreamed of having my own photography studio, and now it's a reality. I've pinched myself several times since being handed the key, just to make sure this isn't some dream.

Walking down the hallway, I open the door to the main area where I'll be taking photos. The windows provide a plethora of natural light, but I'll still need to grab some professional lighting, along with props and other items. I mentally calculate a list of things I need to get as I survey the room. I can see holiday set ups, couple sessions, and maybe even the possibility of boudoir photography happening in this studio.

"Natalie, are you in here?" I walk back out to the reception area to greet Madison. Her office is just across the street, along with Justin and Lucas' new agency. I don't know if Justin realizes he leased the office next to hers, but I'm not saying a word to him about it.

"What are you doing here?" I ask, smiling as she pulls me into a hug.

"You think I was going to miss your first day checking out

the new space?" Her smile fades as she looks around. "It's kind of run down in here, don't you think."

"Nothing a coat of paint and some much needed TLC can't fix." I look at the space around me. "So, shouldn't you be at work?"

"Nah, I'm here to help you today. Boss gave me the day, since I just finished up with a tough client." She winks at me as she goes to bring her stuff into one of the offices. "Which one are you using for your office?"

"The one in the back." She nods before taking off down the hallway.

"This space is huge. I'm so proud of you." She yells from the back. I smile as I take her words in. I'm proud of me too. I wasn't sure if I'd ever get to this point, especially with the hospital bills. I follow her back to where my office will be, wanting to put down my stuff somewhere. Grabbing my notebook and a pen out of my purse before setting it down, I turn to make my way back to the lobby. First thing I'll need to do is get furniture.

Paint marks my cheeks, my arms, and even my legs haven't been spared. The front lobby area looks amazing with the light gray I chose for the walls. Madison paired it with a deep gray for the trim. It looks classy and beautiful. I've been in the big room for two days now. I got the accent wall painted yesterday. Today, I'm working on the rest of the walls. Setting the paint roller down, I wipe the sweat from my brow using the sleeve that doesn't have paint all over it.

"Looks good in here." I jump a foot in the air as the voice penetrates the silence I've been accustomed to since I started working in here. Turning, I see Lucas standing at the door.

"You scared the shit out of me." He looks sheepish as he holds his hands up in front of him.

"Sorry. I thought you heard me come in." He walks into the room, turning in a full circle as he checks out what I've gotten done.

"What are you doing here, Lucas?" I didn't even know he knew I was here. I haven't responded to his note, or the coffee cups. My heart isn't ready for the talk I know we need to have.

"I know I said I'd wait, but Natalie, I'm in hell without you." Tears threaten as he talks. His eyes come up to meet mine, and I can see the torment in them, the pain he's holding onto.

"Lucas..." He holds his hand up, stopping me from talking.

"I don't deserve the opportunity to talk to you, to touch you, to hold you. I don't deserve anything from you. But I'm here anyway, because I can't live without you. I was a fucking fool to walk away from you, Natalie. I didn't realize what I was doing at the time, but the minute I figured it out, I wanted to beat my own ass for the pain I caused you." The tears that I was desperately trying to hold back are falling freely down my face with each word he says. I can hear the pain in his voice and it's killing me inside. "I know I broke my promise to you and there's nothing I can do to change that."

"Why did you walk away?" I ask. I'm not sure I'm ready for the answer, but it's been killing me not knowing why.

"I watched you close up the minute you heard about Ethan and it had me questioning if you were still in love with him. I was holding onto anger that wasn't even directed at you. Lauren going to the press only amplified it. I saw that picture and all I saw was you holding something back from me, from us. And then the article that went with it, it stung." I nod my head as I listen. I get it. I did close off after I heard from Ethan's lawyer. And it wasn't because I was in love with him.

"Can I speak now?" My words are laced with the anguish in my heart. He nods his head at me, and I swallow the lump in my throat. "I wasn't still in love with him, nowhere near it. But Ethan was still Savannah's father. And knowing that he didn't have an opportunity to change for her, to become the father she deserved. It messed with me. And then there was you. And you're my rock, but I felt like I couldn't discuss it with you until I figured it out in my own head."

"I'm so fucking sorry," he whispers. He steps closer to me, but I hold my hand up showing him I'm not done.

"I went to my therapist, yes. But it was because I feared telling you everything that I went through with him. I was scared that you'd walk away from me after seeing how broken I really am." Tears fall down his cheeks as he watches me, his hands in his pockets. "But I opened myself up to you, I told you all the dark and dirty things."

"I..." I hold my hand up again.

"I'm not done, Lucas. Let me finish." He nods at me, rocking back on his heel as I prepare to finish what I was saying. "You walked away from me, Lucas. And while I understand your reasoning, it hurt me. Ethan broke me, Lucas, but you. You shattered me." The tears are freely falling from both of our eyes as we stand here staring at each other. All of my words are out, everything I had to say to him.

He closes his eyes and takes a deep breath. When he opens them, I see so much torment swirling that it kills me inside that I did that to him. He nods his head at me and turns to the door. He doesn't take a step, doesn't move. My head falls as I wait for the inevitable, for him to finally walk away once and for all.

"I said I wouldn't walk away again." His words reach me, and I hiccup as the sobs take over, my body shaking as I try to breathe through the pain. "But I will, if that's what you want." I don't want that, but I'm so fucking scared. "Just say the word, Natalie." I bring my head up and meet his eyes. He's turned to where he's looking at me again.

"I don't want..." Before I can even say anything else, he's rushing to me, pulling me into him. My arms instantly go around his body, holding him as tightly as he's holding me.

"I'm so fucking sorry, baby. But I'm not walking away from you, ever again. I was a fucking fool." I pull back from him as he continues his little spiel. Without thinking, I move my hand, cradling the back of his head and pull his lips to mine. His words stop as his mouth meets mine.

There's an intensity to this kiss, a fire that was barely alive is now a burning inferno as he moves his hands to cradle my neck, moving me to where he can explore my mouth better. Everything about this kiss marks me as his. His tongue licks my lower lip, begging for entrance and I have no choice but to open for him. The moment his tongue touches mine, we moan together. His other hand moves to my lower back, pulling my body even closer to him than I was before. He breaks the kiss but doesn't pull his face away from mine.

"I love you, Natalie Renee." The tears that slowed down start falling freely all over again at his admission.

"I love you, too." I whisper. He closes the distance between our mouths again, this time his kiss is passionate and slow. I don't know which kiss I prefer, the burning one from earlier or this one. They both signify so much to our relationship, to what we've been missing over the time we were apart.

I pull back from the kiss as I try to catch my breath. He rests his forehead on mine as he does the same.

"What time is it?" I ask, my head swimming from the intensity of the kisses we shared. I pull my head from his and check my watch. "Shit, I have to get ready to get Savi." He cradles my face with his hands, forcing my eyes to his.

"Speaking of Savi, we need to talk to her about this."

"Um, are you sure?"

"I've never been so sure of anything. I'm in love with you, Natalie. She needs to know." I sigh as he pecks my lips softly. "Bring her to my house for dinner tonight."

"Okay." I say, my eyes closing as I feel his forehead rest against mine.

# Chapter Thirty-One

LUCAS

Putting the spaghetti noodles into the boiling water, a sense of peace washes over me at the normalcy of making dinner for Natalie and Savi. I know Natalie still has some fears, but I'm hoping that tonight helps alleviate some of them. Ethan did a number on her through the course of their marriage, stripping her down so much. And then I went and fucked up her trust in me by walking away.

The timer beeps pulling me out of my own thoughts. I grab the garlic bread out of the oven and set it down on the island before stirring the noodles to make sure they aren't sticking together. My meat sauce is simmering and my whole house smells like an Italian restaurant. I hear the front door open and then small feet barreling through the hallway. I pull the oven mitts off and prepare myself to be knocked over.

"Lucy," Savi yells as she runs through the house and straight into my legs.

"Savannah Marie, I told you to knock." I can only laugh at the exasperation in Natalie's voice.

"Lucy says I don't have to." I stifle my grin as Natalie rounds the corner and stares me down. She's dressed comfortably, a soft sweater covering her top half and yoga pants on the bottom half.

"He did, did he?" Savi simply nods as she continues to hug my legs. Natalie shakes her head as she comes in the kitchen and puts her bag down on one of the bar stools. Grabbing Savi under her arms, I lift her up and hug her to my chest.

"Hi, sweet girl. Did you have a good day?" I kiss her cheek and smile at Natalie as she watches us.

"I had the best day ever." Setting her down, she goes on to tell us everything that happened. While she's talking, I grab the wine glass I set out earlier and fill it. "And then, Mommy came, and said we're having dinner here. So, it really, really was the best day." I smile as Savi climbs into her seat at the island.

"That does sound like the best day." Walking over to Natalie, I offer her the wine glass. When she goes to take it, I pull it back and pucker my lips to her. She looks at Savi and back at me before taking a deep breath. Before she even has a chance to react, I pull her into me and lay a big kiss right on her lips.

"You're kissing Mommy." My lips curve into a smile against Natalie's lips. I kiss her once more before pulling back. Her eyes are wide and watching me, but there's a smile playing on her lips.

"I did. Is that okay?" I turn to Savi, who's watching us with the biggest smile on her face.

"This is the best day ever," she screams out, standing so she can jump from the stool to me but a single look from her mom has her sitting her butt right back down. Winking at Natalie, I pull her into my side and walk us over to Savi, who reaches for me. Picking her up, I hold both of them close to me.

Once dinner is finished, I put on a movie for Savi as I sit in the kitchen watching Natalie collect all the dirty dishes. She refused to let me clean, saying that as the cook, it was only fair that she did the cleaning. Her face shows a million different emotions as she rinses each dish before placing it in the dishwasher. My eyes track her movements as she bends over, her tight pants showing off the shape of her ass in a way that has me wanting to bite it. I pull my eyes off her ass and look to her face. It's scrunched in confusion as she continues working in silence.

"What's on your mind, baby?" My voice pulls her from her thoughts, and she looks to me.

"Did you have to kiss me in front of her?"

"Baby, she's three. I don't think a full sit-down lecture would've worked." I give her my best smile, hoping it helps ease some of the tension from her shoulders. Standing, I walk around the island and come up behind her. Wrapping my arms around her stomach, I settle my chin on her shoulder. "I haven't kissed you since this morning. If you thought I was going to wait until after we told her to get my lips on yours, then you haven't been paying attention."

"Lucas." My name is a whisper on her lips as a blush forms on her chest and works its way up her neck. I take the dish from her hand and put it back into the sink before I turn her to where she's looking at me.

"I'm right here, baby, and I'm not walking away from you again." Before she can even form a response, my lips are on hers.

After putting Savi to bed in the guest room I set up for her, I sit on the couch with Natalie. She's nursing the same glass of wine she had with dinner. Taking the glass, I set it on the coffee table before pulling her onto my lap, her legs straddling mine. A laugh escapes her as I settle her in place and before she can react, I seal my lips over hers.

She kisses me back with just as much passion, small moans escaping as she leans into me. Pulling back from me, I notice her eyes are hooded with lust from the momentum of that kiss. Grabbing her under the ass, I press my lips to hers again. I stand and move us to the bedroom. Dropping her onto the bed, I break the kiss as I hover over her. Her eyes stay closed as I watch her breathe in and out.

"Is this okay?" My words draw her eyes open as she stares back at me. She nods her head as she breathes in deep, her eyes tracking my movements as I move over her, my hips thrusting lightly into her core as she lays here. Closing the distance between us, I seal my mouth over hers. A gasp leaves her, and I take full advantage and slip my tongue in, my need to show her just how much I love her possessing me.

Laying her back, I break the kiss and lean my forehead against hers, both of us doing our best to catch our breath. I close my eyes, doing my best to control the urge to own her, mark her as mine. Just as I get myself under control, I feel her hands cradle my face, forcing my eyes to open.

"You don't have to hold back with me, Lucas." My eyebrows scrunch together in confusion as she leans up to kiss me gently. *How did she know I was holding back on her?* "You won't break me." It's those words that finally break through the last of my resolve. Sitting up, I remove her shirt, rolling her over so she's on her stomach. Trailing my fingers up her arms, I grab her hands and bring them up to the headboard, hooking her fingers around the beams.

"Keep those hands right there." I whisper into her skin as I kiss her bare shoulder. I feel her shiver under my touch as I trail my fingers back down her arms, her back. Wrapping my arms around her stomach, I reach the band of her pants and start pulling them down. I gasp in shock as I pull them down, noticing the thong settling nicely between her ass cheeks. I kiss each piece of skin I uncover as I move her pants off of her legs.

"You have the most beautiful body." My words are whispered as continue my light feather kisses. "Do you know what you do to me? Just how much you affect me?"

Pulling her pants all the way off, I feel her intake of breath as I take my hands and squeeze the globes of her ass. I smack them lightly, gaining a hiss in response as I massage them afterwards. Wrapping my hands around her hips, I pull her up to where she's on her knees. I can't pull my eyes off of her. Her shapely ass is primed and gorgeous, a light handprint forming on the left cheek. The sight of that mark only intensifies my need to own her. Undressing as quick as I can, I watch as her breathing becomes more erratic the longer I take.

"You look so fucking good like this." I whisper as I kiss her just above her ass. She lifts her head and meets my eyes.

Seeing the lust in her hooded eyes has all the blood that was in my brain rushing down, only making me pulse harder with need. She watches me over her shoulder. Without taking my eyes off her, I grab my cock at the base, pulling on it lightly to relieve some of the tension. Her legs are quivering as she holds herself in place, her breathing ragged. I can see her pussy glisten with the juices coming from it.

Settling myself behind her, I grab her hips with need, my fingers biting into her skin, marking her. Moving the tip of my cock to her entrance, I gather the juices before lightly pushing inside and retreating before trailing it to her clit, pushing on it gently. The movement elicits a moan from her. She removes one of her hands and I slap her ass in response, causing her to jump and squeal in response. She moans as I massage the spot I slapped.

"What did I say about your hands, baby?" She quickly puts her hand back, hooking her fingers onto the headboard. Going back to what I was doing, I continue my assault on her clit with the head of my dick. I can feel her entire body shaking with each push at her entrance, making my way further in with each turn I take between her clit and her opening. I can feel my own body shaking as I continue to hold myself back from taking her as hard as I want to.

Just as I'm about to push a little further into her, I feel her push back on me, impaling herself on me all the way to the hilt. She screams into the pillow beneath her as I bottom out, the angle making her pussy that much tighter.

"Fuck, baby. Why did you do that?" I can feel her body shaking around me, her pussy quivering around my cock. She pulls herself off and then slams herself back, and my eyes roll back at the intense pleasure this is causing all over my body.

"Stop holding back, Lucas. I trust you." Her words are mumbled into the pillows as she pulls herself from me and pushes back against me again and again, forcing me to take control before I empty myself into her. Grabbing her hips, I stop her movements and look at the sight of her below me, my cock inside of her.

"You're better than any fantasy I could ever come up with, Natalie. I fucking love looking at you like this, your beautiful ass up in the air with my cock deep inside of your pussy." My words bring another moan out of her, making her wiggle against me. Holding tightly to her hips, I pull back and push in, the sound of my balls slapping against her are masked only by her moans with each thrust I make. "You like that, baby?"

"Mmhmm." Her moan is muffled by the pillow her face is planted in, my hard thrusting not allowing her much movement.

"Fuck baby, you look so fucking good." Knowing I won't last much longer like this, I wrap my arm around her hips, my fingers finding her clit and stroking it as I continue pounding into her. Her moans take over completely as she detonates all around me, her pussy quivering and pulsing so much that it pulls my orgasm from me. She bites into the pillow, trying to keep herself quiet as I empty myself into her and fall onto her, my hands landing on each side of her, so I won't crush her.

Rolling off to the side, I take in the woman breathing hard beside me. Her face is flushed, but she's smiling. Pushing the hair out of her face, I lean in for a kiss before pulling her into me.

"That was amazing." My words are labored as I try to catch my breath.

Opening a new business has been the craziest fucking thing I've ever done in my life. I thought my life was constantly on the go as a model, but it has nothing on this. Natalie helps as much as she can, but with her own workload and Savi, we spend more time apart than together. The few moments we can be together, it's like all the walls have crumbled and nothing is holding us back anymore. The buzzing of my phone pulls me out of that memory just as my cock hardens at the thought of her on her knees in front of me.

**Natalie:** Hi baby. Where are you?

**Lucas:** Be home in a bit.

"Dude, how long is this going to take?" I turn to see Justin standing off to the side, looking pissed about having to do this with me. I didn't want to bring him, but the asshole wouldn't take no for an answer when I told him I had shit to take care of.

"I told you that you didn't have to come with me." Rolling my eyes, I go back to looking at the display in front of me. I never thought I'd get to this point in my life, looking at rings. When I was with Lauren, it was never about marriage, just convenience. But now that I have Natalie, I can't picture life without her. Just as I'm about to give up and try another store, I spot a ring that has me looking twice. It's breathtaking in its simplicity, and right below it, a matching smaller ring. I grab the attention of the store attendant, asking her to take them out so I can inspect them closer.

The setting for the larger one looks like a twisted vine with rose gold and white gold enveloping together towards the center diamond, smaller diamonds accenting the white gold on the front. The one below has smaller diamonds making the shape of a heart, with infinity symbols tied into the heart and going around to the back of it. Holding them both feels like kismet and I know that these are the rings that I'll use for my girls. Somehow, I managed to get both of their ring sizes without them realizing it. Took some work, but I finally did.

"I think these are the ones." The lady smiles before pulling out her order pad.

"Why am I even here? I didn't sign up for this shit." Justin throws his hands in the air and walks to the other side of the store. I try my best to ignore him, the lady at the counter's stifling a smile but she gives me her full attention.

"The Infinity Collection. Beautiful choice." Smiling, I give her all the information about what stones I want for each ring, including having each engraved with a special message for my girls.

"This is why I'm never settling down. This frou-frou bullshit is for the fucking birds. Ring shopping. Next thing you know, you're going to be asking me to stand up beside you at your wedding." He rolls his eyes, but when his eyes catch mine, he gulps, loudly. "Fuck." He stalks out of the shop without waiting to see if I'm done. The lady behind the counter can no longer hold back the smile she's been desperately trying to hide.

"Your friend's something else."

"You can say that again."

"You going to bring this up when he finally falls?" She giggles a little as I smirk at her. Little does she know that Justin has already fallen, he's just too damn stubborn and hard-headed to realize it yet.

"I'll be sitting ringside watching it all go down." She shakes her head and finalizes my order. After making the full payment, I walk out ten minutes later knowing that this is the step I want to take. I just need to figure out when and how I am going to do this.

The moment I've been waiting for is finally here. I told Natalie I needed her help with a shoot and she's on her way now. Instead of meeting her at my new office, I'm at the cafe across the street. She doesn't know this, but I finished furnishing the studio she bought. When I'd seen her vision for it, I knew I wanted to help somehow. Madison was able to get me the list of everything she was wanting for the space and slowly, I've been getting things for her. Madison has kept her busy, along with the outdoor sessions, so it's been easy keeping her from finding out. At this moment, all our friends are currently in there waiting to surprise her.

Leaning against the building, I keep an eye out for her as I scan my phone, trying to look as nonchalant as possible. My nerves are eating at me. *What if she says no? What if this is too soon?* All I can think about is spending the rest of my life with her and Savannah. The past few months have only had me falling deeper and deeper with her. She's my sun, my stars, my moon, my everything. Without her, without Savi, life is just incomplete. There's no life without them.

Looking up, I watch as she walks down the street. She

hasn't noticed me yet, but I can't take my eyes off her. She's in a cute sundress today. White with blue lilies all over it, her skin's tanned from her time in the sun and wisps of her blonde hair frame her face as it falls out of the ponytail she has in. Her camera bag is slung over her shoulder and she holds it protectively against her. She's breathtaking. She finally notices me standing here and the most radiant smile lights up her face.

"Hey there beautiful." I close the distance between us and pull her into me, kissing her forehead. She wraps her arms around me and nestles her face into my chest. I hold her for a few minutes before pulling back and kissing her like my life depends on it. I can feel the love she has for me in the way she kisses and today's no different. *She won't say no.*

"What are you doing over here? I thought we were meeting at your office?" I grab her hand and pull her off to the side with me, so we don't continue to block anyone from walking on the sidewalk.

"Do you trust me?" Her smile turns to confusion as she searches my face. Smiling, I kiss her again, erasing any doubt from her mind the best that I can.

"Of course, I trust you, Lucas. What's going on?" She's looking around, probably checking to see if she is being punked or something. Pulling the blindfold out of my pocket, I hold it up for her to look at.

"I need to put this on you." Her eyes come to mine, darkening with desire as she tries to hide it in my hand.

"Lucas, we are in public." I laugh out loud at her whispered words.

"Oh, baby, if I had known you'd be okay with using this in the bedroom, I'd have brought it out a long time ago. But this isn't for that. I just need you to trust me." She grabs the blindfold from me, her cheeks crimson from the blush creeping up her neck at her outburst and my response.

"I do trust you, Lucas." She hands the blindfold back to

me. Turning her around, I place it on her eyes and bring it to where I can tie it. Her body tightens the instant I start tying it and it takes all I have not to pull it back off and fill her in on everything I have planned. Leaning in, I find her ear.

"Trust me." She relaxes into me and nods. She's chewing on her bottom lip again, but as much as I'd love to pull it out with my teeth, I can't. Not right now anyways. Pulling her along, I make sure she doesn't trip as we make the short walk next door to the studio filled with the furniture she's been wanting.

Taking a deep breath, I open the door and lead her in. *She won't say no.*

## Natalie

I've never been blindfolded in my entire life. I trust Lucas with everything I am, but I never imagined something like this happening. My mind is running over a million different scenarios. *What the hell's going on?*

"Baby, relax. I'm right here." His voice soothes me, even with my nerves shot. I have no idea what's going on, but as long as he's right here, that's all that matters. Lucas is the best thing to ever happen to me, aside from Savannah. He's the gentle waves in a stormy sea. I'm so hopelessly in love with him. "You ready, baby?" I nod my head, unable to speak.

The blindfold comes off and I blink my eyes to adjust to the light coming into the windows. *This isn't his office.* I turn around to take in my surroundings. The last time I was in my studio, I was waiting on furniture. Turning a full circle, I see a reception area full of the furniture I was wanting to use. There's a coffee bar, a couch, and a mini refrigerator. Several of my photos from my website have been printed on canvas, showcasing my work throughout the room.

"W-w-what did you do?" My words stumble as they come out of my mouth. I can't even think coherently, let alone form words.

"That's not all, let's keep going." He takes my hand, leading me through each room. They are all decorated with everything that I need to make this studio work. We approach the door for the studio itself. He releases my hand and gestures for me to walk in.

Opening the door, I cover my mouth as I look around. In the corner by the windows are Madison, Justin and Savi. As soon as she sees me, Savi runs and hooks herself to my legs. I can't move, can't breathe. This is beyond any expectation I ever had. "Lucas, what is this?"

"Well, Madison helped me out. This is your dream, baby. And I am so proud of you for making it happen." Tears form in my eyes as he explains how they all worked together to put this together for me.

"You did this? For me? But why?" He kisses me lightly on the mouth before slowly dropping to one knee. "W-w-what are you doing?" I whisper but he only smirks at me as he takes my hand.

"Natalie, we met when we were eight years old and you became my best friend. For years, you remained that best friend. I didn't get the girl then. I was too stupid, too dumb, to see just what was right in front of me. And then you walked back into my life. And you weren't alone. You had this sweet girl with you. I fell in love with Savannah the moment she smiled that toothless smile at me. And through all of that, our friendship grew. My feelings grew. You're the light of my life, my best friend, my soulmate. I love you more and more with each passing day and I couldn't imagine life without you in it, without either of you in it." Letting go of our hands, he reaches into his pockets and pulls not one, but two velvet boxes out of his pocket. Looking to me, he grabs my hand. "I've been searching for the words to say when I did this, but none could ever fit because there are no words that can describe the love that I have for you. Natalie Renee, will you do me the honor of becoming my wife?"

Tears fall down my face as I watch this man open the velvet box meant for me. The design looks like a twisted vine with rose gold and white gold enveloping together towards the center diamond, smaller diamonds accenting the white gold on the front. A simple diamond sits front and center. I can't even form words after hearing everything he said so all I do is nod instead. The smile he gives me is blinding as he removes the ring from the box and places it on my finger. He kisses the back of it and mouths *I love you* to me.

Grabbing Savannah's hand, he looks to her. "Savannah Marie, if your mother is the light of my life, then you, my sweet girl, are the stars and the moon. I love you and you're so very precious to me, and to your mother. You deserve all the good things in life, all the beauty that this life holds. Will you do me the honor of becoming my daughter?" Savannah throws herself into his arms, pushing him onto his butt from his kneeling position. She's suffocating him with how hard she's holding onto him.

"Does this mean you get to be my daddy now?" Lucas chokes as tears form in his eyes and he looks to me. My own tears are steadily falling at the sight in front of me. His eyes search mine, questioning how to answer this question. Kneeling, I pull her back from him slightly before taking her face into mine.

"Is that what you want?" I ask her quietly.

"I want that more than anything, Mama." Looking to Lucas, all I see is love shining in his eyes as he watches us. He pulls the small ring out of the other box and places it on her finger, and I can't help but fall even more in love with him as I take in the infinity design that is surrounding a heart made of small stones.

"I would love to be your daddy." His words are choked with emotion as he says them. Pulling us both into him, he holds us on the floor. I feel his lips at my ear. "I love you, Natalie." Pulling back, I kiss him lightly on the lips.

"I love you too, Lucas. Always."

The End

*Fall Into Me* - Brantley Gilbert

*All of Me* - John Legend

*Dear Daughter* - Halestorm

*I Won't Give Up* - Jason Mraz

*Marry Me* - Train

*Like I'm Gonna Lose You* - Meghan Trainor feat John Legend

*Stay* - Rihanna

*All or Nothing* - O-Town

*My Everything* - 98 Degrees

*I Knew I Loved You* - Savage Garden

*All My Life* - K-Ci & JoJo

*I Can Love You Like That* - All-4-One

*Wait For You* - Elliott Yamin

*Because You Loved Me* - Celine Dion

*Do I Have To Cry For You* - Nick Carter

First, I want to thank my husband. Your unending support made this possible. Thank you my love. I love you forever and always.

To my kids. You drive me insane, but you make me a better person. I love you three with all my heart. You won't know about these books, and even when you're old enough to know, we will all pretend that you don't. It's just better that way. Trust me on this.

To my best friend, Stephanie. I love you so much! Thank you for the venting sessions, the spiraling when I didn't think I could do this. I appreciate you more than words can say. Ride or die

To my author wifeys, Emily and AK. Y'all are rockstars and I am so thankful that you are both in my corner. Here's to glitter to make it shiny, knives because we're stabby, cupcakes for the sweetness and traveling to see the world. I love you girls.

To Jodi, thank you for taking me under your wing and helping me with all the things and taking time to answer all my questions.

To Maria, Jamie, Nicole, Claire, Zoey, Heather and Brittney. Thank you for taking a chance on a new author and bringing me under your wings. You support has been amazing and I'm so blessed to know y'all.

To my beta readers. Y'all are the true MVP. Thank you for helping me make this story what it is. I appreciate each and every one of you. Lucas and Natalie are here because of you.

To my cover designer, Kate. This cover is everything. I am absolutely in love with it. Thank you for bringing Lucas and Natalie to life.

To my editor, Saxony. Thank you for helping me make this story powerful. I couldn't have done this without your unwavering love and support for this story.

To RWR, thank you for the push to make this story happen. This book wouldn't be here if y'all hadn't pushed me to turn that 3k prologue into more.

And a big thank you to YOU, the reader. I'm so very grateful that you took a chance on me, on my words. If you loved my story, I'd appreciate if you left a review for me. It's not required but reviews help authors like me get our books out to more readers.

To keep up to date with all my upcoming releases, you can join my Facebook Reader's Group - Norma Marie's Readers Retreat or you can sign up for my newsletter at www.norma-marieauthor.com/newsletter.

Norma Marie is a contemporary romance author who believes in love that heals. With hero's full of devotion and heroines who find their worth after trauma, her stories will encompass you in swoon worthy moments that steal your breath away.

Residing in Clarksville, TN with her small zoo, Norma Marie can often be found in her craft room playing in glitter and inks or writing stories full of hope and passion. She's a lover of romance and when she isn't covered in glitter or sitting behind her desk bringing her stories to life, she's often sitting on her deck with her kindle and a  white chocolate mocha from Starbucks.

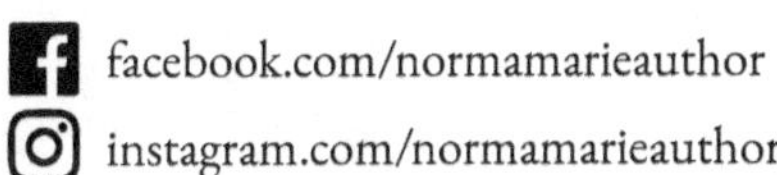

facebook.com/normamarieauthor

instagram.com/normamarieauthor